The Luke Steel Chronicles

By Ken Roche

 New Generation **Publishing**

About the author

Ken Roche is a Writer/Backpacker/Adventurer from the south eastern Irish port city of Cork. He has trekked through the golden triangle, lived in the hills of Jamaica and crossed the badlands of India as well as numerous other locations around the globe.

He is also a survivor of the Boxing Day tsunami in Thailand.

For James and Olive

Contents

The Stranger

Whatever happened to the good old days of terrorists like Carlos the Jackal or the IRA? The stranger said to me in an loud American accent, in truth I wasn't sure if the guy was talking to me. All I knew for certain was whoever he was, where-ever he was from, well he was just plain dumb. I was queuing to go through the metal detector of HM Customs in London Heathrow! So I really didn't need this in case, well I'm sure you know just why I didn't need it. Thou he had said it in my general direction.

I'd thought it best to just ignore him. You see the unmistakeably stench of hard liqueur coming directly from him was my main reason for suspecting he was talking to me, but it equally could of been from the strong joint I had put together before leaving home and had just smoked outside before coming to get my flight. Either way I just continued to stare ahead pretending not to hear him, like you do with strangers you consider maybe a bit.. Unstable I guess is the correct description, besides to talk like that, is this place, nowadays, defiantly puts him in that category.

My names Luke and back then I was just a normal happy-go-lucky middle-class Brit embarking on the gap year thing, with a wallet full of cards and a brain more empty than space time or wait was that time space? Anyhow it was my first time if I am to be honest that I had ever even heard of Carlos the Jackal. The IRA yes Carlos the Jackal no. Later on I would in fact remember seeing Carlos face on TV but was just not able to put the name to the face at that moment in time.

In fact if you had shown me a picture of him and said this guy was Che Guevara's best mate I would have been none the wiser, as to me they all had that look back in the day, you know the look right? Still I wasn't going to inquire at this particular time about him and did the drunk seem like the best person to ask? Hell no. It was also the first time I was to hear about the mystical ancient mountain city of Lhasa! A place I'd also seen in pictures but again did not know the name.

I was about to hear about both of them on the same night and from the same stranger! In fact there was a lot I was going to learn about from this point onwards, most were good, some were bad, others real bad. I managed a wry smile and nodded to the American just to seem to agree with his growing frustration at the length of time it now took to clear HM customs and excise. Which was what was clearly annoying him, but knowing full well the implications of such a stupid comment in this day and age can in fact ruin your holiday plans before they have even begun! Unfortunately nobody seemed to have told him this.

The guy seemed to manage to keep his mouth shut long enough to get himself through customs unnoticed! A miracle I'm sure you'd agree and to my joy I watched him disappear into the crowd, soon enough I too found myself flowing along with the tide of human traffic. The twinge of excitement boiled inside as I picked up my bag. Just in case I'm deemed a complete loon by passing strangers I hopelessly try to suppress my smile. I bounce to my departure gate with eyes like an Ibizan acid house refugee and a grin to match, eventually I reach my departures gate and queue with the rest of my fellow 'quirky' passengers.

Now look if I'm honest I don't know why I choose Kathmandu! Honestly I don't, not there's anything wrong with Kathmandu but of all the exotic places I could have gone in the world say France or Italy etc I choose

Kathmandu. My only personal issue was I had always considered myself somewhat of a romantic type, and I really could of done with maybe a few lessons from our continental neighbours on that front as I matured. But you know that gangster movie where the guy says, I don't know why but as long as I can remember I had always wanted to be a gangster? Well it was sort of like that except deep down I had always wanted to be a backpacker! Strange I know but this is not the movies it is reality after all.

An adventurer, to see the world from the streets. Not an SAS type adventurer but to not know what lay around the next corner, to smoke more weed than an Amsterdam coffee shop connoisseur. To not know when or where you're next meal or bed for the night might be. As I slipped into my seat I became overcome with anxiousness, a type familiar to all seasoned lone travellers! That feeling of butterfly's in the stomach. The combination the fear of flying, and feeling of impending doom which lurks in the darkest parts of your subconscious screaming 'this is your last chance to get off this flight is jinxed'

I reassured myself. Easy lad it's not a war zone you're going too! You're going somewhere you can grab a cold beer smoke weed, chat to interesting cultured and enlightened folks, from which maybe just maybe you will learn. After all doing the Gap year jaunt was one thing! Doing it on your own to somewhere as far off the beaten track as Kathmandu placed you in a entirely different league from say the ones that all go in a group to work on a sheep farm in Australia.

It's all good I smiled to myself! Illuminated and chilled by the fat funky joint I had earlier smoked, all of a sudden I heard a voice, not any old voice but a familiar one.....what the..I have heard that voice before. Slowly I looked up and to my absolute horror see it's the drunk! As I look up he looks down at me ....Holding a ticket in his hand. You know in horror movies when the face begins zooming in and out? Well that's exactly what happened.

Our eyes locked! Vivid and intensely, momentarily frozen in time until I spotted his pupils dilate. Yup this is sixty seven c my seat al-right! He said before proceeding to belch loudly as he chucked his bag in the overhead locker, slams it shut and plonked himself down next to me, his elbow banging mine off the arm rest as he got comfy! Rude fuck-wad...Great, now I get to listen to this guy all night. I pick up the in-flight magazine and flick through it cursing myself for not buying a book to keep myself occupied.

Man I sure as hell hope they're going to serve us a dam drink real soon? Again with no one else around I get the distinct impression he is saying it to me trying to start a conversation maybe? But why me? It's always me! Twice in one night picked on by the sloppy drunk. Itching for me to respond, rubbing his hands on his thighs. I got a thirst on me like no one would believe; he says turning to face me directly this time as he finishes his sentence! Well what about you sir don't yawl agree?

You look like yawl need a stiff drink too brother? Yawl awful quite there mister going travelling buddy? A backpacker dude or em maybe you're still young enough to be doing the gap year thing? He says squinting his eyes as he monitor's my face. Eh yeah sure of course I am doing the gap year thing, I stutter being left with no choose but to answer.

Don't worry! Huh, worry about what man? I am certain they will get around to it soon....Huh excuse me mister? The drink you said you want a drink and I'm sure they will get around to serving soon. Oh yeah sorry buddy I've had a few already...No way I nod slowly looking at him. Whey hey he laughs and nods with the big proud grin that uniquely ignorant boastful drunkards the world over seem to possess. Like drinking yourself into oblivion is something to be proud of.

So is it your first time going to Kathmandu? Yes 'God why didn't I buy a book' well I'm telling you brother yawl going have one a hell of a time. I am? Where the hell is the god dam stewardess? He says pressing the call button. I realised he was just another nervous flyer who needed to get drunk to fly. How many times have you been there? I asked. Oh I've lost count! All I know is it's the top of the world man, he says with a grin. As for the hashish it is some of the cleanest purest, strongest shit you will ever smoke! What the fuck? Did he just say what I think he said? It's that obvious I'm a stoner.

Then leaning in close in a hushed tone says, yawl be careful now hear! I've warned you I'm serious it's strong! It is? I leaned closer to him. I mean for real? Yup especially that soft black stuff steer clear of that. We both leaned back into our seats. This was quite a shock to me as he certainly didn't look like a stoner but the template classic drunk.

But this was aeroplane talk, where I would learn in the coming year's complete strangers would tell you the most personal stuff. You see when you are seated next to someone alone for ten or more hours on a plane it's like planes become pay as you go shrink sofas. Where individuals offload secrets they couldn't or wouldn't dare tell someone they know, but as they know they will never see you again you're the perfect human confession box! Free Counselling if you will.

Talking about all sorts of personal stuff with strangers once the booze gets flowing then the altitude kicks in and you completely lose control of your sense of reality. In a few hours you will be gone your separate ways, yet at the time it seemed so up close, so personal, so special.

I've had women tell me of their husbands affairs or indeed their own or how the family fortune was squandered by a older brother or mother or guys casually tell me that they sleep with hookers and that they don't feel an ounce of remorse as their wife won't do this or that with them, so it's their fault their doing it.

And it's no time to come over all chat show host, just agree is the best policy. Yeah just agree is my motto! Funny thing is, those same people upon landing time will suddenly shut up stiffen up and walk away from you as soon as they hit customs the paranoid fucks. I heard they mix in a little opium to make it a bit more minding bending, he whispers. Huh? Oh I was daydreaming. But hey I've never seen it been done myself! Nor can I figure out why they would do that when it's only going to cost them more and not make any more profit right? Eh yes mate? I guess that's just another backpacker myth huh? Eh..yeah eh I guess so.

Why does he keep talking about drugs? Do I look like a user? I hope customs don't think so when the plane lands! Eventually he's served a drink then takes a swig that would put a pirate to shame; still it seems to chill him out. Names Brandon, Brandon Huckabee from Detroit Michigan he says offering his hand which I shake. Luke, Luke Steel, Err from London! Not altogether used or comfortable with the American way of introducing yourself using name and city and state.

So what's the plan Luke? Huh? Your plan what is it? You got a plan right? He knocks back another sip of liqueur! How long are you planning on going on vacation? It's a gap year thing. OK so where yawl going to see? Yawl know what's your plan man? He laughs ignoring my protest that it isn't a vacation! Yawl even have an itinerary? Well Err actually I don't really have a plan as such, instantly feeling utterly stupid judging by Brandon's horrified expression. Look I got a year off so I was planning on just seeing where it takes me.

Oh a sprite of adventure? He smiles nodding his head, I like it I like your style my man, you remind me of when I was younger. I do? Yeah sure..Stick a pin in a map, that was me boy! We both laugh. Tibet! Tibet! Tibet he says staring at his head rest in front of him, that sacred land of myths and mysteries! It cast's its magnetic mystical spell over all who enter Luke, making some whizzing motion with his hand like a wizard! All I can do is state at him. Oh yeah buddy yes sir and not only to travellers but long before backpackers or those doing the gap year thing ever even heard of it.

Spies, missionaries, warriors and adventures, scholars mystics, astrologers and truth seekers have all felt its magnetic web of intrigue draw them there for thousands of years my friend, but very very very few have made it Luke, with even fewer returning to tell the tale. But hey don't let my ramblings put you off he laughs. Err okay you're not, please continue Brandon.

Yawl sure? Yes. OK look it's one of the most extremely remote and fascinating parts of the world brother, it seems to of been granted to be a place of complete timeless splendour Luke! Complete timelessness like you wouldn't believe man, the land where time itself stands still. Really? Yeah, look for thousands of years Tibet has captivated the minds of men! That land way beyond the mighty Himalayas on the highest plateau of the world, the forgotten land, the land of mystery and intrigue forgotten not just by man but by Mother Nature itself.

Where I should go? Any must see? He knocks back

13

another sip as he thinks. Well all I can say is I don't know how anyone can find say more than four or five days in Kathmandu interesting. That bad eh? No not really, the opposite in fact but it's just such a fascinating part of the world, with such a lot to see, but it isn't going to come to you man! No-sir-e, you must get out there and find it yourself! Some starters then? I sit upright looking at him he looks back at me! OK he smiles, if I were you I'd get myself over to Lhasa! Definitely.

Number one see Lhasa! Err Lhasa? You have not even heard of the place? Nope! And you're flying to Tibet tonight? Uh huh I nod. Jesus H Christ where have you been all your life? I shrug ...OK look it's an old city, a place of pilgrimage to some. Enchantment to others! Real nice place though no matter who you are. Anyway make sure you go by road! You go right over the fucking Himalayas man, it takes a few days driving but dam what a ride he laughs, trust me you will never forget it! Never.

I trust you mate! He smiles back. I feel I can trust Brandon even though I thought the opposite only an hour ago, but warmness an instant fondness has over taken me about the guy, he seems, well he seems genuine. So this gap year Luke is it literally a year? Yup! Then make your way over to the mouth of, I mean I should say the source of the Mekong river and catch a slow boat downstream! Yeah? Sure why not? You're planning on seeing Thailand at some point right? I guess, of course you are the gap year folks all do Thailand.

Wouldn't be a proper gap year in Asia without doing Thailand brother that's for sure, well I don't know many first time travellers who sailed into Thailand from high up in the Tibetan plateaus, the foothills of the Himalayas itself and down on the Mighty Mekong.

Man by the time you get to Thailand's beaches you

will be the toast and envy of every backpacker, every bar and hostel every idle boast by every moronic boastful dick can be wiped out in one swoop by your intro alone. I bet yawl every cutie will dig you for it too. Here take this card Luke if you ever get into trouble or need advice about anything, call me ok, don't be afraid to contact me, and also take this one as well he says holding up another card.

Who is this? I ask taking a look at the card? Mr. Koo! Mr who? Mr Koo, he is a Em let me see he is what you might consider a fixer over in Xining! Where? Xining -its inside China..China? What? Well it is where you're going to have to go to get to the Mekong! Now Hold on Brandon I never said I was going to..going to what Luke? He laughs....Go trekking up mountains and stuff! Hey it's up to you man it's completely up to you; you got the card, now you have Mr Koo too, if you need him............................... Mr Koo ....I say quietly to myself! This might just be an adventure I won't forget after all.

Kathmandu

I cleared customs without a second glimpse, so much for paranoia. I had lost Brandon or he had lost me. As I readied myself to go out into my brave new world he walked past. Hey kid good luck, hope you have a great one he said as he shook my hand one last time, and don't be afraid to email me if you need anything ok.

Then as quick as he appeared he disappeared into the scrum of people in the arrivals hall. Just like every other overly friendly person I would ever speak to on a plane when it came to walking through customs they don't want to know. I grinned shrugged and took out my copy of the traveller's holy bible going to the just arrived section on Kathmandu. 'When getting a taxi into town from the airport agree to pay no more than five dollars' ok got it. I took a deep breath and made my move.

As soon as I was in the public hall I was surrounded by a tide of people all offering their services. The faces zoomed in and out some holding up flyers or waving offers on hotels excursions etc! Politely declining them eventually I make it out. A little guy catches my eye by doing nothing more than walking casually next to me. I thought we just happened to be going in the same direction but any time I'd look at him he would smile. Somehow he stood out from the crowd, his easy going manner? I'm not sure, but after I asked him what he wanted he explained he was just another taxi driver looking for a fare.

He agreed to bring me into town for the five dollars quoted in the book. As we navigated our way into town he asked which hotel? The majestic please! Why the Majestic? A friend recommended it. Are you sure you haven't been reading the traveller holy bible? He laughed looking back at me in the rear view mirror. No. I lied! Why what's wrong with the Majestic?

Very noisy, has a mosque nearby so you get call to prayer unless you like getting up early, he smiles. Not really I say looking out at the soldiers standing about with rifles! Look my friend I can get a much better place for half that money.

OK tell you what, you bring me to have a look at the Majestic first and maybe then you can take me to see the ones your recommending? No problem Mr. Half hour later I walk out of the majestic and pause on the steps as I light up a cigarette, guess he was right about that. OK Luke give the guy a chance I tell myself, best hurry thou as it's going to be dark in a few hours and I don't fancy driving around Kathmandu with a complete stranger jet-lagged in the dark.

I jump back into the cab, what's your name again? Mo! Now to most westerners the name mo means just that, a name nothing more. But from living in London I know from my Afghan friends that Mo is short for Mohammed so is the guy is thinking I might be freaked out by knowing he is a Muslim? I couldn't care less what he is or what he believes in. Mo take me to this hotel you are recommending. Five minutes later we arrive Mo puts the car in brake, he turns around and looking straight at me says. OK when you go in you say you wan see room ok? Do not care about price ok! Then you say ok I will think it then you come back car me? Err ok.

OK and if you like I will get you a very special discount from my friend ok. Err ok! I Followed Mo's instructions. The staff showed me two rooms with stunning views, the waiter smiled as he opened the rooms back door leading out onto the stunning hotel grounds, at the back of which was a small lake. The asking price is a justified one hundred US dollars a night. I decline as instructed. OK Mo I did as you said! You like huh?

Well yes but how much? Fifty per cent he grins. Half, he makes a chopping motion with his hand. OK we go my friend house! OK matey. After twenty minutes driving the sun was beginning to set and set fast! How much further? No problem my friend no problem.

Suddenly he drove off the main road and down a side road. With no tarmac and littered in holes we drove along the bumpy road for a few minutes.

Now I'm totally lost. Then a crowd of men perhaps two hundred strong came into sight in the distance. My stomach heaved, they are gathered under a single yellow street lamp. It's dark, pitch dark now as nightfall arrives faster or so it seems in Asia. He slowed the car down to a crawl in case he hit anyone. As we passed dozens of bearded faces peer in at the westerner. I look the other way to avoid eye contact and notice the street lamp above is being swarmed by thousands of mosquitoes all buzzing around it! Sometimes you notice the strangest things when under pressure.

Err what's going on here Mo with the crowd? Oh they have been to pray! He says looking back at me via his rear view mirror, all I see is his eyes! Pray? Yes Pray, Church? Mosque! The bumpy ride comes to an abrupt halt. He parks and gets out tapping his hand on the roof indicating for me to get out and to follow him. Into a dark building! I exit the car look around me taking in my surroundings and up at the building. It would be considered maybe a squat or a derelict crack house in a ghetto type neighbourhood back home.

A lightless outside stairwell leading up to various flats in a four story block is where he is disappearing into, he beckons me to follow! I gaze up briefly once more before taking the decision to follow! Not that I had any choice at this point. It was then I realised I had in fact made the classic traveller error in a strange land, and for what? To save money. Suddenly I realised how stupid I had been to come here with him. Fucking Jet-lag, I told myself desperately trying to balance not showing fear or acting aggressive. I was very much aware that I could now loose all my money, clothes or even my life.

Err Mo I shout after him. Yes? My bags in the car, should I take them? This neighbourhood don't look too..Mo laughs no worry my friend. It's OK now come come Luke. Again repeating the words as he skips swiftly up the steps, disappearing around a corner and out of sight. I take a last long look around me, deserted streets dark dusty and dingy with dogs barking, and the smell of burning rubbish with the odd street light in the distance with flies swarming all over it.

Welcome to Kathmandu I muttered. I follow him in! Slowly I climbed the dark wet mosquito infested steps, it's very dark and I can just about make out the steps. I was bitten on the arms and legs by the mosquitoes before even reaching the door on which Mo is knocking. He looks at me and smiles and gently he sways his head from side to side! Inshallah he will be home! Inshallah I need a joint.

This is it, the handle slowly turns then the door swings open! Revealing... a teenage girl! I smile and try to look normal. The young girl shouts out to someone before Mo ushers me inside, now I'm standing in some family's home. An old wise man appears! No other way to describe him as that's exactly what you would call him if you saw him, his hair is long and silver with a smiling brown skinned leather cracked face.

Tea? I accept and he calls out to who I presume to be his wife, he speaks to Mo then produces a briefcase

19

filled with forms which he begins filling in. I am not going to be killed today after all... He looks up at me from the floor where he has sat cross legged, and then he speaks in the little English he knows! How man days you Mr? He asks pointing at my chest with the pen.

Two! OK? I ask holding up two fingers! OK ok the old man say's scribbling. Mo is happily chatting to the family! He needs your passport. Huh oh ok I hand them over, he bows copy's the serial numbers on my passport on to his forms then hands them back. You sign.... he says loudly handing me a pen! I sign, he tears along the edge and hands me back the slips. I hand him the cash and it's a done deal. The tea is served, quickly we drink up. We say our goodbyes and within minutes are back on the road.

In no time we are at the hotel. On arrival I grab my bags from the car, then accompanied by Mo walk into the very same hotel and go to the very same receptionist I spoke to an hour earlier. I produce the recites the wise one had given me, the woman smiles and accepts! I book in, sign the forms quick flash of the old passport, and I'm handed the keys to my room.

OK Mr you want me to take you for some food you? Smiles Mo! Can you give me an hour? No problem, see you then. I put down my bags, lay on the bed and turn the TV on, this place is crazy I laugh to myself. Soldiers guns half price rooms, the travelling is done for now after my twelve hour flight, now the fun begins. Brandon then Mo who else? I relax as I begin rolling a joint of tobacco and mix in a little grass I had stuffed into a sock in my bag, not the most sensible move I admit but when you're a stoner like me sensibilities are a luxury you can seldom afford.

I open the window and smoke the joint looking at the amazing multi coloured garden lit up by the hotels night lights! With weed your mind wonders....your brain expands. I meditate as the cranial nerve endings crystals collide with the THC crystals of the weed and my minds portals are opened. Enlightened and Illuminated I enter what is known as level one of the psychedelic experience....the left and right side of the brains commutation channels switch over.

The magnetic becomes electric, the masculine becoming feminine! You see Entheogens takes you to places you haven't been, and never can go to without.....the colours of the garden changed becoming a visual master piece Van Gogh himself would have been proud of! Then the what if's arrive! What if MO was Al Qaeda! What time is it? Wonder what time is it back home? I wonder how mom and dad are doing. How did Brandon know I was a stoner! Who really was Brandon Huckabee? Was he the CIA? I laughed at myself fucking jet lag. Who cares your safe now Luke. You made it I tell myself as I lie back on my bed, if only I knew.

The Top of the World

The phone rang! Hello Mr Luke? Yes! You come now. Why? Hello hello! That wasn't an hour was it? Emerging into the warm evening air a few minutes later Mo approached. OK Mr Luke where you wan go tonight huh? Do you know a good place for dinner? I pull out and open up the traveller bible. Err what or where is Thamel Mo? No Mr Luke you no want to go Thamel not at night. No? Too much trouble, soldiers, police, he says pulling a face.

Bad vibes Eh? You want dinner OK I bring you to the legend of Kathmandu Mr Luke! A short drive later we pulled up outside a narrow row of wooden buildings, five or six stories high. They look like they could all fall down at any moment, if from nothing else but from the sheer number of bulky thick telephone cables that seem to line every street in the city.

Mo pulls up the handbrake! You see the legend of Kathmandu! It is? Yes.... All I see is shops plus it looks like business is over for the day! No you look... what that small door in between two shops? Yes is open, bar and restaurant upstairs very good you love! Sure? Yes sure I give you The Rum-doddle! Mo says with a huge grin and wave of the hand.

Looks sort of dodgy to me. In there you will meet all kind of traveller from west, south east and north. Err its actually oh never mind Mo. Some will say crazy things..Like what? He looks around to see if anyone's listening, makes a gesture to indicate I come closer Some may tell you they have seen the Yeti he whispers nodding while staring into my eyes with a dead serious expression, so serious in fact that I am bound to take it as such and not burst into fits of laughter which I really struggle not to do.

A Yeti? I mean the one and only? Yes! Again I stifle the urge to laugh. Yeti I repeat thinking am I hearing things or has the joint and jet lag combo mashed my mind so much that now I am hearing things. Yes the fucking Yeti! Mo says getting real excited; he is a big huge snow monster half human half ape! Puffing out his own chest to get his point across! White furry body.

Yes Mo look yes ok I've heard of the yeti! Calm down its cool. I will go and check it out. I exit the car and look over at the crumbling building. OK Luke now you go have good time, drink lots of Everest beer. I will wait here no problem.

Did he say Everest beer? I wonder as I saunter across the street and look at the front door and creaking old wooden staircase! Can't be as bad as the old wise mans house I tell myself and walk up and open the door, as I do soft seventies style reggae is playing giving it a nice ambient vibe. It's filled with tourists mainly! The accents hit me hard and fast.

I hear Canadians loud Americans over friendly Aussie's whilst some quite Japanese sit in the corner! Nationalities from just about everywhere in between. All sharing story's of adventure from the back packer trails. I waltz in and I grab a seat and take in my surroundings. From behind the bar the waitress shouts, what would you like? Err an Everest? I shout back.

She comes over and flings down a rather odd looking beer mat. White and in the shape of a foot print! Yeti's footprint and she places my Everest on top! I look up at her but say nothing just smile. The walls are not adorned with pictures of past drunkenness and revelry but the Yeti beer mats she just put down, thousands of them which people sign before they go off trekking up the mountains or the big one climbing Everest itself.

They write their names dates and nationalities on them, some even colour in their nation's flag! You can see Italian Greek Israeli and a whole heap of other nation's flags drawn on the beer mats. This is ground zero for the Mt Everest crowd, the last pit stop of normality humanity and luxury before taking that final plunge into the unknown! The last opportunity to live and savour the good times before the possibility that the grim reaper might just make an appearance in the coming days.

A sign on a wall proclaims **Namaste** 'This is the best bar in the world' that's original I tell myself. It is.... Huh oh you frightened me! Sorry didn't mean too, where are you from? The waitress asks. London! OK we get quite a few from there! Really? Yeah, want something to eat? Yeti burger and fries, you got it mate she laughed.

Everest beer and a Yeti burger...don't get better than this I laughed taking a swig of my grog.   Looking around I watched as the Japanese got up and went upstairs followed by the big loud mouth Canadian! I knew he was a Canadian as he was wearing a massive maple leaf t-shirt and was boasting about something or other as I came in. In fact he was one of the first people I heard.

My food arrived and it looked like a regular burger in case you're wondering, nice but I kind of felt a bit let down. I wanted it to taste I don't know, different, the waitress came back. Anything else? No thank you, actually err excuse me yes there is something, what is it? What's up the stairs? I asked pointing up! Our roof terrace! Feel free to go up if you want. So I did and walked out into a fantastic view. Hey dude welcome to the top of the world! Bawled out the Canadian with a big grin. I smiled and grabbed a seat and took in the view without saying a word. But clearly my lips were moving as next thing I knew I'm being asked.

Who are you talking to dude? Huh who me? No brother I'm talking to the abominable snowman, he says with a grin. Was I talking to myself again? Its ten thousand feet up here bro and your talking to yourself, says the heavily stoned and tattooed Japanese dude. Sorry mate it's the jet-lag! No worries bro but if you ask me it's this altitude. Once you don't start answering yourself back you know, having arguments and shit then it's all good! We all laugh.

Smoke? He offers me the joint in his hand! I gratefully accept it with a nod and a smile; and suck on it. Unbeknown I've just inhaled a lungful of the sweetest black Nepalese! Holy shit I splutter in between fits of coughing, blowing back out the sweet tasting smoke through my nose and mouth, what the hell is that? I ask. He leans forward..His eyes blazing red...it's one hundred percent pure Nepalese temple ball my friend. He says slowly, then from inside his pocket he takes out a round lump about the size of a tennis ball, unwraps the cling-film to revile a sticky ball of black hashish that glistens in the moonlight. Like a star in the night sky it sparkles, the aroma hitting me like an invisible wave as it wafts upwards.

Whoa fucking hell mate look at the size of that! I blurt out sending myself into a slight coughing fit, mind if I take a closer look? I pass the joint over to the giggling Japanese girl next to him. She takes one puff then hands it straight back to me, confused I offer it back to the tattooed guy, but he declines as he re-warps the temple ball. So I look towards the Canadian who shakes his head, so with no one else wanting it I stick it back in my mouth and consider it all mine, nice...

Names Mitsu, Mitsu? I repeat making sure I got it correct, as in Mitsubishi? Yup. OK my names Luke pleased to make your acquaintance! Mitsu laughs! What? Luke sky-walker! He tells the girl something in Japanese, then yet again she giggles. Looking away from me she indicates for him to put some hash in a joint she's been rolling, he gently heats the ball before sprinkling a little on top of the tobacco she's holding. Never thought of my name like that before to be honest I say stubbing out the joint he gave me.

Err how much did that big boy cost you? I say indicating towards the ball of hashish he is juggling in his hand. About a hundred US dollars, he shrugs! Not sure the cost in rupees or yen or whatever, can't be bothered to work it out! The girl spark's up the joint, yet again takes one drag before passing it to me. I look at Mitsu but he looks away, so I continue to smoke even though I can feel I'm going to get completely wasted. But in case it is some initiation at worst or downright anti-social at best I just get on it.

That must be the size of an orange, we watch as he juggles it up and down in the air!

Must be about......Five ounces I reckon. Yeah..too dam bad he won't shear any of it, says a voice. Turning I see the big Canadian smile. As his monstrous frame stands and moves towards us! Shove up he barks, as he moves in closer and squeezes his giant backside in between us. Well can I have a toke off of that baby or what brother he asks taking a swig from a beer in his left hand. I look at Mitsu who nods.

I pass it to him and he inhales a month's worth! We watch in silence as the joint literally burns half way down. With sparks and ash dropping while he keeps on sucking till his giant lungs are expanded to bursting point! Blowing it back out he nods his head in satisfaction, not bad not bad at all, looking both left and right at both of us with a grin on his face, but the shit we got back in Canada! It is way better........ I am sure it is mate.

So what are you doing here bro, climbing Everest? Nah. I knew it! How? You don't look the type plus you're a smoker, smokers don't do dumb shit like climb Everest! What about you? I asked. Me? Fucking adventure man, fucking adventure and lots of it he laughed as did the others, right on Mitsu smiled and high fived me, well that makes four of us then.

Names Barry he says shaking our hands! Luke I nod. Mitsu! And this is Natsumi! Don't say much does she? I say to Mitsu! Nah the old English isn't too hot. I thought you guys knew each other? Nope! So how did you get all the way up here Barry? Planes trains and auto-mo fucking-bales he replies mimicking a deep southern accent! I can only laugh I'm so stoned... I should have seen that coming! Hell yeah Barry shouts.

When did you arrive up here then? Today! Three days ago Mitsu says. Wow so you guys just got into town then? When are you heading back to Canada Mitsu asks, Few weeks I suppose. Been travelling about long? He then either ignores me or didn't hear my question and stares up at the stars, it was a fantastically clear night sky I must admit, and with so many stars it was impossible to count.

So I too just looked up for a while! It was bliss. A guy once told me. Barry said pointing up at the heavens! That what we see when we look up at the night sky, is the atoms of the brain of the creator. What all trillions of them? Yeah every one of them is inside us Luke, think of it like when you look at strands of DNA..... It's where we come from, and if the portals, the star gates are open, we ascend and we go home. If not we are bounced back down by Saturn! The lord of rings.......Whoa mate that's heavy! Isn't it Mitsu added.

27

Yeah, sorry about the head fuck guys. Anyway I am going to try and make my money last me until April! It should be a bit warmer back home by then. I'm sort of getting used to the heat now, he smiles as he stubbed out the joint. Oh shit! What? I have a taxi waiting outside for me, guys I forgot all about him. I must dash....what the hell for? Don't know to be honest.

Well then get the hell rid of him! You don't need him to figure your way around here.

All right then I will, but tonight I need a good night's rest so I will get him to take me back to the hotel, you guys back here tomorrow? I will be here around lunch time Barry replies. We only get up at that time! So to us it will be breakfast time jokes Mitsu.

OK cool see you guys later. I go down the stairs into the bar and I pay the bill, as I wait for my change I feel a vibe that all's gone quite, looking around at the men next to me. All in their early forties, two have beards one has a goatee, they look strangely out of place. Like I don't know but definitely not the climbing type that leave's the hippy type but they don't sort of look that way either. Dam I am stoned and judging people again, the waitress hands me my change, it's a creeper is it? She laughs! Huh what is? She winks, the penny drops, yeah I smile and leave...

On the street below stoned and ever so slightly baffled I stare up at the sky! The Atoms are the ....Man what a night! I see a car headlight flashing me. Its Mo, did you enjoy the rummy doggle? Yes it was fun I answer as we drove off down the narrow streets. Now you got to understand driving albeit either as a passenger or not is one of the most surreal things one could ever do in this life when completely stoned on Nepalese temple ball.

But to do it in Kathmandu is literally out of this

world! We pass a place with lots of soldiers hanging about. That is Durbar square! Tomorrow I can take you there lots of...Err yes about tomorrow... actually I will be going to eh I mean I will be able to make my own way tomorrow. OK up to you he answers with a tingle of disappointment in his voice.

We pull up outside the hotel after what seemed like ages and I gave him the ten dollars we agreed. Thank you for your services Mo but I am going to be here a long time and need my money to last. I hope you understand. You have been a great help today thank you. I understand Luke I hope enjoy my country. We shake hands. And as would become the norm I'd learn to accept during my travels I'd, meet someone. They're in your life for a few short hours, days a week maybe, then gone just like that! Just as quick as they came into my life they would vanish. Never to be seen again except in memory.

He jumped into his car, waved then drove off into the night. Leaving one very tired and weary plus superbly stoned safe and grateful soul standing on the hotel steps. Next morning I woke looking at the ceiling starved. I showered and went downstairs for breakfast. As I Passed the receptionist she looks, so I smile, she bows, the breakfast room I then discover had its doors locked. What's wrong with the breakfast room?

Nothing is wrong. She answered! Well it isn't open...That's because the staff are not here.

Oh why not? Because it's five am! Only then did I check the time. My watch is not adjusted yet I mumble. I can send coffee to your room if you want? Err yes I mean no. Not really wanting to go back into my room plus I'd already showered so I accept the coffee offer but request for it outside in the garden. Why not! She said with a smile.

I walk outside passing the old bell boy sleeping on the ground. It's just after five so the crickets are still making noise, as are the geckos running about. A shine spreads across the lawn forming the morning dew. I sit on a bench and take in my first morning in Asia! A waiter arrives with my coffee and I slowly sip it as I watch the sun rise.

Then for some reason out of nowhere my grandfather comes to mind. Whoosh... in an instant I'm catapulted back to my childhood, as a kid I grew up in a large house with both my parents and grandparents, unconventional I know but it worked for us and we were all one big happy family. As the eldest I can remember more than my siblings those good times.

My grandfather used to run his own grocery store and would be up around dawn, never later to have a cup of strong black coffee accompanied by a cigarette. This was his breakfast. I would quietly get up to sit with him at dawn every morning while everyone else was sleeping! Even today I like to get up before everyone else for some unknown reason.

Sitting there I'd study him silently smoking his cigarette! Whilst he looked straight ahead in deep thought, in the movies old guys always seem to have some wise words for the young but not my grandpa. Neither of us ever spoke at that hour, so we used to both just sit there staring at nothing, with me happy to experience being up when everyone else wasn't, him I suppose grateful that the little feller wasn't asking him questions at this hour.

He would always spill a little coffee down the side of his cup, until a small pool was floating on the saucer, he would then hand the saucer to me! Holding it with both my little hands I would happily slurp it down my five year old throat! My taste for stimulants began young I guess you could say.

I smiled as the tiny makings of a tear formed in my eye as I thought of him that morning. How strange the human mind when something as simple as a quite coffee alone can bring back such a vivid memory you thought was once locked away and gone forever! I visit his grave when I can, but strangely never ever thought of our shared coffee mornings till my first morning in Kathmandu.

A bell ringing brings me back to reality and turning around I see the receptionist wave to indicate the breakfast hall is open. I was outside in deep thought nearly an hour wow! I ate and then grabbed a few bits from my room before exiting the hotel with a local map in my hand and cash in my pocket. I set about exploring Kathmandu on foot.

I make my way to the local markets to purchase some more bits and pieces then I go walk about the famous Durbar square! Saw the big bell and famous big drum! Then lunchtime I decide to hit the rum doggle to see what's up. What a difference day time makes! No crowds at the counter. No loud drunks boasting and no eyeballing in fact it's completely empty.

Hello I say to the waitress! Hi, behind me the door swings open and in walks the big man himself! Hey Barry how are you? He nods grunts orders a coffee and sits down next to me. Make it two coffee's. Look I understand this might sound strange Luke, but I just don't want go home man, you understand? Like never? Yeah like never, the waitress brings the coffee, why mate what's up?

Luke I've learned on my travels, this journey this voyage of self-discovery, is we have all been lied to from day one man! Eh ok...Look listen to me Luke! When you travel, on your own for long enough your mind! It will change bro. It will, it opens up allowing new things in, things that previously you would not entertain. The stuff you will see and experience...you have just begun to travel on your own correct? Yeah correct mate.

We are all human Luke remember that. Err sure.....the only differences are in the way we look and communicate. I mean we all want a nice life, no war in our country shelter food that's it right? Err I guess.... But this system is designed to programme us how to think man, you don't get it yet but you will, how we react, how we view the world around us the people in it! Barry I am kind of getting lost here.

That same system is designed to make us believe that we need shit we do not really need Luke! Banging his fist down on the table...Whoa dude chill! Listen ok sorry I didn't mean to ...but but I've seen so many bad things, Like what? Like suffering and... OK back home I've got this big screen TV, a four wheel drive. I could go on man. I really could but I have quite literally got tons and tons of shit that I basically do not need, you know to really survive.

Of course Barry mate but needing and wanting or surviving are completely different things. Luke we are born and raised in the west to be consumers, to be consumer slaves! Debt slaves if you will. Just keep on buying shit. Encouraged to keep up with the Jones's by this evil monster called capitalism....oh ok I see, you do? Yeah.....

Our masters are corporations! Know what a Corp is Luke? Not really but I am sure your...it's like a person but it's not. It's dead as in corpse and it can sue you or it can be sued, it can get a loan, it can even get a fucking mortgage can you believe that shit? But ultimately if the shit hits the fan, it's got its board of guys on it making the moves so no one dude goes down! It's like a perfect criminal. They will destroy a nations natural resources like the machine it is, no heart no feelings just profit and we my friend are their fucking slaves.

But these are things that make our world easier, more convenient Barry! True, or so it seems in this illusion they have created. Luke the system has made modern day slaves out of every man woman and child on the planet! You can't see that yet but you will. They keep the people in the third world dirt poor, so they have to make this shit for us, just so to be able to survive. They are born to be the big Corps worker slaves, like ants.

That's a bit much Barry! Not so Luke, not at all, when you consider we too are slaves of the Corporations. We are? Of course, but we are the consumer slaves, we work ourselves needlessly hard but not to survive. No..... we are the lucky ones we work just to buy more shit we don't need, we're as they work themselves hard just to survive, whilst our politicians fool us into thinking these are just badly run countries, with tin pot economic advisers.

Then we have democracy which is basically mob rule as fifty one percent of the populace can tell the other forty nine percent what to do, and hey it's real easy to fool most of the people. So hey presto we are indoctrinated into believing we have real democracy! We don't? Hell no bro if we had democracy it would be like if eighty percent voted for something. I hear you bro honest I do. You don't! I do. Do you realise we are the only living creature that pays to live on our planet? You do realise that don't you? Never thought much about it to be honest but now you mention it.

Guess if I spoke to my granddad now, you know if he was still around and told him hey at night time the family don't talk no more, we sit in darkened rooms staring into screens he would think the worlds gone crazy! Barry lights up a smoke. He'd be right Luke! He'd be Dam right...Think about it who wants to fucking work? I mean there's a fucked up concept if ever there was one. Know what job stands for? Tell me Barry. 'just over broke' because that's the way the bastards will keep you.

Humans need food shelter and chill with their family end of fucking story! You got a point Baz! But no sir, media hammers home the message on a daily basis about how he is a hard worker or she is a hard worker! Must work harder! Not working hard enough. But who's going to raise the kids mind the family, teach them etc? Err the state I suggest! Correct and they teach them to be consumers with no time for meditating on just why the fuck we are here or where we even came from. Or more importantly! Where we must return too.

Where we must return to? The door swings open! Mitsu and Natsumi walk in. Hey swashbucklers says Mitsu taking off his shades, placing his smart phone, MP3 and other assorted bits on the table. See what I mean? Barry winks. I smile. They order a Japanese breakfast! What did you get up to this morning or did you just chill in the hotel? Stay in the hotel are you kidding me? Been on the road since sunrise mate, been to the square then up to see the statue of Vishnu or someone! In and out of temples the lot you name it I have done it well at least I think I have. Yeah there are enough temples in this place to keep you busy for year's man, if that's your thing.

Temple this, Pagoda that! Says Barry, he is loud at times, rude at others but inside I sense a deeply rational yet unconventionally Illuminated individual, an eccentric modern day philosopher, a rebel crusader battling the moral scales of justice balancing his soul on one hand, heart on the other. Either that or the guilt complex of a western consumer slave that will recede in time once he is on home soil. Last day in Kathmandu announces Mitsu! Are you going home? No we are off across the mountains in the morning! Where too? To Lhasa! OK by bus or what? I think it's by bus. Why do you want to come? If we all go we can get a jeep, works out cheaper.

Then I remember Brandon telling me go to Lhasa! What'd you think? Natsumi pokes my side laughing. Err yeah sure I'm into it! OK good but the guide said each Jeep needs a minimum of four. I will go if you need an extra body Barry says! What really? Yup! Besides I haven't seen Lhasa! Are you serious? Does a yak fart? Err yes, of course I'm serious I'm game if you are Luke! Mitsu stood up...I sense adventure people. I sense big time adventure and as such declare a toast to adventure and err coffee.

Joys of Backpacking

The taxi pulled up outside the tour shop and the startled owner looked up from his computer as we rush in! Hi Mitsu! My friends and I would like to go to Lhasa! To Lhasa? Yes, by Jeep....Eh ok I must just make a call, he speaks as he looks us over then put's the phone down, it will cost one thousand dollar! No problem we tell him. I need deposit! No problem we hand over some cash and promise to come back later with the rest. ..OK, Jeep will collect you five thirty from your hotel in the morning! Don't be late. But you must pay me before eight tonight to confirm.

Also you must have two passport sized photos each for Chinese border! He smiles.

We look at him, then each other then back at him! Chinese administrators, very tough he smiles. Outside we make plans to link up later; we shake hands and go our separate ways.

After walking around town I find a place to get my photos. Then after a short international call service were I chatted about the usual stuff telling them I am safe, no attempted kidnappings and so on. I mention I've meet folks and we're going off on an adventure of sorts. I just don't make it sound that way. Then I decide to chill have a coffee and reflect on the words and voices of my family. I have a smoke, sip an espresso watching the world walk past. I feel the day's activities have caught up with me and with jet-lag lurking like a hyena waiting to pounce the nicotine and caffeine double whammy was just what I needed.

I make my way over to the shop and pay the balance. OK. Its seven day journey! Seven days? Yes what you think this is Luke a picnic? But err..All fares, he interrupts, as well as best available guest-house's breakfasts are included, as are the local guide and translator service. Translator service what do you mean translator service? His eyebrow rises, jeep driver can translate OK.

But what …Now all you pay is sixty dollars! Sixty more for what? Chinese immigration…OK Luke everything else up to you. Now good luck and make sure you are outside hotel at five thirty! But em…it a long drive to Chinese border Mr and if it's closed you sleep in the Jeep! Very cold, most uncomfortable, you no like trust me. He gave me his card. Anyone give you trouble…. contact me! Thanks Bro.

Back in my room I roll a joint, lie back on the bed staring at the ceiling smoking with the breeze gently shaking the curtains. I find myself drifting off to another world, this 'other world' is back home, my real life back home. I see it…like a crystal ball…hey there's my family my friends but strangely it seems like, like another world to me, another time place dimension call it what you like. It's like I could be watching someone else's life, a surreal out of body type experience I can't describe.

All I can do is laugh as I vividly watch myself going about my daily life. Barry got a point you know! We have been brainwashed, conditioned to think a certain way! Years later on reflection I realised that when you travel, especially on your own and I mean really travel…. for a long period of time to a far off lands, what you leave behind is… another dimension, your soul stays at home, but your body the physical that's what actually travel's. Ever notice how every person that's ever emigrated will talk to you about the good old days back home? Their soul is still there, it never even left.

I smile every time someone younger than me talks about the good old days, for them yes they are, but only in 'their reality, their concept of time' it will always will be the good old days to them! They have punched through the apple....Creating the wormhole that is travel-time or time-travel depending on your perspective. Travelling be it backpacking or whatever is the ultimate freedom, a freedom from studies or work, from a partner or spouse maybe or from kids or even parents, it is the ultimate human freedom.

That life back home has only hit the pause button momentarily, eagerly awaiting your return to continue like you never even left, of course the memories and experience's that you return with will also never leave you. That's part of the whole wormhole effect...then it comes to me in a flash, in an instant out of nowhere I realise..Man I'm stoned, and fall into a deep sweet sleep.

The phone rings! Hello....speaking clocking fuck, time to go, quick wash, packed last night! Downstairs checking out when on the button transport arrives! The driver hops out, all five feet of him! He smiles I smile. I am your tour guide he says grabbing my bags placing them in the back of the Jeep. Come come we hab no time to lose.. man ....jump!

I jump in, a short detour later to pick up Barry, Mitsu and Nat and were on the road out of Kathmandu as the driver floors it. Getting out of Kathmandu is a nightmare after six in the morning, so I am trying to get us all out and onto the main highway before rush hour, he shouts. These little narrow streets you see go for at least ten km before highway. So we cannot lose vital time to reach border.

OK dude....Yes no problem Mr, besides we also have to make up time in case of natural disaster! Disaster? I shout..What kind of disaster? Landslides! Oh I thought when you said disaster you, oh never mind, a landslide isn't that bad is it? I say looking at Mitsu ...That's all you think, he says under his breath looking out his window as the Jeep snakes its way through the maze of ancient narrow lanes. Passing workers and monks in bright orange robes out early to collect their alms.

This morning is the first time I have actually felt like a proper traveller. This here is the real deal, sense and sensibilities out the window, as I'm off into the unknown the un-travelled in search of adventure with strangers I have only just met. To an eventual outcome I cannot possibly fathom! Now we're talking adventure I tell myself as we stop for Gas. I get out take a deep breath staring at the long wide road ahead, it rises up and up into the mountains, disappearing into the clouds or fog, we will be there a few hours' time I tell myself! I hope it's a good ride.

Looking over at Barry I see one of the points he tried so hard to make me understand yesterday! Barry I was blind but now I can see! Huh? I'm glad I meet you guys. Luke. Yes? Drink some fucking coffee. How long more to the Chinese border? I ask the driver, maybe four hours, depends on Buddha! OK not bad...Somehow we make it to the border on time entering over a dodgy bridge with the biggest Chinese flag in bright red you ever saw with the immortal words Welcome to China... No Photos allowed.

Then for six days we travel unwashed in cramped conditions, smoking our brains out. Eradicating Mitsu temple ball to the point that we could barely speak at times. Well ok most of the time and at those moments we would observe and meditate in silence as we travelled through wild and exotic lands and funky named places like....The La-Lung-la pass or the Kam-Ba-La Pass....Shigatse and narrowly missing such local cultural delights such as the 'exorcism' festival! We laughed in the face of plunging temperatures horrific death deifying roads, vultures and some of the worst food imaginable! You name it we faced it, and you're wondering why we got stoned? Bless you Mother Nature for Marijuana.

Yamdrok Tso

On the last day we arrived at lake Yam-Drok Tso. We walked up the hill a few hundred feet
from where the Jeeps were parked below, so we could check out the lake from a good vantage point! We left Nat inside talking to the driver as she wasn't interested in the view.

This beautiful turquoise lake is situated at an altitude of a little over four thousand four hundred meters above sea level, the largest freshwater lake south of the Himalayas. In fact when looked on from the above nearby mountains it appears like a holy sapphire! Situated in between snow-capped mountains it offers heavenly tranquillity to those seeking it, a place so alluring to the human eye it's hard to describe. The distant sound of yak's bells and howling wind competed for dominance as we took in the surrounding landscape.

To die-hard stoners like ourselves it was all the more awesome. Mitsu took out his water bong out of his rucksack and filled it with water from a nearby stream flowing down from the Himalayas! I stood in awe knowing I would never witness this again and savoured every last second. Looking out as far as the eye could see this amazingly beautiful land, like something from another world or sci-fi movie, no trees just this beautiful timeless lake that seemed to just sit still, like an Oasis.

Mitsu produced his shrinking ball of glistening black Nepalese, heated it enough for it to begin to crumble into a fluffy gold powder....its luscious smell wafting through the crisp clear Himalayan air, the beautiful aroma that only comes from unprocessed unadulterated hashish. I ripped up a cigarette and sprinkled some of it onto the foil that he had been placed on the bong....doing my bit as he placed the once black but now golden brown hashish powder atop.

He lit it, taking a huge lungful before quickly passing it on. Now for anyone who never used a bong the only real issue with bongs is unlike a joint they go out in seconds, so you got to keep the flame more or less constant till it's gone. The hit is instant and can be very powerful and at times almost too intense depending on the type smoked! Whoa bro that's hit me like, like, like I don't know what! Barry said as he grinned from ear to ear. I grin too because I know how he is feeling deep inside. Mitsu grins as well as we do a three wise monkey impersonation.

Stubbornly and with eyes blazing red. Barry this time absolutely packs out the bong, adding even more hashish sprinkling in several lumps that would easily cost ten bucks each back home! My mental reply being Nooooo please haven't we had enough for fucks sake? But no words come out! Going to have to front this out...yeah just leave them smoke it first I tell myself, then I can pretend to smoke but blow it out the corner of my mouth. Yeah then they'll be too out of it to realise if I inhaled or blew it back out via my nose, smoking but not inhaling. If ever there was a understated phrase and original sentence you got to give Bill Clinton the kudos he deserves when he made that one up. I wonder did he even realise just how much he was writing himself into the annals of Marijuana culture when he said it.

Now I don't know if Barry was so stoned he didn't know what he was doing or just plain old bravado? But I watched in amazement nonetheless as he brought this monster to life, a mushroom cloud of smoke rose up high around his head. We took it in turns to pass it around. I did always consider myself a team player, so now sitting content we laughed and joked about silly things grinning like escaped loons from an asylum. It was then I noticed something peculiar...the once louder and louder clanging sound of the yaks bells had ceased.

Something told me look behind but before I could an almighty roar from a man with a deep loud voice. Shouting in an accent I couldn't comprehend, scary deep angry violent hate filled words slash...slash. Our grins faded as we looked at each other in terror as we stumbled from our seats.. Looking at each other we began to shake, mouths open, what did he say?

Holding onto each other in fear. He continued! Slash slash-his-eye......he bawled in short fast bursts.... Dudes talking about slashing people's eyes out and shit. Barry said as he picked up a big rock from the ground. I panicked copying that move by also picking one up....In front of us was a Dread. A Rasta-man, the accent that's confusing us was Jamaican! He bawled out again with Barry now about to lose all rational thinking.

He dropped the stone and picked up a huge rock hoisting it over his head instead with both hands. Mitsu points his bong at him...But the guy wasn't aggressive I could see he posed no threat, hang on guys.....what Barry asked. It's happiness we are hearing. Listen...Realising the smoke and the altitude had made things awkward, foggy to figure out at times. Then with his arms outstretched he again said the same words yet this time it was more audible.

Barry. What? Put the fucking rock down! Are you so fucking out of it Luke that....Look mate he means no harm! What? I'm serious mate trust me..Trust you? We met three fucking days ago now we're in the middle of the wilderness with a madman screaming murder and you want me to trust you! He is not a madman. Well he looks like one to me and Barry..Barry...it's cool trust me ok. I look him in the eye, please mate lower the rock.

43

But what if he's a terrorist Luke? He isn't a terrorist Mitsu I say grinding my teeth! Just how the fuck do you know? Cause em well... look he is smiling for one! What the fucks that got to do with it Luke? Terrorists smile all the time! He is not a total fucking loon and besides what's a Rasta doing here? He actually looks glad or slightly happy I think to see us.

Selassie I. he smiles placing his hand across his chest! OK time out Barry. But what is a dread doing right now, here in the middle of Tibet wondering about on a fucking yak? In fact just what the fuck would anyone be doing just wondering about here? Well you could just ask what the fuck we are doing here? We're not wondering about alone on a fucking yak are we bro? Man this stuff is too strong I am beginning to trip out and Imagine shit......

Selassie I he repeats as the sound bounces and echoes all around the lake and nearby hills repeating itself over and over to the point that several minutes later we could still hear it. Selassie I. Hi there my names....... greetings in the name of his imperial majesty emperor Haile Selassie I King of Kings, Lord of Lords, the Conquering Lion of the Tribe OF Judah.... Jah ...RasTaFari.....we stare at him mouths hanging open, he smiles a massive beaming smile back at us. I don't know about you guys but that's the most intense buzz I'd ever just had...What?

Greetings baldhead.......Huh, who me? I point at my chest with one hand whilst rubbing my head subconsciously with the other! Yes you sir. The three of us just stare back at this guy though our bloodshot eyes, dry mouths open. The Rastafarian with his locks hidden beneath a white beanie hat stands. Yup most intense hit ever Barry says nodding his head! Err so who is this guy? Mitsu says whispering through the corner of his mouth? He is a dread. I know what he is Barry just not who why or fucking what the hell he doing here.

Look Mitsu I've just about had it with your rudeness...You have, have you? Yes I have, and why the fuck are you whispering? I don't know if he is more surprised to find us or we him? Dressed all in white his hand connected to a rope which is attached to his yak! Who carries all his worldly possessions. He has painted the yaks horns red green and gold, the colours of Ethiopia.

Greetings I. Err hello, is all I can think of saying back. Good-day.... Barry says but it's Mitsu who is more straight to the point in asking what we are all thinking! Just who the hell are you? My name is Gilbert he says taking a bow! Gilbert? Yeah man but you can call me Ras! So which is it then? Gilbert or Ras? Well Mr Ras do you think it's cool to creep up on people when... then ignoring Barry's and Mitsu line of questioning, upon seeing the bong grins a mischievous grin! Herbalist I? Yet you speak with the tongue of a soldier of Babylon, Huh?

Me say me see you are herbalist I? He says pointing at our chests one by one! His eyes scanning our faces. Oh err yeah were caners alright dude. Barry laughs, the same herb as spoken about in the scriptures I? Excuse me...I reply. Yes sir and for 'the sheep shall hear of the Father.....and return to the pasture' he says with his huge grin. What did he mean em... I ask looking around but their sat staring straight ahead of them.

Can me beg you a smoke from the chill-um? Indicating for the pipe to be handed to him! Me nah smoke long time, he grinned....with no one else seemingly able to understanding what he was saying, I begun to translate, Mitsu he wants to smoke the bong mate. How do you know? Because I'm from London! What has that got to do with anything? Look trust me

45

give him the bong. I don't have time to explain. Luke trust is an expensive luxury and I'm fast running out of cash and...............................

'And the wolves in sheep's clothing cannot fool us,
for their very souls are at stake.....
for the wicked shall perish off the face of the Earth.....
but the righteousness shall be forever''

he said interrupting our conversation as he walked back and forth. At which point Mitsu handed over the bong, would you like some hash with that? I got some nice temple ball.

Respect. We watched as he slowly and carefully.... almost religiously began filling the bong, stopping occasionally mumbling words sometimes upwards to the sky! We all looked up, then back down, back up. Then at each other, then look back at him again, all very funky deep cool shit but we didn't understand a single bit of what he was actually talking about when he did talk.

Mankind must learn to respect the herb you understand? We nod back mouths open. You see what was trans-muted down here to mother earth by Jah, to work in cohort with the soul. The souls of man, of Solomon, to help nurture Solomon's temple. This here sacred herb was given a divine purpose, this simple peaceful plant you understand. This gift must be respected....... Jah Rastafari: Eternal God Selassie I. He passed along the bong to me. I indulged before passing it.

For when the time had appeared for Jah to return. The supreme angel commanded the chariot of heaven to meet him.... And when the chariot appeared unto Elijah, he ascended and returned to his throne in heaven where he reigned from the beginning and shall do unto the end of time. King of kings. God of gods.

Where are you from Ras? Barry asks.....Mount

Zion...Holy mount Zion! What in Israel? Or Egypt? I think you'll find mount zion is just outside Jerusalem! Shut up Mitsu Mount Zion is in the Sinai desert everyone knows that! No its not. Yes it is! Where else does the zion bit come from? You see Sinai....zion..quite easy to figure out really duh...My head darts back and forth between the two......Bullshit man Zion and Sinai don't sound anything alike! Yeah man there are a few of them it's true! Ras say's getting involved in the debate. But the Chinaman is most correct. Huh chinaman? Bro I am Japanese.

But the one written about in the bible, he continues without even acknowledging Mitsu's complaint. It is just a little bit just outside Kingston! Kingston? Inquires Barry. Yeah man. Jamaica? Yeah man! Objection! Huh? No its not! I bark, it can't be, the one in the bible is in, well it's in Jerusalem I think. No disrepute..I mean eh respect but I tend not to argue unless I'm almost certain I'm correct, and I am pretty fucking certain, in fact it might even have been the original name of the city.

Do not let Babylon mash up your mind man. He says passionately looking at me. For you see they want you to believe nothing good can come out a Jamaica yeah know! Oh I see. But that a wicked lie man! He hisses angrily. Then lowering his voice to the point we're we need to strain and move closer to listen to him he continues. Holy mount zion ....is not a place brethren, he laughs with smoke slowly exiting both nostrils. Mount Zion ...holy mount zion is a state of consciousness! A state of mind he says pointing at his temple. This place here right now. He says standing up waving his staff about, it could be Mount Zion if you so want it to be.

Calm down Barry says. See you there big man, Jah send you here you know. Who me? Barry asks. Yeah man. I do not think so dude he says with a little laugh and shake of his head. He squats down in front of and facing Barry. Trust me brother it is of no accident this all happen you know. What happened? This place here he says looking around the hills..This very time right now right here for us all to meet. It is of no coincident at all brethren! No? I ask.....Yeah man in the midst of all this someone hands me a joint. I smoke it before offering it to Ras.

Ras or Gilbert willingly accepts taking it as soon as I offer it! Why have we met here? I ask. We have arrived at this particular moment in time at this very special place for a very special reason! What reason do you think Ras? Who knows man except Jah himself, or maybe for me to impart Selassie I teachings upon you at this time. He says smiling looking at each of us. Not at this time mate and defiantly not at this altitude. What did he say? Mitsu elbows me! Nothing! Very well then man, maybe your nah ready for enlightenment just yet but you soon will be.

He finishes off the joint. But you know it cool, when you're ready you will know. Then leaning back against a boulder he looks out yonder into the distance squinting his eyes. You do know this place here that lake below, it's the most sacred place in all Tibet? Yeah we heard that.... Yet this lake itself has no source of incoming water? Nor does it have any outlet for this very same water already in it to depart! Really? Yeah man the water bearer himself....Aquarius must deliver it, the people they come from all over this land here called Ti-bet and further afield just to drink this pure holy water.

It is said this lake it's the sister of the Buddha himself, you know why.....the people they come drink huh? Bet you can't tell me why....OK we can't. Why do they come Ras? Mitsu asks! Guidance! Guidance? Yeah man he nods....because to drink from this lake...this holy water gives the ultimate guidance as well as protection...From what? I ask looking around feeling a sudden cold chill....from what you seek protections what else? All manner of good and evil spirits...the duppies man and me a duppie conqueror.

Want to come with us? I say looking over at the others who nod approval. Why not Barry replies, the more the merrier Mitsu adds. What about Betty? I ask looking at the yak and then back at Ras as Nat begins shouting up at us to hurry. Come on guys we must go Mitsu says as he stands up, it will be dark soon. Ras yeah man? He replies looking at the Yak. Emancipate her! Mitsu laughs, come on guys lets go.

So it came that four became five. We drove and drove and then drove some more. We smoked and smoked and then smoked even more as we went up hills with landscapes resembling lunar surfaces before going nose first down gorges, across river beds with lush green vegetation. Up and around winding mountain cliff's we drove with drops so steep you didn't want to look down. Then a little after midnight the road once again became a highway and soon after a city came into site an ancient mystical city, we had arrived.

Lhasa

As we passed the city boundaries the driver slowed down to avoid arousing the security forces attention. Allowing us to see life after dark in this mystical place. The first thing you see upon entering Lhasa is the vast white fortress that soars high over one of the world's highest cities. Built into a hill it overlooks and dominates the city, a truly amazing sight that sends goose bumps over all who see it. As it has done I suspect for a very long time.

That's the Potala palace! Says Ras I was here last week. It was built in the seventh century by king Gampo......It holds the tombs of seven Dali Lama's man....Does it? Asks Barry, like mummies bro? Actually it is called the Forbidden City! Interrupts the driver, as the monks... they did not trust foreigners. But Lhasa translated directly into English does in fact mean holy city. We are now at an altitude of twelve thousand feet plus at this moment in time we are technically sitting in the middle of a river valley he-he. Can you believe that? All this and this high up yet we are actually in a valley.

None one speaks. All silent in our thoughts looking out the window as we drive to the hotel. Yes my friends the city you are now in is actually built on the bottom of a river, a basin. Right in the heart of the Himalayas! Cool huh? He says shaking his head; let me get this straight Barry say's. You're telling me we are twelve thousand feet above sea level? Yes....But were actually in the middle of a valley? Yes........Shit... hear that guys? Think about that for a moment! We are Barry, trust me we are.

We drove through the deserted dimly lit streets, coming to a halt outside a hotel. We jump out and I look up a bright pink neon sign, it illuminates the street with one word.... Oasis. Same star quality I hope. It's been a long journey, words cannot describe how much I'm looking forward to a bath and a bed man, Ras tells me as we walk into the foyer. My bath can wait till morning because I'm shattered I reply. The hotel has a small public area, a giant old fan hovers overhead spinning around very slowly making a faint humming sound. In the background behind and to the right of the reception desk is a narrow metal stairs built into the back wall of the building, at first glance I thought it were a fire escape but it's the main staircase.

The only stairs! Yes I can confirm that all in all the Oasis hotel gives a dangerously exotic and intoxicating vibe. Eventually the bell boy leads us up the narrow staircase and into a big street facing room. It has five single beds and one old brown bedside cabinet in between them, a cheap old green curtain is all that keeps the streets neo glare from blinding all who enter the room. We chuck our bags on the floor in one big heap.

Myself Ras and Barry jump on the beds we like and Nat makes for the toilet with her bag. Mitsu chucks the remaining lump of hash on the battered old table; don't just look at it, skin up! Ras and Barry both make a grab for it with Ras winning. Barry grins at him as he stretches back on the be.! He breaks off just enough and tosses the rest across to Barry who laughs as he builds a joint.

Ras prepares a chill-um, within minutes it's simultaneously being passed around as is the joint that Barry rolled! Nat comes out of the toilet and gets into bed without uttering a word, within seconds we hear her snoring. All the stress of the journey seem to just fade away in a haze of sweet smoke. Soon we're so stoned we can't even talk, then one by one we crash till all that's left is the sound of snoring. Looks like I'm the last man standing I tell myself as I out the light. I stare at the neon glare from the street outside within no time I too drift off.

I awoke to humming. Morning Ras! Luke the Elohim has blessed us with yet another day on this here his most divine of creations mother earth! He said pulling back the curtain leaving in a blinding sunlight! Ras fucking hell man... Glory be to the Faada and to the maker of

I-ration, as it were in the I-ginnin are now an shall be forever world without end.

Selah" JAH RASTAFARI.....

After breakfast we venture out onto the streets of Lhasa. No sooner had we began walking when an ever so shifty man appears walking next to me he smiles at me I smile back. Then he smiles some more so I return the courtesy and as I knew would happen from my first meeting with MO he then began a polite conversation asking the usual questions that travellers get asked. But find hard to decipher if it's of genuine interest and friendliness or a hustle...

Where are you from?

How long you have been here?

How long are you going to stay?

Is it your first time here?

Where are you going now?

Every seasoned traveller worth his salt will know those particular questions can be translated to roughly mean the following..

Which currency are you using/exchange rate?

How much of your money you may of already spent?

How much time have I left to hustle you?

Are you wise to the scams?

Can I begin hustling you today?

Talking to no one person in particular although walking next to me he spoke to the group as a whole.

Mitsu answered him first informing him we were headed to the Polata Palace then after a few steps the man stops introduces himself as Mr Cheng. Then announces he is a tour guide and it's our lucky day! We decline and keep walking. He stops following us at this point but thou shouts. You will not get into the Palace without me, will see my friends. But it's cool I will wait for you by the spin café ok.

We arrive at the queue to the entrance of the palace as a long procession of tourists from the four corners of the globe builds with the majority being Chinese! Eventually we get to the entrance gate. The solider on guard stops us and points at a sign, on it are written several different languages. In the middle is English and it bluntly reads Foreigners must be accompanied by a local guide at all times.......... Maximum number of sightseers daily is two thousand.............

Eventually after walking back down we find Cheng. Agree to hire his services for the day and he escorts us around the palace then later offers us herb, how much man? Ras says to him..... How much will we get and even then only if it's a bargain because money is short, besides the police could bust us and .... no problem with police Rasta. They no problem just keep it all on the down-lo my friend. You tell me how much you need? ... Need? We nah need nothing man! Hashish or weed? Mitus interrupts....... up to you, hashish is good with me Barry nods. Me a weed man myself you know Ras grins...A compromise is reached. The deal brokered and Cheng agrees to bring some of each at about eight o'clock.

The Israelites

Back at the hotel we washed and were back on the streets in no time. We browsed about town to kill some time till our eight o'clock rendezvous with Cheng! In the market Barry purchased some trinkets whilst I buy a pipe! Ras got stocked up on cigarette papers and after that we shuffled towards the café, ignoring the numerous calls and whistles from the ladies of the night working the dozens of massage parlours that have seemingly sprung up since nightfall. We walked into the café and the Thai owner waves indicating that a table is available in that direction, so we go flow towards a large table.

Soft ambient music to soothe the soul seeps from speakers you cannot see, creating the illusion that the walls themselves are breathing music, red lighting adds an exotic look. We sit as directed and as we do notice seated next to us is a man. An unusual looking man! Personally I spotted him the minute I walked in but I don't like to stare. Now I can get a much better look without him thinking I'm being confrontational. Deep in meditation with his legs crossed in a yoga style posture he chills on the cushions. Eyes closed a look of peace and contentment, he radiates an inner calmness that affects all around him including us.

Not sure if he is in a trance stoned or both. White with his head shaved to the bone and bronzed from being exposed to the sun's rays! Which confirms my assumption he has been in Asia a little while longer than myself. I guess him to be around thirty years of age. Wearing wine coloured robes and sandals in a style associated with Buddhism it was easy to understand why no-one even noticed he was there until they had almost sat down on him.

We relax and began chatting with most of the conversation speculating on what kind of herbs Cheng will bring and what time! Then as I go to answer out of nowhere a breathtakingly beautiful woman appears at the door! She slowly walks past us almost in slow-in-motion; she joins the man meditating next to Ras.

Early twenties her skin an amazing shade of olive, long dark caramel coloured hair that glistens as it flows all the way down her slender and shapely back. She greets the man, her bright white teeth illuminating the room! Then leaning across the table she whispers to him, the outline of her stunning figure which is covered by her blue sarong and matching top is clearly evident.

That palace today was like something straight out of a wizard movie wasn't it Luke? Nat says out loud, suddenly waking me out of the trance this woman seems to of put me in. Huh? Then I noticed the woman and her companion also heard Nat saying this. Embarrassed I stare at the table. It's more spiritual if I can be so bold as to interrupt? The shaven headed man says in my direction. Err sure be as bold as you like! I mean why not eh? I stutter still unable to make eye contact. After-all wizards are just superstition. Depends on your belief man! True and what do you believe in friend?

Ras Tafari......Which is what exactly friend? I mean obviously I know what a Rasta looks like but tell me more..........Mmm Ras strokes his chin. His Imperial Majesty Haile Selassie I of Ethiopia is.....The King of Kings. The Lord of Lords and the lion is the symbol of Ras-tafari. For the lion represents Haile Selassie I who is the 'Conquering Lion of Judah' and these here, my dreadlocks represent that very same lion's mane....

And for it was written in *Psalm 104:14* He causeth the grass for the cattle, and herb for the services of man. Rastafari....but a man himself cannot rule. A spiritual leader can only do so and that man is the "Conquering Lion of the Tribe of Judah" and that my friend is it. In a nutshell of course for there is lots more but you get the basic understanding? Yes I hear you say's the man smiling. For that is the thing about life man. The body itself may be hard! It physical he says slapping his hand on the table in front of him to make his point. But like a radio if you pull the plug, the radio it die man.

Once the electricity that is life is severed. The umbilical cord that is mother nature which keeps us here, in this reality..this realm? the man suggests with a grin. Yeah man this realm it disappears! Ashes to ashes..atoms to atoms...you see I believe that we as humans we are spiritual beings! Spiritual and physical beings the unique combination of our creators design, and due to some strange reason for some untold reason gravitate towards this earth to live out a physical existence before returning....home? Barry suggests.

Well yes home the physical turns to dust for sure but the Soul.......Oh the soul is always there man! It stays around for eternity and sometimes it flows to other places then It...it is in another realm or dimension he says looking up. Unable for us mortals to even begin to comprehend such complexity...sometimes in light sometimes in the darkness but for ever present. You see the body is a vessel transporting the soul and its revelation is revealed through Jah-Rastafari.

This realm you talk of, that dimension where is it? The woman asks! Destiny! Its Destiny we all have our own, our individual date with destiny our fate. Some may say we a go Zion, to paradise or heaven or back home where we came from. Maybe not who knows? For it all depends..The man smiles and puts forward his hand...Ras takes it warmly. My name is Aaron, and this is my sister Sara! We are pleased to meet you. And myself you. Ras is I! Hello Aaron and hello to your beautiful sister! Let me introduce you to my friends here. This is Luke! Hello I smile thoroughly confused trying to decipher what Ras had just been talking about. It all made perfect sense in an unusual way! A way I never heard described before.

Over there that sorry looking chap? Well that is Barry he's Canadian! Ras says with a wry expression; don't ask if he is American it upsets him. And then this lot to my left is Mitsu and Nat! And you sir, where are you from? Ras puts the question we have all been wondering since we first saw them. Israel Sara and I we are Israeli! I in I man the land of the almighty! Ras smiles. The birthplace of Yesus Kristos himself! Who? Aaron asks, Yesus Kristos! Please allow me to explain. The messiah was Yesus Kristos as master and saviour. Haile Selassie I as divinely chosen by the creator to represent him on earth.

OK in plain words you see due to the stigma associated with slavery and thus the false pagan use of the name Jesus by the enslavers. Well we the Rasta-man prefer the usage of the original name. How was it false? I ask. Simple Luke, not practicing what they preached! It is therefore preferred to use the ancient name of The Messiah...Yahshuwah, Yahoshua, Yahshua or Yesus Kristos! Oh wow I didn't know that...Yesus Kristos! Say's Aaron. We have learned something new every day we have been in Tibet! I was supposed to go to Israel you know but end up here instead man. Pity Ras it's a beautiful place don't let the things you hear put you off my friend you would love it. Yeah man karma or destiny which is it? The lord works in mysterious ways, Sara smiles. I and I man for this is true my lady.

We too were drawn to this place by a powerful force we find hard to explain Aaron adds

Mitsu then asks what's so hard to explain about coming to Tibet? I agree with Mitsu Aaron. I mean us lot here! We just got stoned and thought it would be fun to come here. It's much more serious than that for us Luke, more a quest Sara adds. A search for the truth, if I can be as bold to call it such. I listen as best I can. But in my mind I cannot stop noticing Sara's beauty over her words as she converses with Ras. Suddenly I am jealous of his worldly spiritual knowledge and vow to learn as much about the topic I have for most of my life neglected though selfishness and ignorance.

Why so what exactly are you searching for? Ras asks. the tomb of...of Yesus Kristos!

Aaron says looking around judging our reactions. I choke a little on my peppermint tea!

Really? I say looking at them. As really is just about all I can think of saying. I can't think of anything else remotely intelligent to counter the statement with even though to my ears it's the most preposterous statement I've heard EVER.

That's a bold statement man! Ras says radiating his cool confident tone that I could never pull off. Yes he studied here with the monks in a monastery for several years before returning to Canaan! Aaron explains. On the outside I'm like Ice nodding away giving the impression I too am a somewhat spiritual guru...But inside my response is more akin to....what the fuck you talking about Jesus Tomb in Tibet?

This is deep man! You're telling me. 'not able to hold back and with limited spiritual knowledge I blurt out' ok wait just a second and let me get this straight. You want me to believe that Jesus Christ himself the man! Was here in Lhasa? What else that he studied Buddhism in the Portola Palace too? I say laughing... then I notice no one else is laughing! They are all just staring straight at me.

I am not telling you what to believe nor should you take my word or anyone else's word for anything Luke! Aaron says looking into my eyes creating a hypnotic like effect on me. For I am just a stranger to you and you in turn to I. I and I man adds Ras...but whatever you choose to do Luke, research it research what I am saying here tonight my friend and you will see. I am not saying he was a Buddhist a Hindu or whatever. The pieces are there it's up to you to put the jigsaw together.

Think of it like this if you will, the ancient world was a place of great travel mystery and exploration, and you certainly didn't need a passport or anything like that to move around. You see back then the world was in fact, well it was what we would today term a very cosmopolitan place. Cities would be full of travellers and explorers of every nationality comings goings. Of course it was also a time of chieftain's and warlords of different tribes and clans. Much like today's stock markets they traded, bartered exchanged goods and services. They would of learnt from each other's cultures exciting new ideas concepts and faiths. It was after the time of Hermes and of students visiting places like Athens and Alexandria to study.

So how do you think did he got here? I ask...walked it most likely! Sara replies to me. Yes at a pace of say ten miles a day it could be done in around a year or so.

Fair enough but why here? The birth story remember that Luke? Jesus birth story? Yes the three wise men that came from the east? They were merchants supposedly but in all reality they had to be astrologers! Yeah sure I remember that story. Well I am pretty sure Jesus or Yesus would of grown up listening and knowing all about them from his parents storytelling. Eh well.. I mean surely they must of told him all about them right? The manger,

59

no room and the three wise men, well of course I suppose they must.

So in a way it makes perfect sense that he would at the very least be a bit curious wouldn't you think? Suppose! Well obviously he must off been. ok so anyway you think he was sort of finding his roots or something? But why Tibet of all places? Yes you could sort of put it like that if you want? Aaron says, not my particular way of putting it but none the less I understand where you're coming from. Nor is it just here in Tibet either.

No? No! Well to say I'm intrigued is a slight understatement I laughed. We gathered quietly around the table in a circle with everyone's imagination now captured by our new acquaints, as the Israelis began outlying their amazing theory ....Luke we think he came here towards the end of his travels not the at beginning, before returning home to begin his ministry! But if he was on his way home when you assume he was here, then where do you think he was before he came here? Well the evidence suggests it all points to the fact that he was well....in fact in India.

INDIA! I blurt out? Leaning forward and being a bit more subtle. Whoa are you mad Aaron I laughed? No not in the slightest well not the last time I checked! Now I've heard it all India. Come-on? Well actually it was Kashmir. Definitely yes....No seriously Luke he was definitely in Kashmir of that we are one hundred percent certain! Kashmir? Where's that? Asks Nat. It's where the world's best hash is produced? Says Mitsu....that statement is open to ridicule I laugh but right now we have more serious topic at hand...Yes Luke and maybe even as far south as Orissa too! Where? It's in northern India! For what the hashish? Asks Barry..Can you lot forget the smoking for a second, for just a few minutes? I laughed.

Luke seriously we know we only just met you guys but there has been a massive cover-up and manipulation of the facts regarding one of the most influential people who ever walked the planet. How long for? Not sure...the last eighteen hundred years at least of that we are convinced! I and I man. Definitely man Babylon has been cooking the books about the Elohim now long time man..Long time! Aaron laughs with his sister you know the word Elohim Ras? Yeah man...I am impressed Rastaman we are impressed.

Think about it guys! Aaron says. No record exists of anything he himself ever wrote! Nothing not a single page! And if he did write down anything which you would think he must of done at certain points in his life, it hasn't survived. Aaron looks around at us tapping his fingers.

Yet here is a man that even the history of time itself. I mean our clocks calendars everything has been influenced by him and yet absolutely nothing, zero, zilch that can be actually attributed to him personally is documented to study or read! Stuff written by others yes him no. I mean call me a conspiracy nut for questioning the official story but come on.

Isn't that to do with the Gregorian calendar? Yes Luke and don't forget both the Julian's and flavian's involvement. But what did he look like? Sara says looking around at everyone in our circle. His height, hair, eyes? Nothing all we get is he was a Jewish guy with long hair a beard about average height and if you believe that then we can find a thousand clones doing yoga on Goa's beaches every Christmas.

It's almost laughable if it weren't such an obvious con, few records of his childhood and even less again about his family! Had he brothers or Sisters? Was he an only child? Surely not! In those times it was perfectly normal for a family to have up to a dozen kids! But all we get told is he had a mate called Lazarus! Exactly Luke. Yet nothing about where he was or what he was up to between thirteen and thirty. Ask a church man Barry smirks.

Please, the church that's laughable they can't even agree if he was a Nazarene or a Galilean! As Aaron continued his rant Ras says in my ear. Bwoy me know there was a reason me come here you know? Huh oh yeah I nod mesmerized and totally unsure what to think except to say nothing and just smile. Yes that's correct Ras the gospel! Huh what you talking about Luke? It tells us one just one transitional verse! It says 'and Jesus grew in wisdom and statue and in favour of god and man' that's it, next thing he is thirty years old at the river Jordan and being baptised by his elder cousin John! I mean come on guys wake up, where the hell was he? who were his influences? Aaron asks looking at our blank expressions.

I never thought of it like that did you Mitsu? Nope, so who do you think is behind this conspiracy? The Vatican, why the Vatican I ask? Because it propagates the lies! Aaron answers, by now I'm totally entranced in this spider's web of intrigue. They stole the biggest obelisk in all of Egypt, well Caesar did and no one even knows how he managed to pull that one off without breaking it into bits. But he did it. What's an obelisk? Nat asks....it's that big pillar thing like they have in Washington DC Ras informs her......

I mean after all he was just a thug who ran a fire brigade racket! Who what I missed that? Julius Caesar he was the original Gangster. Mafia call it what you like...they built the Vatican in the city of seven hills of Rome put lions in it and plonked the Obelisk bang in the centre of saint peters square. What do you think Luke?

Sara asks me. I don't know what to think to be honest, why err what do you think Sara?

The Romans killed Jesus Luke. Not the Jews! Well no actually the Jew's did kill him Sara sorry if that offends you but Pontius Pilate had twice been reprimanded by Caesar for going too harshly on the Jews. Then he did everything within the limits of his office to spare Jesus from execution! I do know a little bit of history. She laughed. Caesar was a gangster who ran a fire brigade protection racket for years when he was young and if you didn't pay up your business got torched. He was the original mafia. What don't you understand about that? Well eh nothing, was he? I mean for real he did that shit? Yes, they both barked.

Our discussion is interrupted by the arrival of two male travellers who walk in loudly and boisterously as well as holding hands! Both Aussies. Bret was a little less than six foot with an athletic build and tightly cut curly brown hair. Holding his hand his boyfriend I would be very soon finding out was Scooby. A little shorter with blond hair blue eyes, a double for a Hollywood hair dresser or make-up artist type. Camp as they come. They sat either side of Sara after exchanging kisses then set about the usual gossip.

Scooby. Brett you must meet our new found friends! Aaron tells them, these are our fellow travellers, this is Ras Luke Mitsu Nat and Barry! Guys Brett and Scooby, G'day people they wave! We mumble our hellos. Hey mister where have you been? Huh that voice sounds familiar I think to myself but by this stage I was completely absolutely intoxicated by the mixture and fascination of what they had just told us, looking up I realised, hey Mr Cheng!

Oh shit dude sorry I mean we forgot all about you, OK it ok people forget Mr Cheng all...... the time. Push up he says as he sits himself in between Ras and Barry, he looks at the owner looking at him, then smiles and causally requests a coffee in what seems to be his general nonchalant mannerism. The owner prepares his coffee; he then quickly takes something from under his armpit.

This is for you he says handing Ras a folded newspaper. Ras carefully places it between his legs under the table looks around to check if anyone is watching. Opening it and looking inside he sees it is full of fresh marijuana bud. Still on the stalks, how much weight is here? A quarter pound maybe! I am not sure Cheng answers looking around himself nervously.

A quarter pound man? Maybe more a startled Cheng adds. What am I going to do with a quarter pound of weed man? Don't ask me Mr Marley! What who? Mr Brett this is for you he says as he hands over a block of soft rubbery looking black hashish, you're delivering to them too? Barry giggles shaking his head, shit man look at that giggles Mitsu. That block is at least the same shape and size as a TV REMOTE CONTROL! Holy shit that much would keep a busy Amsterdam tourist coffee shop going for a week! I joke as Aaron looks at me, ok maybe not a whole week. Scooby takes it and gently bends it till it cracks a little in the centre revealing the inside to be a dark green colour, smelling it he looks at me and smiles.

Oh man smell this! He says to me Mmm smells nice, Nice nice? Its Fucking Awesome dude. So you guys know each other? Barry says to Cheng looking at Brett, Oh yes long time he laughs. This is not the place for us to casually be smelling weed! We're all going to be in a world of shit if we get busted you do realise that don't you? Cheng is universally thanked by all with cash rewards coming at him from all angles under the table.

He smiles his eyes illuminated with dollar signs. No thank you Mr thank you, no my pleasure thank you.

Then he puts forward his next suggestion from his list of must dos for us while in Lhasa.

Now whom can I interest in accompanying me on a visit to the pink lady? Cheng announces.....amidst much laughter I tell him we will pass on that one I think bro.

Well don't look at us. I don't think they will be getting much business Scooby says in such a camp manner that even Cheng himself laughs. Scooby and Brett see likeable characters, complete opposite of Aaron and Sara who are whilst strange and deep to listen to intoxicating and beautiful to look at! Yet their cool cause hey they smoke the sacred herb and anyone that smokes the herb is safe in my books.

What is happening to me I drift off thinking? Here I am someone who only a few days ago would not even smile at strangers not to mention talk to them. Yet since I got here my concept of humanity conciseness and understanding of true tolerance towards others has definitely shifted! Looking across at Barry I see he was correct.

Guys thank you for the coffee but I must depart this fine establishment! Cheng says whilst clearly indicating for someone to pay his tab. Of course if you meet anyone looking for any kind of entertainment or if any of you gentlemen we're to change his mind you can find me at the PINK LADY we all say out loud to him before he can say it. Everyone laughs all around the café.

Aaron and Sara then invite us to come to their place for a smoke and to chat further! We have a big room rented up the street with cushions and floor space aplenty. So after dinner we went to the room where Aaron and Sara we're staying. With lots of fresh Hashish and Marijuana to test we wasted no time in getting to work. I rolled a joint. Brett prepared a bong! Ras rolled a joint of nothing but green buds and no tobacco. The Israelis had a chillum and soon the room was filled with an amazing mixture of aromas that wouldn't be out of place at the annual Amsterdam Cannabis cup tournament.

Sara had hooked an mp3 player up to some speakers and switched on some Tibetan ambient music. A slow distant drumming with the sound of a woman chanting. It set the tone and background for things to come...Nice.

She leaned over and quietly spoke with her brother, they both then looked around at us smiling, he then produced a small box from under a bed and removed what looked like wrapped sweets. Hey guys I want you all to try these! What are they? This is called K one hundred Luke....Oh I respond. Desperately doing a mental search for where or rather if I have ever even heard of it before.

Seriously man what's this stuff. Me nah deal with Babylon's toxins Ras says studying one closely. No laughs Sara. K one hundred is a unique mixture of Entheogens! What's that in English? Asks Barry. Why it's a mind illuminating gateway enhancer she laughs. In other words they can open the door or the portal if you like to the process of consciously being able to experience dual realities at once. OK its dried Himalayan mushrooms laughs Aaron. The famous Amanita Muscaria to be precise, not a psilocybin type shroom that makes you trip but Muscimol which can give both a trip and outer body experience.

The fly agaric? Mitsu quizzes. Yes it is, that's another name for it, but K has been mixed with king cobra venom and the purest Kashmiri hash oil, all compressed into an after dinner type mint! He laughs. Ah why didn't you say? Barry pops it into his mouth faster than a frog catching a passing mosquito and gulps it down as do the others. Now my mental response went something all the lines of king fucking cobra venom magic fucking mushrooms hashish oil and all in the one hit? You got to be fucking kidding me.

Something wrong Luke? Err oh nothing Sara. Good I thought you were talking to yourself there for a moment. Who me nah, so what will happen Sara? You know if I take it. Don't worry Luke, it will just release your third dimensional thinking. Oh ok, err how do I do that? The best way to release this outdated thinking is to accept the flow of unconditional love that I am sending you right now. You are? I am she smiled, now go ahead take it.

I pop it into my mouth and crunch down hard, a disgusting bitter taste instantly soak into my taste buds.

Sara smiles at me. I attempt a smile back in her direction, within seconds I feel my muscles relax then turn to jelly before they go dead as complete paralysis sets in! My vision becomes blurred as sweat glands open all across my body. First my back then my chest armpits forehead. My mouth and throat slowly and completely dry up! You're no longer grounded ones Aaron announces laughing. Come resonate friends, your now ascending ones.

I slowly looked around as I sensed my facial muscles freeze up and tighten! All I could make out was this blurred mass of multi-coloured faces swaying in tune with the rhythm of the music in the background. A slow swirling fan overhead seemed to eat the smoke and under which lay a Tibetan cushion that smiled over at me. I smiled back laughing as my heart suddenly began to thump in a strange synchronism of sorts! The drug produced a synchrony of my brain waves to the actual beat of the music.

I'm hyperventilating I realised but so far gone, so out

67

of my mind, so out of control of my senses. I'm too gone to even have a panic attack. Then out of nowhere water begins to drip onto my lips. I begin thanking whoever it is that is giving it to me. Then I realise hearing laughter that no one is giving me any water its sweat! My sweat and its dripping off the tip of my nose having come down from my forehead.

I can't say how long this awful feeling lasted but then as fast as it began it disappeared. Then without further ado the euphoric effect 'or heightened arousal and sense of general well-being to me and you' section of the trip kicked in..... and I'm fucking buzzing! Your path to mother earth is open Sara smiled at me. It is? It is. Yeah man shouts Ras grabbing my hand and shaking it wildly. I take a swig of water and compose myself and look around grinning like a loon. I stare in amazement at my companions.

Your eyes look wild, giggles Sara. Do they? Yes she says handing me a joint as she sways to the music. Holy shit! What Luke? You're so beautiful! The room erupts into fits of laughter as Sara blushes, why thank you Luke no probs. I smirk as I stuffed the joint into what after all must of looked like the most ridiculous cheesy grin on the planet. I sucked the fumes deep down into my lungs holding both arms outstretched and smile. Then and only then........like wet gremlins after midnight....the party began.

I took a few drags off a joint then passed it to Aaron who is quietly studying the room's occupants. Scooby is showing Nat how to roll a joint. Aaron, we almost forgot to tell you, guess who myself and Brett meet today? I have no idea do tell me. Well not exactly met but you know! He is off his face! Brett says laughing, I am not! He says slapping Brett's arm well ok perhaps just a bit hee hee. Well we found this cool little company offering excursions.

This little gem of a place. Anyway cut a long story short they are doing the most amazing excursion. What is it? I ask. Well it's a strange one! Brett says looking at me, definitely not to everyone's taste I know. But we are going aren't we Scooby? Too bloody right we are mate! Not one's for lounging on bloody loungers in Bali mate. but we are going to travel to the source of the Mekong River. Right to the point of where it all began! Get the fuck out of here! Mitsu shouts. Wow, you're journeying to the source?

Aaron smiles, that is awesome, amazingly awesome in fact, how long does it take? I ask He begins to answer but I drift off as he begins talking to me, it hits me like a slap in the face! Who are we? What are we? Where are we going? Where did we come from?

All rather De-Ja-Vu Brandon Huckabee from Detroit Michigan appears...Advising me to do just that, go to the Mekong, journey to its source Luke, journey to the source of a river that in one way shape or form helps sustain a billion humans.

So vivid and clear it's not de-ja-vu I tell myself. It's just a recollection of a past event! A conversation with a stranger, a bit of advice, nothing more. I'm just spaced out or am I? I lie down and get comfy, could be telepathy I tell myself as everything feels so strange and soft. I begin to hear voices faintly in the distant! The voices are like whispers at first scary panicky upset cries, talking about vomit and puke, lots of puke, it gets louder and louder it's an australian voice puke....Puke, Puke, LUKE!!!! Aggghhh.

Luke, are you bloody deaf mate? Err what? Well err yeah kind of, only a little thou, too many nightclubs when I was a teenager I think Brett, you know standing around too near the speakers smoking with your mates!

Mate, don't do that shit again will you? What shit? Forget it mate. Err ok. By the way, the answer to your question. It will take a few days but you got to be prepared to rough it. I nod, as the last leg cannot be done by a four wheeler! Really? Apparently so mate then it's going be yak time, are you listening to me Luke? Huh? Yeah yeah of course. Mitsu again sensing my discomfort steps in to help, cool that will be one for the grand-kids eh? He says nodding at me. Oh yeah I smile and nod.

Imagine being able to cup your hands together like so! Scooby says clasping his hands together to then drink a cool clean clear mouthful of water from the source of the Mekong itself! Untouched by mankind or pollution.....He is making it sound better than holy water eh.. Barry say's. So how much are these boys charging you guys for this trip? Barry asks. Five hundred each! Why got you thinking? Sort of well I have been travelling around Asia for over a year now and it's something I was thinking would be cool. Plus I want to get back to Thailand before the weather turns and it would be possible to get there by land I guess if I headed in that general direction. Cool...so fancy coming with us into China then?

What do you think Mitsu are you game? Are you serious Barry? Is he serious? Luke, Ras. Someone please tell me if Baz is serious! Are serious Barry? Mitsu wants to know. Of course I'm fucking serious man why does everyone always think I'm not serious? No we don't, yes you did you said that back in oh never mind. Look it sounds a totally awesome plan to me, think about it bro after seeing more temples tomorrow what else is there to do unless you're a temple spotter! Sure you can smoke your brains out but then what huh? Routine yes Ras correct pure routine is all that will be left man.

You will fall into a routine, just another routine of

counting the days till you go home! No more enlightening blissful experiences, no new horizons, no more adventure, no more finding funky death trap hotels with mega views run by maniacs, used by groupies junkies or sex tourists, no more err... Self-discovery? Yes self discovery, that's a good one Luke, self-discovery and lots of it bro.

No more the objective mind and senses suspended! No more new enlightenment which places you on a new plane of existence. No more putting in your order for the reality to which you wish to resonate. Sara adds as we look at each other, Sara? Yes Luke, you're awesome.

You know what sealed it for us? Scooby says, get this but the source itself was only discovered in nineteen ninety four, can yeah fucking believe that? Hey guys how totally awesome is that? Only twenty or so years ago that's after they said they had landed on the bloody moon. Seriously is that how long it took them to find the source of the Mekong River?

Is that true? That they only found it a few years ago? Hundred percent matey! Awesome or what? Yup awesome, two hundred years after Henri Mouhot was given the job of finding it, who? A famous French explorer but even he couldn't locate it. OK but in his defence he did stumble across and discover the Angkor Wat along the way! So we can't totally disrespect the guy now can we?

But I can sort of understand him getting a wee-bit distracted and forgive him! Wait Angkor is AWESOME dude have you been Luke? Nope. I was in Angkor Wat! Barry shouts. Awesome eh... yeah awesome, so you mean to tell me that the guy who found the lost city of Angkor was actually on his way to do this journey? Got it in one big fellah! I'm fucking going man that's all there is too it, count me in bro. I'm not sure about that

71

lot over there, but me def.

Aaron don't tell me you're considering going too? Sara says looking at him, why? Because that sort of counts me in as well don't it she laughs switching her eyes towards me. The son of god didn't go to the Mekong too did he? Nat asks with eyebrows raised! No no as far as my research suggests he only studied in a place called the Himis monastery it is Ladkah. But

Don't worry it is in the opposite direction! Aaron winks, it was a joke! Oh.

You really believe in what you're saying huh? I say to both of them. Well put it this way the evidence is mounting up! Sara says. You mean there's more Brett asks? Of course and lots of it! Aaron laughs. Such as? Scooby says sparking up a fully packed bong! Technically all religions are correct cause the say the same thing...Huh says Ras..more or less, but these books, they are still here today in the palace Aaron continues... all written in Sanskrit so it will have to be translated of course. So why has no one translated it already? Natsumi asks.....Because the scripts can only be touched and opened by the Dalai Lama himself! Sara replies. WHAT? But he is.. Exiled we know! Aaron laughs, this just gets better and better, I stutter..

Seriously only the Dali lama himself can have a look? And he hasn't been around here for what? Fifty years man! Ras says. Well that sounds awfully convenient, oh and don't tell me, the scriptures they cannot go to him? He has got to come to them correct? Exactly Luke! I knew it. I just knew you were going to tell me that, I say as I out my joint in the ashtray. This is all beginning to sound like some bad movie plot eh Luke? Barry jokes, yeah next thing they're going to want us to ride shotgun while they break in or something and we laugh out loud...

Deep man this is very deep stuff you know? Barry looks at me, all roads lead to Rome eh....Indeed it seems! I didn't sleep properly for days! Sara ads, when I found out the significance of all this! Yeah but why Tibet? Mitsu asks? Shaking his head, because looking on a map it made more sense for him to go straight into India as it seems to just go in a straight line across from Jerusalem to India! He did! That is what he did, says Sara, Well I think he did.

I think he would of had to of joined up with one of the trade caravans that at that time moved mainly between Palestine and Kashmir, were not talking just one a year Luke, and from there he would have been able to travel into India, Nepal, Tibet....I see. There's a temple there that even at the time when Jesus was alive it would of been old even to him, it's a place where say the Hindu version of the pope, sorry but that is the best way I can think of describing him or a very holy man at any rate, well its where he resides! If I wasn't mind boggled enough by all these revelations not to mention the snake venom entheogen potion Sara then revealed more.

But being himself he couldn't help but open his mouth, for when he saw suffering or injustice! Even if it got him into big trouble he would take a stand. Trouble? Why? How? Barry inquires I mean how could JC get in trouble? JC as you call him, well despite the public image he was in fact at times downright rude, even to his parents! But here he basically started to upset the higher caste Indians over the treatment of the lower castes, and that's serious shit in India! Brett says looking at the rest of us! From then on his time there was numbered and was a marked man.

So he had to go, moving north ...high up into Tibet, then later on he arrived here in Lhasa! Rumour has it the Hindu ruling elite had even attempted to have him

73

killed! What? Someone was planning a hit on Jesus? Barry jokes...Do you mind mate? Well it wouldn't of been the first time someone wanted him out of the way now would it Luke? Look I am interested in what she has to say, chill bro I am digging it too.

Anyway he was tipped off and left under the cover of darkness, just like he had left Jerusalem at night all those years before eh? Of course, Sara smiles but maybe that's just all hear-say! As there really is no firm evidence to back that all up. OK time out time out! Enough my head is hurting, can we just go back to talking about something easy? Scooby-bless him, conveniently changed the subject, right OK then, who is coming with Brett and myself to find the source of the Mekong delta hmm? he says looking around the room! Everyone's hand shoot up.

Hey bro looks like our adventures have only just begun! Barry says to me. I smile as more joints are rolled, pipes filled as smoke and laughter fills the air as storeys of past busts by cops! Tales of faraway exciting lands are exchanged, as are ways to conceal stashes to get past evil customs officers. Ras explains the Rastafarian belief system to Aaron who was as astonished as I was to be honest to learn that at the turn of the last century Marcus Garvey a Jamaican, had a prophecy that a King would come from the east and he would be the reincarnation of Jesus! Several years later in the sixties a man of compassion, wisdom and understanding did in fact arrive.

And when it was discovered by the western media that he was in fact the two hundred and twenty fifth descendent in a direct Ethiopian royal linage dating from Menelik1 they 'the media' went nuts. Menelik of course was the first son of King Solomon and the Queen of Sheba and legend has it he was the chosen one of his father to bring and protect for safe keeping the ark of the covenant to Ethiopia –which coincidently was also the first official Christian country! And of course you all know King Solomon was the son of king David of Jerusalem, of course you do.

You see with maybe the exception of Ethiopia itself did the Rastafarian faith take hold. You see that is why Rasta consider Africa home! Jamaica and the west in general is hell or Babylon! As it's controlled by evil corporations the meat industry big Pharma and so on, and the time of freedom was when we were taken as free enlightened people from the kingdom of Ethiopia which was in fact Zion and to Zion we must one day return.

On and on the various conversations went, but for me my head was interested in the story Aaron and his sister had told. Personally I found the tales of cover ups and plots, of silk routes, of assassination attempts and manipulation much more intriguing! Looking over I noticed Mitsu Nat and Sara converse deeply about religion while Scooby Brett and Barry were talking about the beauty of watching the sunset on remote Thai beaches! Nice to know not everyone here was obsessed with religion, it was a perfect mix of people.

Everybody! Scooby cried out.... In the morning we must all meet at the café nine am sharp ok? Seriously people we need to be at the tour guides office to sort it, we don't have much time guys, so no one be late got it? Brett and Scooby go in one direction and we go in the opposite. Later on in our room I found it difficult to sleep! Very quite there Mitsu what's up? Barry asked, Huh oh just in deep thought that's all! He answers staring up at the ceiling! All roads lead to Rome eh! Barry chuckles, yeah he laughs all roads lead to Rome..... It is, it appears to be the truest saying ever.

All jokes aside I say looking at Ras looking at Barry

looking at Mitsu staring at the ceiling. That Aaron....he is a pretty clued up guy don't you think? I put forth my drug induced analysis forward for further consideration! Yeah man him knowledgeable big time, both guidance as well as wisdom flow fort from deep within I and from him heart too. But you got to forget about it right now or you nah get no sleep man.

I lay awake staring at the ceiling watching the occasional shadow creep across it from the headlights of a lonely passing car on the street below. I leaned over and stole one of Mitsu cigarettes from our shared bedside cabinet, not because I even bloody wanted one but because well I didn't but I needed something to fiddle with. A Rubik's cube would of been nice. I recalled reading a book one time about drinking lots of orange juice if someone consumed to much magic mushrooms and had a bad trip as it would 'bring you down.

But where do you get fresh orange juice in Tibet. At this hour, in the Oasis hotel?

MR Bahadur

Early next morning we piled into the travel agents like zombies. Brett, how are you today? I am great makodia Are you ready to go on your trip? Yes but I have a small problem. Which is? Tell uncle makodia. They want to come too can you arrange it? Does a yak fart? My friend anything is possible with uncle makodia anything you know that, how many people you got? em how many we got? Seven, seven of them, seven huh leave it with me call back in two hrs ok.

Two hours later we storm the shop again! Hey Scooby good news man, good news my lucky friends the transport, driver you need and everything else you may also need, well that's there too he laughs! So these are your friends huh? He inquires pointing at me with a biro, Yes this is everyone, this rag-tag dishevelled crew! OK guys listen up and listen good. I do not know how well travelled you are! Nor do I really care what I do care about is my drivers and Jeeps. I don't know if Scooby has told you the logistical nightmare your about to part take of actually let me phrase that another way.. Just how fucking dangerous this journey is! But what is of the utmost importance is that you always and I cannot stress this enough always do what my friend here bahadur tells you to do.

It was then we saw him, tall square jawed with a sinewy physique and not one of us had even noticed him standing in the shadows until he moved, about fifty years of age with a scared face, he looked every bit the stereotypical Hollywood Asian baddie. A chameleon in man-made surroundings and hopefully would also be in mother nature's if called upon! Mr bahadur do you want to say a few words? Hello he smiled, my name as you now know is Mr bahadur! He said in near word perfect English. I understand you guys are on holiday and looking for adventure? Well you have come to the right place.

No bungee jumping or white water rafting crap here, but realise this, you guys are going to be pioneers of the excursion Mr makodia is offering and if it is a success, it will become part of the regular traveller circuit and you can boast to all you friends how you were the first to try it. What if it's not a success? I ask, then makodia is taking your next of kin details, so they will get your body! If it is possible to recover it he smiled. Funny, you're a funny guy I say laughing, he isn't laughing man Mitsu says to me with a grim expression! I thought he would say no more excursions or something? Barry says shaking his head.

Isn't that correct makodia? Huh? The bodies. Yes yes I take all details of home address so no worries man. Are you sure you want to do this? Sara asks Aaron, of course, it will be fine don't worry. OK makodia continues this adventure to locate the source of the Mekong and I will be honest here most of us Tibetans couldn't give a shit where it is. But it's located in the inner heartland of the highest and most inhospitable part of the central Asian highlands, which makes it just about one of the most if not "the" most inhospitable places on earth.

Hundreds of kilometres from any settlements! That means any 'humans' in case you're wondering, make no mistake friends with the exception of maybe the Antarctic. It's harder to find a more desolate place on the entire planet...Understand? Because I'm looking at a few speechless people right now! We understand I alone say looking directly at him. Good he grins back...The region itself, he says rolling out a old map on the table as we gather around, was part of the far-flung realm of the

Kings of Nang-Chen and is the home of roughly 200000 or so Kham-Ba Nomads who live in the region.

I thought you said there's no human's for hundreds of kilometres? Mitsu points out. Yes but once near the source itself there are very few human's trust me.. Anyway they live a life very similar to that of Neanderthal man dating back thousands and thousands of years. What else do you know about them Ras inquires..I mean are they hostile? The Nomadic mountain warriors of Nang-Chen? Only if you look Chinese and you don't look Chinese he laughs. The Nang-Chen Kham-Bas are divided into maybe twenty five tribe's independent of each other yet united and ferociously opposed to the Chinese takeover.

But opposed specifically to all those who attempt to penetrate their territory Barry laughs. Exactly smiles makodia. It was a joke dude! No joke friend. Why might they think we are part of some invading army? Asks Aaron.... As funny as that might sound to us here it is a very real possibility to tribes that... well let me put it this way...they haven't seen many outsider's.

But should that happen we have developed a contingency plan..Which is? I prompt for more info..I think we can convince them that your scientists! Scientists? I stutter. Yes why not? Well Err well..Because we got no fucking scientist stuff in our bags maybe Scooby points out, you got laptops? makodia asks...

Well yes, perfect then your researchers for the international institute of earthquake prevention...We look at each other! The what? Earthquake prevention. Yes the IIEP he nods, sound good eh? I grin unsure what he is playing at, you just made that up didn't you? Of course I fucking did! How can you prevent an earthquake you can't ha ha. Sound good to you Mr. bahadur? makodia asks.. bahadur laughs. Sounds good to me look forget about tribesmen just show them some graphs if it comes to it, they don't know what computers are ok cool that's all sorted then Mr bahadur, back to you.

I'm not trying to complicate this for you guys, but they have never been under the control of the Dalai Lamas. Most of them even today escape or outright ignore any form of Chinese control, that's why the Chinese Government has been reluctant to authorize foreigners to travel into southern Qinghai you see? Imagine a westerner getting murdered? It would force the Chinese into a direct conflict with them! I point out. Very good what's your name? Luke OK Luke nice to see you got a good head on those shoulders! My old teachers would disagree with you there Mr bahadur.

Look honestly over the past century more than a dozen local expeditions have failed to reach source of the Mekong! The only reason we can try do it today is thanks to technology but it will still be a hard slog, be under no illusion! It's not for the faint hearted and I'm not making this up but in the mid nineties, they discovered a new hybrid breed of hot-blooded horse up there! What? Yeah with enlarged lungs that specifically seemed to of evolved to the terrain. So god only knows what else is up there.

Makodia. Yes? That's enough this is serious business but rewarding, but only if your tough-enough! Oh yeah I'm Chuck Norris's! Barry jokes, not trying to frighten you guys bahadur laughs I just want you all to know what you're getting into ok! Man we aren't afraid of shit! Mitsu laughs! Good oh one last thing, Mr bahadur says, what's that? I smile.

The tribesmen, we might come across along the way well they killed all the early European travellers who attempted to cross their lands, so if we do come across them...you know, don't panic let me do the talking! He

80

winks. Well that's reassuring Barry smiles. Don't let Mr bahadur freak you out guys makodia laughs confidently, he is an ex-Ghurkha solider! He will take very good care of you, just remember do as he say not what he do ok you guys still want to go huh?....HELL YEAH.

Five am sharp the next morning we are outside mekodia's office when several four wheel drives roar up the deserted street at breakneck speed sending dust and stones flying, before screeching to a halt! Shocked and silent we breathe a sigh of relive when out jumps Mr Bahadur. Looking every bit the military man with boots, combats and a baseball cap with 'united states air force' written across it.

A short thick unlit cigar dangles carelessly from his lips complementing his carefully cultivated image. Shit bro I think Bahadur took my chuck norris comment to the next level Barry whispers. Making me laugh but I also couldn't help thinking that if he is as careful in planning our journey as he is with his time keeping and presentation skills then I guess we are in safe hands.

Everyone here? He shouts! Yeah...Everyone ready? Hell yeah! Lets rock n roll! He says clapping his hands, we start chucking rucksacks and sleeping bags up to the drivers on the roof of the Jeeps. Whoever wants to travel in my Jeep get in now, the rest of you get into that one, myself and Barry dive straight in with him. He light's up his cigar then takes a quick drag on it blowing the strong smelling smoke out the window as he watches the other Jeep in his rear view mirror.

Your name... Bahadur! Is it Tibetan? Barry asks him! Nope he says taking another deep drag on the cigar. My only thought is Barry's questions must be annoying him, it's more Indian than Tibetan he eventually responds. Oh ok! Great he answered Barry as I thought as for a moment there was going to be a bad vibe because of

81

Barry's questions! What does it mean? All your names around here have meaning's correct? Oh for fucks sake Barry I say to myself.

Bahadur inhales hard on his cigar then using his thumb he scoops some saliva from his the corner of his mouth as he does so he stares at Barry, grins then presses his thumb on the hot end of the cigar making it sizzle which is immediately accompanied by the distinct smell of burning flesh! My name in English means superman! He revs up the engine...belt up guys! He looks out the window and I see him making eye contact with makodia who is standing at an upstairs window watching us. He gives soldiers salute and we are off and away forever from the ancient city.

The road out of town was good and within no time we're on our way into no man's land. Where we headed today bahadur? Barry asks. Our destination at this time is Dam-Xung County! Dam-Xung-County almost sounds American don't it Luke? Almost Baz! bahadur looks at him, it means good place in Tibetan. It is where south Tibet meets north Tibet. See the mountain? This is the Tangla mountain its glaciers are a source for the Yarlung River which flows from here all the way down into India, through Bangladesh, before finally flowing out into the bay of Bengal. We drive on and on watching amazing landscape after amazing landscape morph into more amazing landscapes. Occasionally passing huge camp like tents! I take the odd photo of the nomads that roam the lands and have done so for thousands of years! We spot remote mystical looking monastery's far off in the distance so many times after a while they cease to amazing and become somehow 'normal' but some are even close enough to be worthy of a photo and well it would be rude not to.

After a few hours we drive up over a snow filled

mountain pass! Bahadur tells us we are at an altitude of sixteen thousand feet! How he knew this I had no idea. But I was willing to take his word for it! So are we in what's it called county yet? I ask Damxung County? Barry replies. Yeah that's the one mate! No. Well how long more? I press him. We passed it already.....what, when?.......right now we're heading towards the heavenly lake....The heavenly lake? I repeat looking at Barry who shrugs and puts a joint together.

Yes Luke, its better known to us Tibetans as "Nam-Tso Lake" I look at Barry. Isn't that where we meet Ras? No that's Yam drok or something. Oh we giggle as we share the joint and the shear subliminal telepathic vibe of 'it's all starting to sound the same point has indeed been reached'.........for moment I thought we were going backwards Baz...Why it is called that? Barry asks Bahadur. You will see my friend! He turns and says to Barry with a grin, you will see.

A few hours later we arrive at the lake and stand in awe! About twenty local nomads that were seated got up and rushed towards us but were immediately repelled by bahadur who shouted something and they backed-off! We walked forward in a trance of our surroundings, no one utters a word not one of us! In front lay a scene truly from another world barley describable "Nam Tso Lake" is as crystal blue as is the sky above.

Encapsulated by the snow-capped mountains that surround it. Five islands stand in the lake with another five by-lands stretching into the lake from different directions, strange rocks steep peaks, natural stone ladders and bizarrely grottos all compete to present all of us or anyone who visits a picture postcard view.

Enchanting with wild yaks, donkeys, hares, deer, goats gazelles! The list goes on, all of whom seem to wander about casually seeking food, along the shore are

83

flocks of migratory birds in their thousands.....It's like a central station for wildlife Barry sighs. A garden of Eden Sara smiles mother nature's garden....

Nam Tso Lake a Garden of Eden tucked away in the land that time forgot eh Luke? More a land that time has never even found! she laughs as her brother approaches. Well it's definitely too cold to be the biblical one Luke! We smile. Look! Mitsu points, that little hill up there. Are you thinking what I'm thinking? Asks Barry I don't know what Mitsu is thinking man but I'd love to go over there to smoke a chillum says Ras! Hey when you lot are ready? Shouts Bahadur, has he got our bags in his hands Scooby says, I believe so. Why is that do you think? I've really no idea. Oh no he is not seriously Mr B what are you doing? Barry shouts out. We camp here tonight! Where? Mr Bahadur points over towards a few big nomadic tents, there! We can stay there? Aaron asks. We are staying there now get your stuff.

Check in Bahadur says nodding as he chucks his rucksack down! See that huge one in grey he points out, that's it over there! Come on guys let's get this done as quickly as we can. Then we can go walkabout! Brett suggests and I couldn't agree more. Approaching the tent a small smiling old man gets up from his seat, the outside of the large tent is covered with hundreds of prayer flags on one side, a dozen or so yaks are tied up and on the other a half dozen dogs are fenced in, he ushers us inside with a smile. A dozen thick wood poles form the structure's column. Loads of sleeping mats are stacked in a neat pile in the corner with blankets in the other corner.

The lake resembles a giant mirror eh? Barry says to me. Yeah like glass I agree as we make our way over to craggy rock, sure enough it has a cave. It's grassy outside so we just sit down there relax and prepare the goodness. None of us have any desire to go exploring caves as we are far too tired so we chat and smoke and await the spectacular sunset that so evidently looms in the distance.

How's the hash? Bahadur jokes as he walks up to us! Strong, why you want a somke? I reply offering him a joint! No my days of that are well and truly over. Yeah? Oh yes, makes me paranoid. I can't enjoy it like I once did! Guess ex military men should stay away from it! Barry says. It certainly doesn't help the demons Barry! Demons? The flashbacks Sara he nods. Look guys the reason I've come up here is to tell you see the Peninsula jutting out into the lake over there? Yes....Well they are home to many sites associated with prominent monks and from different sects all of whom each have their own sacred rocks and trees of spiritual significance. So don't go chucking rocks at them or wandering over there smoking, he laughs.

Soon it was dark, as the sun went down the sky created a glow, a strange glow not like what I get outside my home in London but a combination of vivid colours all blending in with each other, reflecting onto the lake at night. There is something very mystical about sunset in Tibet! Something even more mystical again about sunset over Nam Tso Lake! Then again I suppose it is the highest and thus nearest most of us can get or are ever likely to get to the sun itself.

Soon the warmness and safety of the day faded and was replaced with a cold dark predator filled night with a moonlit sky above it, the sounds of night stirred around us which freaked me out I wasn't ashamed to admit. Time to go? Barry smiled looking around him. Yeah let's split comes the unanimous response. I can smell fish from here can you? Mitsu joked. We staggered back towards base camp and make towards the fire and then I hear a moan. I look at the others! They look at me! Sara smiles so I smile back! Keep walking I mutter.

Barry did you hear that? I ask. Hear what? As we moved just now I heard well I'm not sure what I heard! What exactly? He says looking away from me. Again it comes this time only louder....that! Just keep walking I hear someone suggest; repeating the words I spoke myself moments earlier. Too stoned and nervous or both to place the voice or do anything other than stagger on. Ok time out who the fucked spiked me? Mitsu demands bringing us all to a halt! I know one of you fuckers slipped me some fucking fucked up drug or something! No one slipped you shit now come on. I try reassuring him.

I'm hearing fucking werewolves and shit right about now Luke and I am not moving one fucking inch till I find out whoever the fuck....Then we see it! Looking back horror strikes us as we see a huge brown bear emerge from the very cave we had just been hanging around smoking joints! The bear shakes its head violently before looking down towards us sniffing the air intensely and immediately upon making eye contact let's rip an almighty roar in our direction.

It vibrates around the lake with the force of a bomb! The shock wave arriving milliseconds later as a strange indescribable sensation hits our stomachs! Mitsu is first to run. Hey I yell and run after him! Then everyone began running after me running after Mitsu. I didn't even have to look behind to know everyone else was running as I could feel them coming up on either side of me trying to overtake! Automatically we ran towards the camp-fire, much to the amusement and laughter of the nomads. Within minutes we are by the fire and assured that the mix of dogs, yaks, fire and humans will always keep the bear away. *Shi Kata Ga Nai* Mitsu says and we all laugh.

Dinner! Shouts the old man. Throughout the meal I would glance towards the rock where I could make out the silhouette of the bear sitting in the moonlight watching us, but soon enough I forget about the bear and around the fire someone begun the art of storytelling. The old nomad in whose home we're sleeping tonight tells us how the Chinese occupied the area sixty years ago! My parents hid from the invading army sent from Beijing he said, the Chinese stick mainly to the towns! So the country is still our domain. It will always belong to us Tibetans he says proudly. I ask him what would happen if they ever come here and he drags his finger across his throat.

One time they offered us solar panels he laughed but we just tell them go, we may have no education. But we understand the Chinese mind and what they are up to, how they work move and manipulate! The Chinese are trying to get us Tibetans to be slaves but NEVER he bawls slapping his leg. Besides, he leans forward staring directly into my eyes where am I supposed to put a fucking solar panel? Everyone falls around laughing.

Later unable to sleep as tired as I was I decided it was pointless to continue trying, so I sat up and quietly looking around me saw everyone was asleep. So I tip toe over Mitsu and yet again picked up his smokes. I slide one out and ever so quietly stepped over the drivers to go outside. Then the old nomad's eye shot open! I froze looking at him but he didn't budge an inch, just smiled and closed his eyes.

Outside in the fresh air I behold the tranquillity of this special place, the fire is low but red cinders glow, dam I say quietly to myself looking around. It looks more amazing now than earlier. I squat down pick up a twig with a hot end and light my smoke. I sit taking it all in out of nowhere my grandfather comes to mind again, the way he used to inhale his smoke, for the second time since I arrived in Tibet I think of him, then get the most vivid flashback ever.

I was twelve years old having a sleepover in a friend's house, my mate had a tent pitched out the back garden and we slept in it. For a twelve year old this was adventure, his mom put one of those old plastic alarm clocks with the red digital lights on the window ledge for us to know the time. Sure enough in the middle of the night something woke me. A blanket of cold had covered me. I awoke and though my sleepy eyes was immediately frozen stiff. I looked at the dark shadow peering in at me through a gap in the tent zip! Mr Death! Terrified I looked at my friend for reassurance but he was asleep, the shadow seemed to panic sensing I saw him and disappeared.

Disorientated after a few minutes I crawled towards the entrance to look outside and verify the grim reaper was indeed gone. I looked around he was nowhere to be seen. Once relaxed I looked over at the clock, I can remember quite clearly even today years later that it said four thirty am exactly. I lay back down and eventually fell asleep. Next morning my aunt came to pick me up and I noticed her numbed expression. Instantly I knew what was wrong.

My grandfather whom I had always been very close too had been very ill. She told me my granddad had passed away during the night. I looked at her sadly and then asked what time did he leave us? Around four thirty this morning! Why? nothing I shrugged. I was twelve years old and something I cannot possibly understand woke me that night. A force so powerful I couldn't comprehend! The sprits came to me that night, or maybe it was grandpa saying goodbye.

They say if you punch a twin the other twin will feel the pain, even if they are not in the same country! But you are telling me you're not spiritual? The afterlife that realm of connectivity between this world and the next, the ying and yang heaven paradise call it what you like. In our dreams and through introspection we can see the creations, but trapped in our physical bodies our ability to interact with them is limited. Man chases the elixir of life without even trying to understand just how fucking real the afterlife is! I thought all this to myself outside in the middle of the night in the middle of nowhere in the middle of Tibet.

Early next morning the old man gave out coffee which we drank, hey Barry! Yes Luke? From this morning on I am making a pact! About what? That on the rest of my travels throughout these lands and forever more no matter how long it lasts, where ever it is I promise I will consume without question all which is offered with an open mind! Funky shit bro. Then we hear clapping and turn around and see its Aaron. Very good Luke very good.

Only by emptying your conciseness of judgments and preconceptions can you really open our mind to true knowledge and awaken from the false perfection that is delusions of grandeur! Aaron says. As the greatest enemy of knowledge is not ignorance! So what is it then? It is the illusion of knowledge of course! What else? All aboard shouts bahadur.....to be continued Aaron! Of course Luke.

In no time we're back on the road and all alone with our thoughts to keep us company whilst we stare out the window. The imagery flashing and whizzing by outside was lost in a stoned haze. As a different world passes by one of abundant magnificence and resilience. Quickly it mirages into a picture in your mind then disappearing in a microsecond from your sight outside the window. Only to be instantly alive again in your mind later and forever more when you desire to pluck it from your minds hard drive. Where you subconsciously place it till the end of your life. That's the joy of travelling.

In our journey of self discovery through the land that time forgot we passed a huge blue sign on the highway with massive white numbers and big Chinese writing. You know the kind you get on highways... I assume it is giving some indication as to how many miles it is to somewhere but it isn't. Mr Bahadur tells us once prompted that it is in fact telling us how many meters we are above sea level. But what caches my eye is not the meter signage no matter how surreal that was but the four large eagles sitting atop of it like hoodlums they watch us riding into town! It's their hood of course they are watching us.

The snow-capped Dargo Mountain lies to the west of Nagqu with the Burgyi Mountain to its east. These two mountains guard over the land like two Lions! The central west region is vast as its flat Mr Bahadur soberly added. President Hu Jintao begun his political career here as a general sectary for the communist party Bahadur explains with a certain pride. So what's to do here? I ask...not a lot he laughed.

But you can purchase medicine from plants that only grow here. This is where Chinese the world over source their medicines which they then sell as Chinese medicine! From Beverly-hills to Sydney from the streets of Buenos Aires to London's China town it all comes from Nagqu you learn something new every day. We check into our hotel which turned out to be ok. The manager informed us that we had only just missed the famous festival of exorcism.

I buy some 'Aweto' from a street vendor promising

me it's great for all sorts of future ailment. Everything from opium addiction to living into old age can be sorted out by this one herb he tells me. Then its bedtime and up before dawn and we were out the door and back on the road. The rest of the day was spent driving up and down hills along winding roads. This was the first time since we began our adventure that we were still driving when darkness fell! It felt strange exciting a new buzz and adrenaline rush.....

Sure we had drove into Lhasa in the dark but this was different, that was Lhasa which is a city but out here was nothing! The moon in the sky and wolves howling up at it! I dared to not even think about the temperature outside the jeep! Or the dilemma we would face should we break down! More than once did wild a Tibetan horse suddenly run in front of us. Dashing across what after all must be a new addition to his landscape. A road and our jeep. Reckon he knows where he is going Luke? Barry asked me as he handed me a joint. As we both stared watching him gallop into the darkness. Of course he must know I laughed.

Then out of nowhere we arrived in a city! Just like that. A city alive with people and excitement, of huge entertainment complexes competed with fancy apartment block's each one trying to outdo the last in terms of extravagance and size! Water fountains cinemas and internet cafés all try to entice passersby. The dazzling lights were calling and we had answered. For we had finally arrived in the frontier city we needed to be. The city of Dzato.

DZATO

Back in about oh two thousand the millennium! Bahadur grinned, well this was a little town of dusty street's with maybe a few hundred souls living here. No shit? Barry said looking out at the urban sprawl...Never underestimate the Chinese! He says with a serious look in his eye...Never! OK I won't. Ten years ago the Chinese came here and built a dam, a small hydro-power station up the road but still big enough to power the city and surrounding countryside. Then they used that power to build several more dams all dotted all along the river...The largest being at Man-Wan several hundred miles downstream in south west Yunnan Provence.

Bahadur studied us in his rear view mirror as we navigated the streets. You see above this massive dam the Mekong is basically a gigantic deep reservoir that stretches for miles and miles. The power this alone generates has helped fuel China's boom. They have stolen god's gift to the Tibetans and we must never ever forget that guys! They marched into Tibet in the fifty's knowing perfectly well that in years to come they would need its resources as they could be used as part of their master plan..What plan? I asked. Luke you don't understand the Chinese mentality my friend! He said as we got out of the jeep and walk into our hotel. They don't plan for next year or the year after.

The Chinese will sacrifice anything and anyone to reach their end goals...Certainly seems so Barry says to me. I shrug as I notice a small old man's head pop up from behind a counter. He smiles at Bahadur who greets him with a warm handshake and bows. The man immediately joins in with Bahadur's criticism of the Chinese. I look at the others, anyone got a joint?

It's true and now the rumour is soon they will be allowing a Canadian mining company to dig for gold in Tibet. Don't look at me for fuck's sake Barry laughs! Gold? I blurt out. Everyone's eyes look towards me then realising I have nothing further to add the old man continues...adding oil into the mix! Oil? Cries Mitsu. Oh yeah Bahadur replies, they reckon the mountains up there contain every single thing modern corporations can use to make themselves rich and powerful.

Luke when you go home tell your people. The Chinese their leaders their government they are very dangerous! To who? You me everyone! They are equally very cleaver and they are the masters of the silent assassination. The what? They will spend a hundred years or more stalking you watching you what you have, what your engineers can create. All the time silently desiring it, generation onto generation secretly wanting the same, your lifestyle but never outwardly admitting it. Slowly they will begin creeping up on you bit by bit, waiting until the time is right to pounce like a cobra! He then begins coughing furiously. Are you ok? He nods they don't care how long they have to wait Luke.... OK I smile but still he holds onto me refusing to let go. I'm serious Mr Luke you must warn them...

I will Err I promise. Take heed my friend or in one hundred years your off-spring your children's children will be coming to Beijing and Hong Kong to be taxi drivers or hotel cleaners! They will stop at nothing! Nothing until they rule the entire world he bangs his fist on the counter! People in your government are helping them right now. London? Yes and America everyone is accepting their cheap goods every dam country! Wow that was quite a rant eh! Sara smiles. Yes it was...Him deep man him deep adds Ras... got to be said Barry laughs. What mate? He has a point about the toys.

For the first time in ages tonight I get a room to myself. All that's on TV is a Chinese soap opera until I find the BBC world service channel so I stay tuned into that hoping for some news from back home. Then breaking news comes in that trouble has broken out in Tibet..... Scores of monks are being been beaten up and arrested by the Chinese army! The reporter says with an angry expression.....Bastards.

The Source

The city was eerily deserted and freezing cold the next morning with just about every business shut. So we were on our way off out of the dusty dirty city and into the unknown under a gloomy mist quickly. An hour later in the middle of nowhere we passed a river. Is that the Mekong? I asked. No that's the Dzato river! Bahadur said and he stopped and got out to talk with the other driver, they checked maps and he then jumped back in...There is only one way up and its over this pass! It's not one you want to make a mistake with, he added.

By now we're on a dirt track that whirls its way around the mountain. Are you planning on sharing that or not? Barry said kicking my foot making me realise I was smoking the entire joint. Sorry mate there you go I respond as I pass it to him, stoned and onward we drove or well Bahadur did. Coming up out onto a small little river maybe only a foot deep, then he stopped, what to do now? he spoke to himself...you follow it perhaps? The river I mean but you're the driver, I told him. He laughed follow the river it is then Luke? So we follow the river my man. We rode along the bumpy riverbank until we came across a small village of small mud houses, bahadur got out and spoke to some man who came out suspiciously eyeing me and the others.

We leave after getting directions and it is still only ten am! Then cross a bridge and the compass says were headed west arriving up and onto another plain then we're back on a dirt track which goes on for maybe five mile's! Straight ahead a mountain range morphs into a lion. The guardian of spirituality and adventure I say aloud, huh? Barry says to me. Err nothing mate.

We descend as the compass swings wildly it stops pointing northwards. We drive for the next twenty minutes or so before coming to a point where we can only go left or right. Bahadur goes right the river becomes frozen so we drive on it for a while. Then we drive across a range and down a steep valley before he suddenly screeches to a halt and jumps out without uttering a word. The other Jeep pulls up and the drivers talk. Bahadur pulls open the door and leans in! We're lost.

What the fuck? Everyone jumps out. I thought you come here all the time? Barry says to him ...yes but there are many ways to get here plus at different times of the year...Meaning? I shake my head. Means different weather conditions don't it..So just what the fuck do we do now? Mitsu shouts, don't lose it bahadur tells him! Don't fucking lose it? You're the one that's fucking lost it man! It's no big problem look guys I have it all under control....How?

We will get directions! What the actual fuck bro? Barry screams from fucking who bahadur? The Abonable snowman or a fucking horse? Or don't tell me the local fucking yeti beer sales-rep! I no like your attitude boy! We are in the middle of the fucking Himalayas bro have you lost your senses? A light flurry of dry snow begins to gently fall as Brett take's out his phone to call Makodia. .bahadur shakes his head laughing! What's so funny? Sara asks rubbing her arms shivering. Phones don't work out here! Your technology can't help...Really? Well the fucking jeep's compass thing fucking helped didn't it? Oh Jesus he is right it's not working! Brett says his voice crackling. Look I am ex Ghurkha ...guys this is no problem just a minor issue, you just all need to calm down! Trust me, bahadur and the other driver then began talking.

Just then around a corner we hear a noise. It stops everyone in their tracks as the sounds near. A motorbike comes into view, he waves so we wave he smiles so we smile! He stops and talks with Bahadur. What's he saying Luke? What am I Mitsu a fucking translator? How do I know what! Ok bro shit....Look Mitsu I'm sorry dude but I presume they aren't talking about bikes and stuff know what I'm saying? Luke look I heard the word Mekong mentioned in there more than once so...well I suspect you would as its where were supposedly going.

The biker was pointing and indicating that we should follow him so we followed him! We drove for ages before this guy eventually went off in another direction, waving at us as he did. Then it was more small foot deep rivers, up more hills and onwards we went. Make a joint will you Barry? Ok. He lit it up and eventually passed it to me half smoked.

Bahadur stopped and what should we see but a house! Can you believe it? Bahadur jumps out knocks on the door. A somewhat startled looking old man pokes his head out. I can't fucking believe someone actually lives here do you? Maybe he is like a gamekeeper or what is it eh gatekeeper or something? Mitsu says. Could be Barry agrees! I turn and look at them! Both wiped out from smoking the finest hashish high up in the remotest mountains where the Mekong begins its life and thus creates and sustains untold life beyond. It's not a fucking stately manor were in. Then we burst out laughing.

Push up! Huh? push up bahadur says as he shoves the old boy in next to me. This way that way is just about all I can make out he is telling bahadur as he points and shouts and orders him to follow the stream! What's that? Barry says pointing straight ahead in the distance. We

97

see something glistening like a diamond as we approach a dam like wall of ice maybe fifty feet high. We come to a halt and jump out wetting our feet on the same stream we have been following all along. I trace the trickle of water with my eyes right back up to the wall of ice. This giant ice cube stuck between two muddy hills on either side. A glacier of frozen water! River water! The Mekongs water! We are at the source of the Mekong.

Dza Chu! DZA CHU! He shouts louder.... smiling and pointing at the ice! DZA CHU I ask he nods Dza Chu he repeats grinning. A rush comes from my stomach swirling around my rib cage and up into the back of my neck making the hairs stand and my body shiver! Bahadur Yes? The stream we were driving along was the Mekong all along? Crazy huh. I look around me and notice a small cluster of prayer flags blowing in the wind while the others are jumping and screaming taking photos.

A strange feeling comes over me. I could no longer hear a thing, not a bird in the sky nor a human voice, just a blissful spiritual feeling radiating an inner calmness and content, of amazing consciousness. I walked up to the wall of ice and touched it with my bare hand holding it until a little piece melted. Taking my hand away I cupped a small amount of water no bigger than a teaspoonful I looked up at the wall then drank the melting fluid.

Aaron stood with his arms outstretched palms facing upwards praying, his sister sitting in a yoga posture with her eyes closed looking as calm as she is beautiful. Nearby Ras Scooby and Brett are also sat cross-legged smoking a big fat joint watching all of us watching them. We exchange smiles but say nothing as we all savoir the moment. I remember all of this is being watched over by one old man who helped us get here. Whom we all forgot about the second we arrived. He doesn't get out just stays inside looking out at us smiling.

I picked up a large flat smooth stone. Pulling out a permanent black marker I wrote down our names and nationalities under which I put the date. Then walking over to the prayer flags I place it on top of the stones holding down the lines that the flags are hung.

Someone will see it have no dought about that Luke, especially once I return and tell Makodia. Then again you could come back and find it all alone huh. Who knows my friend who knows... Maybe bahadur but once that's still here I say pointing at the wall of ice. Then I'm happy.

Forty five minutes after we arrive bahadur suggests it's time to go! We need to make it back out onto the main road before dark. So with a finale glimpse of this little known wonder of the world we depart, dropping the old man en route. Three hours later just as darkness began falling we arrive back on the main road and a little later we reach it safely back to DZATO.

Rumour has it there is a fried chicken take away in town! Sara winks as we entered the hotel. So with visions of chicken tempting the senses of the hungry bellies we walk straight back out again to find some. A day spent in the cold smoking weed with only pot noodles in your belly isn't going to cut it. It's not too windy so we have a stroll around and while stretching our legs we come upon a square with some shops, sure enough there was a fried chicken place there. A Chinese fried chicken joint! We storm it.

Wasn't like the real thing was it? Barry says. It passed I laugh back as we walked out. Mitsu then eyed something in a shop window, walked away from us and then goes inside so we followed him. He bartered the price of something while we browsed. Once his deal was done and he got what he wanted a 'Wifi aerial gadget' we leave.

Luke you should get one too. I should? Uh huh this is a very powerful model! Really? do you know how much this is in Japan? Not a clue mate! Don't not even think this model is out yet. To be honest Mitsu I'm too tired for this let alone to go shopping. Then we noticed Barry was no longer with us. Where's Barry gone? Eh not sure says Mitsu looking around. Hey look there he is, Aaron pointed as we walked out of the shop we spotted him across the street talking to some shifty dude.

Upon seeing us he waves beckoning us over! This guy is a sailor, he says nodding in the dudes direction. He smiled and nods at us. Look Barry I'm real tired in fact I think I speak for all of us when I say that and.. Listen hang on a moment he knows another sailor who works on a cargo ship. I thought you said he is a sailor? Mitsu points out as he fumbles with his new toy.... anyway he says his ship is leaving tomorrow evening! And? And he can get us on-fucking board bro....for the right money amigo!

That's what! Whoa Barry slow down, you want to get on-board a cargo ship in China for a back hander to some guy you just meet on the street? Asks Scooby. Yeah what a fluke I met him huh....He's lost it! Scooby laughs, your mates lost it Luke....He's not my mate I protest. Yes he is just... well ok he is my mate I suppose. OK look Barry tomorrow were going one way and one way only, you got it? We're not jumping on some pirate ship in the middle of nowhere.

Besides you can't trust some dude you just met moonlighting as a fixer for a corrupt sailor or is it a sailor moonlighting as an oh forget it...What do you mean Luke? We're going back to Lhasa where else and not on some dodgy cargo ship manned by god knows who.

No mister good crew professional! The man interrupts supporting Barry. I sensed him feeling nervous and with that a passing police car totally spooked him practically making him run off! Bahadur gently grabs Barry by the arm! Look we are leaving in the morning. I have to get back to my boss and my family so I cannot wait about while you go. Hey its cool bahadur just go without me! What? See he's totally lost it alright Scooby says to Bret? Hey bro you know we can't do that! Mitsu steps in..why not Barry laughs? I thought we are part of a team, a family? He says looking at us for approval to which he receives the desired collective nods and grunts.

Besides we can't just leave you wander off into the night with a stranger! Barry looks at all of us shaking his head. Look guys you do not understand! OK educate us Aaron says. Yeah mon your chatting one bag of pure rubbish right now yuh nuh! Ras tells him.

Look tomorrow the ship departs in the evening and in twelve short hours it pulls into the golden triangle brother! Whoa bro did you just say golden triangle? As in where Burma meets Thailand and Laos? I asked. Is there any other? He says with a *mischievous* grin...I look at the others whose faces give away little. Look guys I have a whole lifetime of cold weather waiting for me back in Canada and I've had my fill of wind and snow for a while I think,

Shit! I say to myself looking at my feet,what to do next?

I look at Scooby and Brett and see they are in deep discussion as is Aaron and his sister.

Then I notice so are Mitsu and Natsumi! Barry how long did you say we are on this ship? Dude reckons twelve hours minimum twenty max! Bullshit how can you go from China to Burma or wherever in that short time on a boat? asks Brett. He has a point Barry. I say to him. It OK Mist-errr! the man screams in broken English shattering the calm discussion, having gotten the jest of the argument at hand. The man explains in his broken words, big river, ship hab power no problem for you, twelve hours my fren he says holding up ten fingers. Ship hab POWER he repeats.

What would my granddad do? I ponder in the mist of this argument. He'd say you have come this far now go the rest. There you go Barry says...what did I tell you? No more wind rain and def no more snow for me, its Pinocolada time once again so get the sunscreen out baby. he says rubbing his hands, because big Barry's a coming to town. We all laugh at him...Barry.....Yes Mr Steel? Count me in. I look at Mitsu and Nat who grin, well the sun would be nice! Gimme five I say and as we slap as we look at the others.

Brett and Scooby smile at each other then turn and say all for one and one for all..

We're in Aaron nods as Sara turns and smiles and we all hug. Do a Jamaican need visa for this place mon? Ras grins scratching his chin. Not sure Ras but I'm pretty dam sure a few bucks in the right direction would sort it out. I mean none of us are actually entering or via any official customs port so we're all technically going to be in the same...Boat points out Bahadur it's only then I look at bahadur who laughs as he asks what am I going to tell the boss huh? He will think your all dead! We all laugh.

We agree a price arrange a rendezvous and hey presto we're on our way to Thailand! In the morning we checked out early, bid our farewells with bahadur, shook hands and promised to stay in touch then just like that they were gone! Our contact the sailor arrived and points out which bus to take. The bus driver tells him how long it will take. Then phones a friend to pick us up at the next bus station. We give him half the money in advance whilst promising the rest to the guy helping us board the ship. Then and only then do we get on the bus and he hands me two mobile phone numbers on a bit of paper.

Number me! He says and this friend number you! Any problem call me. I hope this guy don't let us down, Aaron says as he chucks his bags on board. Nah laughs Barry! How do you know? I got his email...You have? Yeah he laughs. What does that prove? Scooby inquires with a tilted head. I told him lots of more tourists are coming after us you know, to do the source thing! And they will definitely want to do this journey too. So I don't think he will rip us off.

As we boarded the bus the driver gave me a ticket. I looked down at it noticing it was written in Chinese and quickly gave up any attempt at deciphering it. Out of curiosity I decide to ask the driver our destination...Huh? The driver laughs at me. You speaking English! Yes I laugh back, why what is so funny? Shangri-la........ Excuse me? Shan-Gri-La he says slowly. Is destination you...I thought that was a hotel? Barry says as he and the others also look at their tickets! Shangri-La sounds exotic laughs Scooby.

From Shangri-La to the Golden Triangle

After spending most of the morning and afternoon on a rattling shaky old bus we finally arrived thirsty and hungry into the frontier town of Shangri-la! A stunning beautiful old town where just about every building nook and cranny was made of wood. Making it a deadly fire hazard waiting to happen. Makes you feel like you've been teleported back in time eh I laughed as we stepped out of our bus and watched it roar off leaving us covered in dust, all alone in yet another strange cities.

Mitsu laughed dusting himself off. The only tourists in a sea of Chinese faces eh Barry grinned at me! Hang on let me phone the number I was given by the sailor, the voice on the other end informed me to stay put! What did he say? Five minutes I shrugged as a hawker approached me almost immediately offering a book. No thanks! Of all the fucking things that I didn't need carrying around with me now was a book I moaned wiping the sweat and dust off my forehead. We stood around smoking and generally discussing what's going to happen next.

It's by James Hilton, the woman hissed in a scornful way startling me from behind. Never heard of him! I fired back, why you don't ask Aaron or Barry? Because he is British like you! Yeah right, still I never heard of him mate! Huh, hey hang on how did you... This book, she goes on is called 'the lost horizon' it is the reason you are here no? Huh? Yes sir Mister, she grins nodding her head...this is why this place is..she waves her arms about.. Why it is called Shangri-Laaaa...come again I mean what or is it? Really are you joking?

No joking Mister this town was called Zhongdian until this guy.....you countryman you..Wrote this book!

104

She slapped her hand across it, making dust fly off as she made her point. Why? He got the Tibetan name wrong! He could not pronounce it! No way Zhongdian does not sound remotely like Shangri-la to me! Barry smirked, con artist! Away you she muttered as she scorned Barry....Shangri-la is Chinese. She says clearly upset by Barry's intrusion in our conversation. This is China! She stamps her foot into the dust.

So you mean to tell me that a name...famous all over the world was named its name because of an Englishman's inability to understand Mandarin? Exactly Mister! How much? Five dollar! Deal I hand her the cash. Even if its bullshit the story she told was worth the five bucks alone guys. Mitsu laughs. Do you know where we can get food? I ask as she hobbles away! Over there she points with her hand without looking back.

By the time we finished the food our man in Shangri-La arrived in an old US army ten ton open back pick-up truck...hey you! Yes you. Barry....Huh..he said you? Did he? No but he's your contact mate jump in...Come-on guys we are late for the ship..A collective 'we are' is shouted towards him as we scrambled up onto the back and he speed off through downtown Shangri-La's dusty streets. Kicking up dust we went with people, chickens, and donkeys alike all running for their lives to survive.

Err can you slow it down just a bit and how did you know we were the correct people? Aaron shouted through the noise and mayhem! The driver looks at him like he is crazy! Says nothing then changes gear and drives faster ignoring the question as he ignores the red lights! Dude doesn't like questions huh? I say to Aaron! Fuck the questions Mitsu says! Just pray.

We drove on for at least another hour without much in the way of conversation with our 'contact'. The truck was not as bad as it could of been thanks to the rice sacks that acted as our cushions in the back and once out in the countryside the breathtakingly beautiful scenery made up for it. Arriving at the cargo terminal just in time to get our boat. The transactions were done with some third party by our driver and we were off the truck up a gangplank and on board in under sixty seconds. Within another minute the boat slowly began moving away from the dock, as soon as our feet touched deck in fact.

Standing on deck we watched as the thousands of workers below marched up and down the ramps like ants to the various docked ships, carrying sacks of rice, grain and goodness only knows what else to the waiting trucks. Our own vessel was filled head to toe with....apples, apples and more apples, bound for Bangkok's market from where they would be distributed all over Thailand! Funny I would have thought the Thai's more than capable of growing a few apples Mitsu jokes to which we all nod.

The crew member allocated to be our concierge showed us an room. Empty except for a few bare mattresses on the ground this was to be our base. It was an empty room but not exactly as it had a small fridge in the corner! Aaron opened it and it was full of plastic jugs filled with. Fucking apple juice, he said picking one up looking and smelling before tasting it.

First time I heard you curse! Did I? Yup! Excuse me Luke! Only under duress and then I don't even realise I'm saying it. Now would anyone like some fucking apple juice? Leaving our bags on deck. I paused and looked at mine, there hardly going to be stolen Luke are they? Brett shruggs! Never know man Ras adds. OK let's sort that out now argues Natsumi so we put them inside the room and arranged them in such a formation that we could all lounge on them like bean bags. After a quick chat with our host we discovered a meal was part of the deal and the on-board cook made a scrumptious dinner of green chicken curry and vegetables. While eating dinner the ship moaned and ground to a halt.

Why do you think we stopped? Sara asked nervously, don't know Dam issue further on downstream is the most likely scenario I said attempting to look knowledgeable for a once. The captain then joined us for dinner. It was all very jovial and it explained why we had stopped if somewhat unorthodox still I must admit it was all good natured fun until..... Sara asked who was at the steering wheel.

The captain looked at her then shrugged. And it was like somebody had mentioned something about some long lost family member that nobody wanted reminding of as the crew just kept looking at their plate. She had clearly made some sort of 'faux pas' yet nobody was quite sure what. Eventually the captain excused himself and left as did the crew members.

Is he ok? Aaron asked the chef now on his own. Yeah yeah Chinese captain him no like question from woman, make him feel stupid in front of men...no good for him...but ok for you....thank fuck for that I added, thought he was going to make us walk the plank! Is it OK to smoke outside? Barry asked him. No problem mister come I join you...outside he noticed Barry rolling a joint and laughed at us as he smoked his ciggie...smoking Ganja is 'he pointed at Barry's Joint' something my grandpa used to do. Young people now, they do not want that they want tablets he said with a look of disgust. Then he chucked his ciggie over board and went back inside.

It was a mild evening on deck but soon enough we had forgotten about the weather as the herbs kicked in and at one stage I felt we were going too fast for a cargo ship and wondered was this the captains way of getting

Sara back! As I pondered this a shooting star shot across the night sky! Look guys I shouted and pointed up. It was a long slow shooter taking a good ten seconds to go from one side of the night sky to the next.

I have never seen one like this have you? I asked Aaron and Barry who were standing next to me. Nope! You know why it was moving that slowly? It is because we are nearer to the equator dude! It is? Of course...then if the shooting star wasn't enough excitement for one night a stunning firefly suddenly and very slowly whizzed past Scooby's face making everyone gasp.

We are getting nearer the tropics eh Barry? Yes sir he smiled. Then he got up briefly just to look overboard and spit into the darkness below. So how hot does this place get man? Ras asked. Real hot bro! Barry answers sitting back down and humid as hell. You can smell it in the air already can't you? Mitsu says looking up at the clear night sky. Filling his lungs with a joint as he did! Yup might as well throw the coats overboard. Natsumi laughed! Nah don't chuck them away! Well we aren't going to need them anytime soon where we're going are we? I pointed out.

Out of nowhere I thought of a really scary story I'd heard of years and years ago. Then thinking it might be fun to tell everyone as it seemed they were all in need of a good old bit of excitement! Who wants to hear a real scary story? Most said yes with Ras mumbling something about duppies and with both Mitsu and Natsumi agreeing with him whilst also mentioning sprits. I generally felt the consensus we're all saying yes except them, and seeing as they choose to stay. I told it as I felt subliminally deep down they wanted to hear it.

Its early seventies in northern England a man and his wife are driving home late one night having visited relatives who had just had a baby on the other side of

Yorkshire. Now the north of England its only about one hundred miles wide at most and is divided by a mountain range called the **Pennines** and that was a big drive back in those days, so the man tells his wife he knew a short cut. Buy using this disused old road that cut deep through a woods it would save them at least two hours so they decided to go for it! But only half an hour later their car runs of petrol.

So the guy says to the wife he will get out and walk for help. It's about a forty minute walk from here to an old public house where they also sell fuel to farmer's. I'll get some and will be back in no time! The wife is not sure but she doesn't feel like getting out into the lonely darkness of the woods and walking so with no alternative options on the table agrees with her husband! So off he goes, she watches as he disappears into the darkness! Grateful of the fact the battery is still giving power so as to be able to see a little from the headlights. Unfortunately no radio broadcasts used to work up the mountains back in those days so she had to sit in silence in the car.

What about car stereos? Asks Sara. Didn't come with cars back then I'm afraid! Tape players? Brett adds...nope....CDs?..Injects Mitsu as he passes me a joint! They hadn't even been invented you twit. Look do you guys mind! Can I continue? As I was saying. So soon enough looking at her watch she sees its nine o'clock. Then its ten, then eleven, by the time it reaches twelve she is frantic with worry, he should have been back hours ago she tells herself. Then to ad to her stress the battery goes dead leaving her not just cold but in total darkness and silence. When all of a sudden BANG!!!

A huge crash instinctively makes her crumble towards the floor, cowering looking up at the ceiling above she begins screaming. A huge dent in the roof stares down at her like something big and heavy has landed on it! Terrified and wide eyed she listens to the sound of the cars rooftop creaking above as it strains from some force or other on top of it. But then as quickly as it begun it stops.

Slowly drops of rain begin to fall gently hitting the roof, at first one every few seconds, then after a minute or two it begins to increase to several drops per second then suddenly another huge bang! A loud crash followed a more dripping sounds, then BANG again more rain drops! Who are you? What do you want? She screams....In this lonely place in the middle of nowhere where no one can hear you scream.

Suddenly fantastic bright lights illuminate the car from every angle! Completely blinding her.

It's like the car has been surrounded by a giant UFO! But the rain is still falling hard on the roof, then she hears a man's voice via a loud speaker...Hello, hey lady, you there in the car. Confused tired and cold her eyes foggy from tears. She looks around her three hundred and sixty degrees twisting and contorting her body to make out where he is trying desperately to figure out which way the voice was coming from.

This is the police do not worry ok you're going to be fine. I want you to slowly get out of the car. OK she says.....BOOM....Ahhh she bawls and screams once more. The newly found safety offered by the man's voice. The sanctuary the police seemingly brought to her desperate situation was again gone! It was now obvious to her even with the cops present something very serious was up. Can you understand me? The man said from the loudspeaker...she nodded..Yes she mumbled. OK I want you to get out and walk towards me, where are you? She stuttered? I can't see you............don't worry once you get out you will hear my voice clearer and just follow it ok.

Crying she opened the door and moved to get out! Mam.....she freezes.....what? she screamed holding up her trembling hands? DO NOT I repeat do not look up at the roof of your car ok just come towards me, do you understand? She nods and proceeds to get out. Slowly she begins walking towards the direction of his voice using her hand to shade her face from the bright blinding lights...She listens as she hears laughter something comes over her and she stops turns and unable to resist the urge she cannot help but look back at the car for one moment longer.

What she sees horrifies her....A patient that has escaped from a nearby mental institution is standing on the roof of her car! Dressed in workmen's overalls with soaking wet matted black hair from the rain, a broad jaw line is slightly camouflaged by his thin beard, a huge and powerfully built ex miner feared throughout Northern England and labelled 'Rabid Jack' by the media. He was originally sentenced to death for murdering an entire family but later reprieved when the death penalty was abolished.

He is standing holding a decapitated and blooded human head in his hands! A demented look strains the escaped madman's face as he studies the head. Closely examining the face of the poor soul he has obviously killed, before clumsily dropping the head over and over on to the roof of the car. A pool of blood covering the rooftop pours down the four sides of the car. Only then it dawns on her as her focus zooms in. It's her husband's head Rabid Jack is holding in his hands! Being dropped and picked up repeatedly like a clumsy child with a new toy the demented psycho laughs each time he drops his his toy! His head ...the woman screams and collapses.

111

So what do you think? huh guys I smiled....Looking around I notice everyone looks horrified numb or generally freaked out. Especially the girls who just stare at me with a blank expressions. Fucked up world we live bro! Mitsu chuckles as he passes a joint to Ras. You know that was the most fucked up shit I've ever heard Luke but kind of a cool story all the same...what was the name of this institution? Sara asks me. Huh I don't know! It was err somewhere in Yorkshire....eh you know it's up the north of England.

I don't like them type of stories man! Ras says shaking his head. No talk that deals with the duppies is good man! Wish I hadn't bothered now I think to myself. Then everyone starts to prepare go to sleep. I haven't upset anyone have I? Personally as much as I think it's sort of a fucked up tale Barry says passing me a joint! It was still a cool fucking story bro. Thanks mate! Seriously Luke! Totally fucking awesome man, he laughs don't think they get it. I thought it was super cool myself so I reckoned this lot would too! Now I wish I hadn't bothered. Don't worry about them Luke. Cheers mate, night Luke, night baz mate.

Last time I will tell them a bedtime story that's for sure! The ungrateful fuck-wads. I hope it keeps them awake all night I say to myself. I look down and notice someone's left the makings of a joint behind! Fuckers were in such a hurry to go. I grab it and one joint together as I rearrange the bags before grabbing a carton of apple juice someone else left.

I chilled as I made myself as comfy as possible. Then I lit up the Dobie as I settled in on the pile of bags I'd made a bed of. Fuck um fucking nerds the lot fuck um. I stare up at the clear sky above and my mind drift's, I noticed the weather has again gotten a tad warmer in the past hour or so. Gazing at nothing in particular sure enough another comet fly's a past, this time all on my own with no one to interrupt this moment I can stare in silence enjoying this magnificent spectacle. It's power holding me in a trance like state, a hostage to its beauty and awesomeness. For the stoner it doesn't get much better than this. Eventually drifting off into a deep ever so sweet sleep brought on by the swinging pendulum that is the sight of our beautiful timeless zodiac above.

I wasn't asleep long when I heard the first footstep's running past my head, only then was it apparent I was covered in sweat. Shit I'm drenched I realised as I kicked off the blanket. The temperature had soared dramatically overnight and my eyes squinted as the hot sunlight burned into them. I could just about make out the voices of the deckhands running about back and forth shouting in Chinese! And it didn't sound like they were celebrating Chinese New Year either! Confused? You bet I was.

I stayed where I was but the more I sensed the panic. I realised for certain this wasn't a health and safety drill! Neither was it some sort of Tai Chi exercise programme the captain had recommended to get the crew in shape....Luke get your shit what the fuck are you doing just sitting there mon? Huh..What Ras I looked up tired eyes squinting and still the slightest bit confused, no actually totally confused! What are you doing mon? He repeated! This time in a louder tone that also now had panic infused in it! Err don't know ...what's going on? I said rubbing my eyes.

What's going on? I tell you wha gwan man! Deh Babylon soon come deh and then a pure gunshot fi blast! What the fuck are you talking about? With that he grabbed my wrists and jerked me upwards towards him! Haven't got time to explain Luke! We must go now. I protested. NOW! I grabbed my bag knowing that

113

Babylon in Rasta talk meant authority of some kind! Thus the spreading panic amongst all aboard. But I was relieved to know at least the ship wasn't fucking sinking! But the fact I'd never heard Ras speaking his native patios or so excitedly before made my panic level's soar.

We began running after the others who we could see had gone running after our on board contact. Who had in turn ran after the chef, to only then realise the chef was topping bags upon bags of suspious looking pills over board! Why you run after me? He yelled as he empted the contents overboard. With that the ship tilted towards an embankment and it was only then I understood how close and narrow a section of waterway we were in... Excellent place for a raid or ambush! Brett grinned..Depends on your perspective! Barry smiled Go.....the chef bawled his face contorted with a mixture of emotions I won't forget in a hurry! With that we all turned around to be confronted by the captains second in command holding a handgun.

Thai commandos are boarding the other side at this very minute to do a drug search, he shouted. All things considered if they find you on board captain get big fine, maybe even prison! Hang on a minute I protested. Shut up you smoke drugs last night. He smiled, we know and if Mr.... If Thai customs find drugs you in big trouble, and us too so you get fucking off our ship now! He pointed at the embankment with his gun, shouted at his men who immediately begun chucking our bags overboard, then pointed the gun at me.

Then we're forcibly directed towards the thick rope ladder hanging overboard.

No way Sara says... It's too dangerous! Aaron holds her and as he is about to say something when we hear the revolver being cocked then pointed directly in her face! OK Aaron screams! With no words spoke I grab her hand to escort her turning around I notice Barry already on the rope making his way down. Wait! I yell at him as she climbs onto his back and they quickly disappear from sight. Don't hang around for the Thai's to find you go in bushes ok. I shout.

No sooner had we got to the bottom and dragged ourselves through the chest high water and mud crawling onto the land, than the ship began tilting back outwards again. No mistake about it this was the captain's cleaver ploy to slow the Thai's whilst giving us time to disappear. We ran with our bags into the bushes and looked up at the ship groaning and straining as it came to a halt. Then we saw commandos dressed in black on deck. Let's get the hell out of here before something bites us Scooby suggested..

I'm not talking about those little buggers either he added looking at the high grass. We walked through the paddy fields passing the water buffalos and the odd field worker, eventually a farmer we came across pointed us in the right direction to town. Fucking mozzies Barry screamed as he slapped his arm. Instantly a red spot appeared, he looked at me....easy know we are back in the tropics eh.........uh huh. I'm so thirsty let's get to this town.

First time Laos? The waitress asked...Err yes! It is actually I smiled back as she looks at the others... Hope you enjoy your stay, she added after taking our order. Seems nice here don't it? Mitsu smiled at me, seems so. We had jumped ship in Laos. Then came upon the dodgiest looking customs outpost ever. Which I got to admit in hindsight was a blessing 'you can pay me twenty dollar each and I stamp passport now or pay five dollar and wait outside for next two hours while I watch American wrestling' smiled the toothless customs officer with the Elvis hairstyle.

The customs checkpoint had a counter on which a TV was positioned for them to watch. Also present was an industrial sized tub of hair wax and a large black handgun! With the customs post itself being just a shed with a corrugated iron roof. Located conveniently at a criss crossing of canals and roads! Here's my twenty I said to him without as much as a 'give me a second to think about it' An hour later we checked into a hotel and were sitting in the hotel café enjoying the view of the rivers and canals that connected the land in front of us.

Well at least we're beginning to finally feel some of that warm weather eh? I smiled as I lounged in a big straw chair trying not to dwell about the past few hours of madness.

Barry sat across from me looking out across the harbour with his new binoculars. How are they? I asked, not bad not bad at all! He said smiling without taking them from his eyes.

Just checking out how far they seem to go. And? And It's looking good dude ...check out that little island a way over there. I ask him pointing at a tiny speck in the distance oh yeah .

Wonder what it's called he says? We call Ko Mekong! Looking up we see it's the waitress.

Why you want to go somewhere? Excursion huh, she nods...well we got to go somewhere says Mitsu smiling at her! She leans into the table and looks about to see if her boss is watching. You guys ever hear about Nam-Ha? It's a Big National Park? Nope I reply looking around at the others who show a collective shake of the heads.

OK you go she smiles! Yeah? I nod. Yeah why not Mr she nods back! How far? One hundred kilometres! Maybe two but it's so cool! Why? Aaron asks. Trust me you will love it! Yeah but why the man said? Barry persists insisting on a more detailed answer! Why what?

Why will we...guys chill....How do we get there? I ask, Get the local bus downtown and when you get there you rent elephants to go into the jungle spend a few days, maybe a week..Its wild she laughs tigers camping, mushroom's all that funky stuff you foreigners love are there waiting for you, trust me you will never forget it.

Did she just say a few days? Sara asks I believe she did, laughs Barry. That means sleeping where exactly? the waitress had begun walking off before Sara's question could be heard or answered! But she also mentioned shrooms! Bret grinned getting out his laptop and confirming its existence.. if my calculations are correct this park is the size of England Luke. Show me that. I take a look, it's nothing of the sort I laugh handing him back his laptop, might give Scotland a run for its money thou but not England.

The waitress brought us our drink. When you reach the park ask for Channarong! Why? Aaron asks her. He is my brother he take good care of you plus he have elephants! Far-rang must be careful. far-rang get lost there one time...never seen again! Shit Aaron says..yes very sad. What did she call him? Sara inquires. Far-rang Scooby says. It's a Thai expression but I think it is spreading.

Did she mention shrooms or was I tripping? Aaron laughed. What do you think Luke? I reckon we should split Barry. Never know if those commandos saw us run through the fields and have some odd arrest type warrant out here just for us which some local cops could pick us up with! And with that we had all agreed that getting out of town was the best option available. Besides it beat hanging around in this town.

Life in Laos is different and everything shuts down at ten pm sharp, it's definitely more backpacker hippie type hang out than party central Barry moaned. It is for the best mon Ras tells him. It's cool man because we are all in bad need of a serious night's sleep. So we congregated for a little while in Aaron and Sara's room as it was the only room with a balcony offering a street view. We smoked a few joints watched the street life below with its constant stream of motorbikes zooming up and down providing enough visual entertainment to compliment the jokes stories and conspiracies being told.

I fell in love that first night in Laos not with a person but with the way locals in general drive casually about without helmets. Nor not a care in the world as they chat with the other riders on the nearest bike next to them as they drive through the streets. With the warm breeze of night gently blowing through their extravagant hairstyles! It was to be something I would always remember after that first night in Laos and stay with me in my heart. What I didn't fall in love with was mosquitoes and geckos.

Ready? Barry asked as he sipped an espresso next morning as I strolled into the restaurant. Yup you? Yup! Once checked out we found ourselves sitting in the shade of the local bus terminal fanning ourselves from the muggy midday heat. Awaiting the bus to Nam-Ha! Eventually it arrived bags grabbed by hustlers which ended up on the roof with a rope tied around them so we didn't care. And we got on board for the grand old price of one American dollar each. For a journey of over one hundred miles you got to admit it was a pretty good deal.

Rattling along out of town I turned towards Ras who gave me a big smile! Ras! Yeah Mon...What's a duppy? He frowned! No seriously mate I'm not being horrible I heard Bob Marley say it on one of his songs and was you know wondering what a duppy is...is a ghost he laughed, really? Yeah man. I blushed as I noticed Sara looking at Nat shaking her head like I was a kid. Myself and Ras

118

gave each other a fist bump and laughed. It took all day to get to Nam Ha as in the end we drove around a never ending series of bendy roads and making frequent stops every few miles for the locals. But it was I must admit the nicest coolest most relaxing journey I'd been on since I left London. And as dusk loomed we drove into town.

Luang Namtha which is the stop off point for Nam Ha wasn't much to write home about. It had the compulsory river which was just about all it had if you asked me. Once checked into a lodge 'also by the river' and sorted out rooms. Our group taking more or less every available one they had. The walls were all woven together from flattened bamboo and looked the most serious health and safety disaster waiting to happen. After dinner we agreed it best to only smoke outside for fear of turning our lodgings into a raging inferno. The river flowed past the lodge was nice and tranquil so we chilled for a while having a smoke while Ras slowly hummed a long forgotten song.

Know the tune man? Yes doesn't everyone replied Aaron! Know what it means? Not really if I am honest I thought it was Err just a tune....no no no man you see the Rasta-man regard Ethiopia as the motherland! And believe we will eventually return. Ah. As such the homeland was seen as a place of fond memories. A place of freedom and life prior to oppression brutality and slavery! Eventually becoming regarded as equal to heaven or Zion to the Rasta-man. Then a swarm of mosquitoes cut the deep conversation short as we ran inside to escape.

In the morning we set off to locate some elephants, naturally the guy the waitress mentioned came to mind but before five minutes had passed he had found us! Hey guys! Hey guys yes you he pointed. I'm Channarong! He announced as we walked along. Where you been? How do we know you're 'the' Channarong? Ras asked him tilting his head! Because the waitress sent you here he smiled. This waitress is your? Sara asked eyeing him suspiously! Wife he smiled. OK she smirks looking at me. So you guys want elephants huh? See what I mean Aaron everyone around here lies! Yeah. Don't fret don't fret? Look Sara take it easy there's plenty of us here, it's not like it's just us two anymore, we are safe! Aaron reassured her

Besides I smiled putting my arm around her, we're out of danger now.

You got good strong elephants man? Ras asked him. Hab. Three, why how many you wann? Not sure but three should cover it Barry tells him. Can we see their condition? Mitsu inquires. In a failing effort to come across as assertive! You know to see if there up to the task at hand! Know what I mean guys? He says winking at me! Ok no problems my friend me come come. We walked after him up the dusty streets.

Rounding a corner of broken old walls that were once buildings we see them. Tied onto a steel pole on the ground. Huge but graceful they stood. This one is Ayanna! He says patting the first one we're shown. And that one over there is Breyanna! he points. Lastly over here he smiles as he strolls over and gently pats her! I give you the baby Ms Ceyanna! He grins as he poses next to her. Nice combo on the names bro! Mitsu jokes Yeah Mon A B and C! We agree the fee and before nine am our bags are hooked onto the elephants and we were up and away on our journey.

Within minutes we're out of town and into the rolling countryside and before long deep into the heart of the Nam-Ha national park! And deeper still into the very heart of the infamous golden triangle itself! So what exactly is there in this forest? Scooby shouts over at Channarong as we slowly ride along. Tigers, Leopards the usual stuff you get in Jungles my friend! Jungles? Shrikes Nat. I mean Parks.

Swaying gently from side to side we enjoy the ride and take in the views. Don't worry guys Barry say's trying to calm the ladies, in Canada we got all sorts of lion's tigers and bears! Really I knew about the Bears but didn't know about Canada having Lions and Tigers mate! Brett tells him. Well that's cause we don't ha ha, we laughed as we entered the jungle which provided the perfect canopy and natures protection from the sun by tress and lots of them.

Lions and Tigers and Bears joked Nat slagging Barry. Lions and Tigers and Bears she repeated laughing at him. Looking at the rest of us laughing, lions and tigers and bears, she continued to sing with Sara joining in ...lions and tigers and bears, then we all begun to chant it as we entered the jungle under a burning hot sun! As the day wore on and with the humidity becoming intense to the point of being unbearable, with all of us sweating profusely except Channarong. We were pleasantly surprised when Cyanna stopped and refused to move.

Channarong halted and as we looked back she begun huffing puffing and kicking up a fuss and making a general racket before turning and strolling off up a path to our left all of her own accord. With the girls jokingly screaming for help and waving at us to save them. As it all seemed fun we laughed too. What's up? Aaron asked Channarong. Oh nothing don't worry she's young maybe a snake or something spook her! It's no problem, he smiled. Come let's follow them.

We turned around to begin following them, why are we following them? Barry asked...I mean where too bro? Yeah man isn't this leading us away from our destination? Ras shout's across from Breyanna. What destination my friend? Channarong laughs. We stop where we stop! Then we camp where we champ, once the elephants have water everything is cool, he said giving the ok hand symbol. Ras looks over at me. I shrug my shoulders. I know mate I thought he had a destination too but he's the guide.

The morning turned into afternoon as we ploughed through the jungle at the slow pace the elephants moved. Offering fantastic photo opportunities and views you would never ever otherwise get to see if you were on foot! Guys it looks just like a wildlife documentary Bret mentioned and it did! We passed around drinks and joint's to each other smoking and laughing as we told jokes and were generally having the time of our life's.

At times we were able to pluck and eat fruit from the trees we passed! A trick I must confess Channarong showed us initially but which we all soon mastered. Mr Channarong how exactly do we find our way back? Mitsu asked about mid-afternoon. We don't! What do you mean man? They do he says pointing at the elephants.

By late-afternoon we stumbled across a small waterfall and Channarong decided it was the perfect spot to make camp for the night. After chaining the elephants up near the water so they could drink, he rolled out a huge tent and we all helped to put it up, well we put rocks on the edge! But it was all good and up within twenty minutes. Do I deliver or do I not deliver Channarong laughed as did his content customers. He then he produced a small gas stove lit it and we boiled packs of noodles for a snack.

After the snack we decided go for a stroll! Channarong can you show us the flora n fauna I asked. Is he going show us the shrooms dude? Barry says elbowing my ribs. Shush don't freak him out mate. I will ask when the time is right! When? Not sure Baz when times right ok? OK! Careful were you put your foot guys! We don't want any accidents Channarong smiled.

As we walked and talked I suddenly got the urge, a strange urge to look over towards a tree. As I did I spotted something move! Totally freaked I instantly looked away spooked and without wanting to seem an idiot I looked again to confirm, nothing! Now I have that strange feeling, you know the one you get deep down in your guts when you feel someone is watching you? But I admit I was afraid of everyone laughing at me, it was hot and I was tired maybe exhausted or worse coming down with something, had I been bitten by some insect?

Still walking but now lagging behind the main group I tripped and staggered over bits of old bark and branches. I felt the hairs on my neck stand and had to force myself not to shiver with Barry and Mitsu just a few feet in front of me. With the others quickly disappearing from sight after Channarong. Again I get the urge so quickly I dart a glance in its direction! Fuck I see it, it's real alright. I'm certain it's not a mirage or something, scared my eyes dart towards the ground...its shadow like and it's moving, moving fast.

It fucking moving I hissed under my breath hoping the lads would hear me without having to scream out loud! You're not imagining things I tell myself. Watching out the corner of my eye but too scared to stare directly at it. Fuck I know one hundred percent we are not just being watched! We're being followed stalked we're someone's or something's pray and that's no delusional stoned conspiracy nor the heat nor is the fucking sugar rush from all the fruit I've been eating all day getting to me. This is for real.

But what or who is watching us I do not know! I'm

123

confused disorientated or am I? Is it the sugar afterall? I'm in a jungle and...a wave of panic engulfs me, causing my body to weaken, as the mind body coordination fails as I desperately try to catch up with the others. My voice stutters whilst the unstable ground makes it impossible to move fast without risking tripping or falling over and thus breaking a bone! With each twig I stood on snaping as I moved getting louder and the obvious need to watch where I stepped of paramount importance. I looked behind me and begun to tremble and shiver as the fear gripped and bit into me like hooks.

With the others barely a few dozen feet ahead I attempt to whistle. But as I did they disappeared down an embankment out of sight. That added to the fact my throat was drying up meant they couldn't hear me! I got to move faster I cursed myself but don't move too fast or you could fall. I don't want to die here! Just then it I watched in horror as it darted between some trees to my left. Jesus help me I cried.

A human or human like figure stalks us. Flashes of the Yeti appear in my mind's eye as do Mo, Mr Cheng, Bahadur, Brandon....it has to be human, surely it cannot be a monkey they're not that large in Asia so it has to be a human! Maybe it's that lost fellow we heard about from the waitress and we are going rescue him? Shit I tripped and fell down on my hands and knees! I balance myself trying my best to stand up as the cry from my mouth due to the pain of a sharp stone jabbing into my kneecap stung me like a needle. As the others come into a slight view in front of me having heard! Everyone stopped and looked at me get up hobbling towards them.

Baz Mitsu guys! You ok Luke? Yeah sure, well no actually look I got bad news! Now don't make it obvious and go staring ok! But I think we are not alone here. Oh great Luke other tourists? Slightly giddy I persist. No but

124

I do not think we're here all alone! OK we heard that bit! Barry says looking around him. Look I understand this may sound crazy but over my shoulders somewhere, last seen at two o'clock as they say in the army. Where Luke? Mitsu asked with a genuinely worried frown. Over there behind the trees I saw someone or something moving about, running, watching us, stalking us.

Well there isn't jack shit to be seen now buddy! Barry says walking off adding....get out of the sun Luke without a hat it could be sunstroke, makes people you know delirious! Huh...what an asshole I think to myself. Hang on a minute. Can you for once just stop acting like a fucking asshole? Or is it you practised so hard it just comes natural now? I shout. It's at least thirty five fucking degrees bro, seriously get some shade Luke, he shouts back.

Wrap a t-shirt around your head, it might help. How about I wrap a fucking python around your neck you fat fuck. Mitsu hangs with me a moment longer before shrugging his shoulders...Don't know Luke but try not to stress dude as it's probably a deer or something you saw. Before walking off after the others. A what? A fucking deer? In Thailand? Are you on drugs Mitsu? We're not in Thailand Luke. And technically yes I am but I prefer to regard them as Entheogens. Oh well forgive me I stand corrected.

I look over at Aaron who gives me a look bordering on pity before adding with a sympathetic smile, is it possible that maybe a coconut fell? Oh whatever mate what fucking ever! Fucking wankers the lot of them! Fucking nerdy wanking fuck-wad wankers! Knew I should have gone travelling with guys I knew. I fucking knew it now look at me stuck in a fucking jungle with a bunch of fucking pussies. I look around the tress once more but don't see anything! Maybe he's correct, maybe it is the sun after-all!

That is it, I tell myself as I hobble after the rest of the group. I'm not going to look in its direction again. As I catch up they're discussing how to get our bearings. With Ras offering his wisdom. I used the night sky as my compass during my Himalayan trekking man...Not much good during daylight is it? Laughs Scooby. That is true man. OK look you lot I am not fucking about alright. Now I know the stupid escaped lunatic story didn't go down too well the other night but seriously I'm not taking the piss this time ok! We are being watched!

I get blank expressions! Look we got to turn back go the way we came and do it now or else.....Oh give it a rest Luke will you? You're actually starting to freak us out and sound a bit crazy now! Sara tells me! Look I am not going crazy from heatstroke or whatever the fuck you think but I swear I saw! BOOM....BOOM ...BOOM Three massive loud explosions rock the ground and blow up earth where we stand, sending birds flying then we hear Channarong screaming Ayanna......Fuck dude the elephants! Brett shouts.

With a look of terror that I'd not previously seen before. Channarong bolts past us pushing both Aaron and Sara onto the ground as he disappears into the jungle out of sight and I suppose towards base camp. Then as more shots rang out our senses returned, and with few options the others ran after him. Leaving me again at the back and on my own again! Hey, I shouted as I too begin running after them. Fucking stupid fuck-wads no one fucking listens to me.

When we arrive at base camp a scene of devastation awaits us. The elephants lay dead in huge pools of blood that has already begun to congeal in the heat! They shot them, they shot them. Channarong repeats weeping. By who? Nat cries as she holds onto Sara terrified! Who are they? I heard strange sounds like shouting Ras says to her. What did you hear? I quiz him. Yee-Ha type shit you know hillbilly stuff man. Channarong begins mumbling and speaking in his native language.

They haven't taken the tusks Mitsu mumbles as I look at him. What mate? He looks at me! As the realisation slowly kicks in! Of course not girl elephants don't have tusks Barry says! Don't they? I've never heard anything so stupid Ras laughs... Females don't have tusks! They don't, you know like Lions the males they have the hair, the females don't! Well female elephant's don't have tusks. Sorry to interrupt your stupid little fucking discussion but if you lot don't fucking listen to me now and get the fuck out of here like I'd suggested ten minutes ago it's us that is going to be on the endangered species list.

He has a point! Adds Aaron. Get it together and stop fucking about! We got to get away from here and quick! Why? Scooby asks......why? Are you fucking retarded why do you think? The blood will attract all sorts from miles around. Lord fucking help me. Look sorry to point out the obvious Scooby and be ever so slightly rude but we GOT TO GET THE FUCK OUT NOW! I hiss with the sweat pouring down the left side of my face and veins pumping up my neck. Calm down Luke! You're scaring the girls! Scooby replies.

Listen mate who ever shot them aren't fucking poachers! I mean do I really have to state the fucking obvious? What do you mean Luke? They have taken out our fucking transport. Now I told you I saw something and they have decided to take away our only means of escape you thick fuck-wad. Luke just relax. Stop telling me to relax when we got gun tooting god knows what out there, that I think want our fucking skins more than the animals! Luke relax we are going to sort this out!

127

How Mitsu how? Dial nine fucking one one? Yeah don't all talk at once. Oh yeah they have been watching us all a fucking long! I say pointing into the bush in a circular movement.

It's us the hillbillies are after not fucking tusks! So perhaps now you stupid fuck-wads will listen to me because the predators out there! Luke how do you know BOOM Boom Boom huge chunks of earth explode rising up directly in front of my foot! Freezing me to the spot as Ras turns looking at me he smiles a nervous smile then starts running again! Where the fuck is he going now? Err...was that a bullet or a shotgun? Someone says. Boom another one hits a big old tree stump. Sending lumps of it high up into the air! Mitsu screams run and all hell breaks loose as everyone begins to run shouting and screaming.

I take off after the others. Jumping over logs fallen trees pushing brambles bush and every other type of obstacle out of my way. Very nearly getting bitten by a snake in the process! Hey where the fuck are we running too? Barry shouts at me. I don't have a fucking clue why are you asking me? Cause you know who it is! WHAT? No I fucking don't mate. Yes you do. No I do not! Yes you do Luke you saw something...did you Luke? Asks Scooby panting...

Thanks for bloody telling us asshole.......What? Look you fucking moron....BOOM Boom boom more bursts of gunfire this time in quick fire rapid and explosions sending piles of debris flying all around...There's more than one gun shooting Aaron shouts! No shit mate genius. We're dead Mitsu cries! Are we dead Luke? Keep fucking running don't stop! So we're all just going to keep on running then? Someone got a better plan? Let's just keep on running eh Barry, then were going to end up getting separated and lost! Uh huh kind of noticed that one mate. So the plan is run around until we end up back where we begun or out of breath? Who fucking voted me president? You know who they are.

Look Barry I do not fucking know ok. Look over there a fallen tree shouts Ras! Good idea get behind that everyone! Like wildebeests to the river's edge we turn and run after Ras then dive head first and jumping over and behind the tree. Startling a small monkey who shrieks before dashing off as we land. Crouching down behind the tree all seems cool. Is everyone here? Aaron asks. As we all look at each other's sweat drenched faces nodding,who was that?

Anyone see anything? I didn't see shit! I lied. Just pure gunshots mon! I deny everything as I don't want to get questioned by everyone. Gunshot mon pure gunshot a fire me tell yuh mon. You're bleeding! Sara says to me, Am I? No he isn't Nat says...you have the elephant's blood all over you Luke that's all!....Shit I'm covered in it, as I look down at myself! Barry and Mitsu stare at me. What the fuck bro! Not cool! You're telling me. No Luke your language. What? You might say de'fug in future. Err whatever mate. Tell you what if we live I will.... happy? Yes. Hope it's not some lost head-hunter tribes bro! Thanks Barry! The girls begin to cry! Lawd Gawd almighty what you mean head-hunters mon?

It's cool Ras. I reassure him, they're not head hunters! How you know eh? Err well for a start they got automatic weapons so that hardly puts them in lost tribe category does it? This is clearly some crazy experiment, a secret Philadelphia type experiment thing gone wrong! Brett argues. So that's why they don't want anybody here! Scooby laughs, we are so stupid. Bet it's the secret service of some secret government. Shut up man. Luke how do you know eh? I don't Ras.

Look girls all I'm saying is it's a fact of life that you

have piracy around these parts! Pirates! What the fuck...Barry shut the fuck up! Shut up mate. No you shut up! I knew we shouldn't of come here, what a stupid idea I can't believe I've been so stupid to allow myself be talked into coming here. What? Now we're all going to be raped and murdered Sara said as she began crying! Barry? What? Do they really shrink heads? Asks Natsumi. See what you've fucking started mate? Fuck you Luke they should of been told the risks bro! What? I hiss back at him. Look no one forced anyone to come here did they? Keep fucking quite you two.

Well did they? You know at times you're full of shit! Whatever dude you're in fucking denial! Look you're only making it worse. How could it get any fucking worse asshole huh? They've taken out our transport, we don't have a clue where we fucking are and we got no weapons and their probably fucking circling us at this very moment watching our mutinous infighting. And if that isn't enough our guide has been swallowed by the jungle! OK calm down Luke look what you think their plan is? Or think they're going to wait till dark? Ras says spitting dirt out his mouth.

Sara listen to me! OK Luke I will try! No one's going to murder neither you nor anyone else here ok. She smiles...thanks...Just then bullets riddle the side of the tree in rapid succession! See they have been moving around us while we talk! I knew it. BOOM! BOOM! BOOM! Shotgun blasts rip huge chunks of wood and earth sending them high into the air with bits of it landing on our faces smothering us in dirt. Panic levels soar to new heights as everyone, myself included tremble from the combined noise of shotgun blasts, ricocheting bullets and wood splintering.

What are we going to do? Aaron says looking at me for guidance. I I don't know I stutter. Why does everyone look at me when things turn to shit? Because you sound like James bond says Scooby. No I fucking don't? Yes you do several of them say together nodding No I do not besides bond is always Scottish or Irish. Maybe says Brett but technically he is English! OK I know. Everyone looks at me with glimmers of hope in their eyes; Here is what we're going to do! Wave a white handkerchief! What? Eh boy what kind of foolishness are you coming out with? This isn't custards last stand yuh nuh? Wave a white flag you think these savages will know what waving a white flag means?

There not fucking savages Ras and feel fucking free to come up with a different suggestion as I'm all ears right now! All fucking ears mate and I don't hear nobody else suggesting shit!

Ras nods...Bang! A two foot long point razor sharp spear hits the ground landing only feet away from where all of us are hiding. This is quickly followed by another few volleys of gunshots! There circling us! Barry bawls spitting out. When did you start this macho spiting thing? Scooby asks....just now why you like it. No.

SPEARS screams Sara, they must be head hunters! How the fuck can they be encircling us? Barry asks plus just how many do you think there are Luke? I saw one for sure! So you did see something then? Scooby says giving me a look of contempt. Don't give me that look ok. Look I tried to tell everyone but you lot would not listen! I say looking at Mitsu for support, he nods yeah it's true but we thought he had heat stroke or something! I second that Barry says spitting again.

Luke! Aaron shouts...this is a life or death situation, use my rag! Ras says pulling out a white handkerchief. Someone grab a stick! Hurry quick man, a large stick is passed to Ras who fastens his white hanky to it! You see here what this is? This is a job for a man with courage! A

131

brave man a warrior who loves his people and friends so much he is willing to put his life before them! A man with true leadership and skills! A man that cares about the women in his life, he says smiling at the girls! Then hands the flag to me! Huh....Here you go Luke? What are you giving it to me for? He smiles nodding. I said why are you giving it to me? Your idea man. My idea? Yeah mon come now Luke go deal with the bad man dem. He says looking straight ahead.

I look around at the lot of them and the exception is Barry who clearly seems for whatever reason to be enjoying himself like its some excursion on acid. The others are clearly terrified! I try to swallow saliva but my throat has dried up. Reluctantly slowly and with absolutely no other option I put up the flag up and wave it about. Shooting has stopped I whisper. Huh? Ras replies, what's going on up there man? I shrug.

Stick your head up and you have a look! Nah man I do my bit already. Me stress too, can't take no more stress right now! You can't take any more stress? Hey Mitsu. What Ras? They're your people man go chat with them! Just how the fuck did you figure there my people? You go fucking talk to them! I can't even speak their language man! Me Jamaican! I am Japanese which in case you didn't already know is about three thousand nautical fucking miles away from here so what makes you think I can speak their lingo bro?

Hello! Hello...Momentarily distracted we all turn around in shook to see Sara walking out from behind the safety of the tree trunk! No...................Sara get back here now Shouts Aaron! Ignoring him she slowly moves forward outstretching her arms with hands open palms facing straight ahead. Leaving whoever it is out there in no dought she was unarmed. Hello we come in peace! Can you hear me? Hello, do you speak English? Have you lost your fucking mind? Aaron hisses after her..ssshhhh be quite I say to him. If they hear you they might think it's a ploy or set up! I tell yeah man if she can't get the people on side none of us can and were all in big trouble man.

We mean you no harm! We come in peace! Can you understand me? She repeats the mantra as she continues slowly moving forward. Then we hear a voice shout back.....in English! Did you hear that? Is that English or am I hearing things? Mitsu says...Hello Sara says, you can speak English ok that's great. Err then there is no need to worry.....I'm not one bit worried sweetie pie not one fucking bit. Of course not err we don't em I mean we only came for em look can I talk to you face to face please? I cannot see you can we I mean can we chat? Would you like coffee and fucking donut's as well lady? To be honest I wouldn't mind some right now.

What do you people want? And who are you working for? Working? We're not working for anyone, she shakes her head confused. Why are you here then? We're tourists! TOURISTS! Yes were tourists! She nods. Now listen here lady I know I sound like a red neck and all but I aren't so fucking dumb to believe yawl came here on or ok look what I mean is who comes to a place like this on fucking-vacation? He's going to whack her you watch! Mitsu says. Do you mind? That's my sister out there trying to save your skin! Sorry Aaron! Asshole! Guys Look! Just then we see a man slowly walk out into the clearing towards Sara carrying some type of shotgun or automatic weapon.

Dark long unkempt hair and a slight beard shorts and sandals are all he is wearing. Bare chested and slim to the point of being able to see ribs but more in a naturally thin slightly athletic way than malnourished. They are talking, what's being said? How do I know mate it's too

133

far away...should we join them? Aaron asks. I do not think that's wise. Why not? Might freak him out...well I'm going she is my sister after all! Aaron no wait until she signals us ok. Signals? We're not in the army Luke.

There has been no rehearsal for this no protocol to follow like we had a plan! Exactly Aaron So we only get one fucking chance and I'm sure when she thinks everything is cool she will wave us over. Hey guys look! Mitsu says. What is it? It's another guy, a bigger stronger guy. We watch as he walks out into the clearing, fitter and carrying an AK47..is that a cowboy hat on his head? Or am I tripping....Strange look alright it must be said Scooby whispers! It goes with his shorts thou laughs Brett.

We sit watching the three of them talking, sometimes making sudden wild hand motions.

With Sara pointing out across the jungle and sometimes towards us. The men in return are shaking heads mostly. Suddenly and without warning one of them punches the other one in the face. Weapons are dropped and the two engage in a fist fight! Sara backs off turns and with a look of desperation gestures for us to stay put! A few quick punches are thrown! The fight ends and the two shake hands. Then it was back to business with Sara.

The men continued to quarrel for at least another five minutes! Sara turns and walks over to us. Good news? What's the story with these guys? I ask. Yes and no. Look they are not going to kill us! That's nice Scooby smiles as do the rest of us. The bad news? Barry inquires err well. Just say it I tell her...We cannot leave! WHAT! Fuck that now you tell them...BOOM BOOM two loud explosions bring us out of our private world as startled we look round to see where the gunshots came from! Follow us or die! One shouts as he spits...What are they

134

like? Aaron asks...err well they seem ok but....strange.

Strange? Can you elaborate? I push for more info! Don't know I think they've been here a very long time and how do you say it in English? Err lost it? You know lost it? Pointing at her head with a spinning finger. Well of course they've lost it man look at them! Ras laughs, they look like Robinson Crusoe man! The important thing is can we deal with them Sara? It might be possible but right now I'm not sure.

Fear begins to engulf my body as I feel like an invisible blanket of cling-film is being tightly woven around me. I can breathe but struggle to concentrate! Luke are you ok? Barry's voice? Huh what? Is that you Baz? Yes! Err yeah I'm fine. Sure? You look eh oh never mind. They're coming over! Barry turns around then makes himself spokesman...nobody say shit ok and whatever you do don't fucking disagree with them.

They stood before us weapons at the ready with unwashed hair. Ras had a point using the term Robinson Crusoe except they were wild eyed and dangerous looking individuals! Whom I suspect would no more blink at the thought of killing us as they did when they killed the elephants! Once they got close enough they looked a unique mix of both escaped convict and missing in action military. The slightly taller one had pulled the spear out and jabbed it into the ground in front of him laughing whilst the other one Mr six pack I mentally named him, chewed on a chunk of raw sugar cane. Both had AK47's casually draped over their shoulders. Looking the stereotypical Vietnam vets on Acid loons, except of course they weren't old enough.

Howdy! Now come on yawl don't start the silent treatment just because we shot your elephants, he said, spitting a huge load of phlegm on to the ground! Stunned no one spoke except me. What's the fucking story mate?

The skinny one raised his gun, easy boy! OK look I don't know who you are, all we do know is we just booked an excursion this morning and! And? go on boy, and we came here. How many people know yawl came out round these here parts? Inquires the other one..Lots! Sara replies, but no one would bring us and now we know why, I half laugh.

NO fucking wonder no one would bring you here Asshole! Screamed Mr six pack in my face! Know why they don't want to bring yawl here pip squeak? I shake my head slowly. Because this here land was a communist 're-education centre' after the end of the Vietnam War! A what? Asks Barry squinting his eyes....Back in seventy five after the war ended anyone with western habits, yawl know drugs sex rock n roll that kind of thing! Smiled skinny scanning our faces with his wild eyes.....Well now they were all sent over here for 're-educating' at least that's what they called it anyway, so most of them folks over there, he says pointing towards Laos.

Had a family member that was here or knew someone that did and judging by the amount of skeletons we found around these here parts, not too dam many went back neither! Skeletons? Shrieked Scooby. You bet kid want to see some? No thanks Nat answers. Maybe yawl want to join um then huh? He says pulling the spear out of the ground. Whoa wait a minute! What? There is no need for that. Oh really? Now sir what would your good name be? Barry! Well now Barry just in case you do not know or maybe we haven't made ourselves entirely clear, but this here is my land, he says looking up at the sky! Before then staring directly into Barry's face. So I make the god dam rules around here got it? I got it. And if I want to fucking bury yawl mother fucker I sure as hell will got it boy? I got it! Loud and clear boy? Loud and clear.

Can I ask you something? What boy? What's your name? My name? He looks over at the other one then looks back. Eddie! He says smiling his brown teeth reflecting in the sun, and this here fine specimen of the male species is Robbie Ray. Howdy! Now ladies and gentlemen Eddie says, please walk this way. Where too? I ask. Come and meet everyone else! Everyone else like who? How many? Yawl will see...what if it's a trap? I ask Barry pretending to cough! Then what? What can we do he hisses? We're at their mercy now Luke! I reckon we will be ok as long as we go with the flow! Why Baz? Because they could of killed us if they wanted.

The Hillbillies

Reluctantly we follow them. Aaron looked over at me, just be cool mate go with the flow! I said in a hushed tone. We walked for ages moving along a series of narrow slightly worn paths through the dense jungle. Marching in silence like prisoners of war! Strangely if not perversely this was accepted by all. Kidnapped yes, free definitely not. In chains no but seriously did they need them? If ever the saying you could run but couldn't hide was more appropriate it was now. For where could we run too?

With each step taken we moved further into the core of the jungle. The bloodlust slaughter of the elephants. The horrific deafening echoing noise of the shooting. Whilst still fresh it gradually faded behind us with each of those steps. Perhaps it was convenient to allow it do so, to ignore the reality of our situation. As an abundance of beauty an oasis itself slowly opened itself up. Every new step forward into the jungle reviled itself further. Peeling away layers so to speak until gradually the animalistic sounds became less obvious. The coconut's falling from above though, was a sound I personally never got used to.

Guys I remember reading one time that if you lose your eyesight your other sense's become more acute to compensate. I said as we watched another coconut go thump into the ground. It's the survival instinct, touch, sound, smell, taste etc Mitsu replied sensing my discomfort. But sound is number one! Well I guess that's true bro because in here right now. I feel like I have the awareness of one of those American GIs they secretly tested LSD on during the Vietnam War! Barry smirked.

I sensed every twig and branch that was stepped on

before it happened. Every insect that moved I noticed. Every bead of human sweat that dripped from someone's nose onto a leaf below I spotted fall. I saw, sensed tasted almost before it even happened and judging by the looks on everyone else's face I certainly wasn't the only one having a bad trip! You can be forgiven for assuming that once under the natural canopy and shade the jungle offer, as perpetrated by nature documentaries on TV that you would be nice and cool. Protected in the shade it offers from the sun. Mother Nature's air-con and to a certain extent that is true. Especially in very hot climates in summer time. But herein lays the problem! The hot air, it too is caught inside nature's canopy like you and unless there is an air-flow system for which to extract it, it's going nowhere.

It lingers and sticks to you like glue and you exert any form of physical activity at all! And I mean at all, then it's like you are in a Sauna. And so it seemed the deeper in the jungle we went the more humid it became. We were saturated in sweat to such an extent that at one point it became difficult to walk! Robbie laughed as he noticed us struggling. That's why I don't wear jack shit fellers, he spat! Eddie giggliing with him! Eventually after a few hours it dried and became less of a problem. Look at this guys Mitsu said. I looked over as he pointed over there on the tree! The skinny green thing you see it?

I focused in on the general area he gestured towards but saw nothing but then it moved! A luminous green snake no thicker than my thumb but at least six feet long. Ever so slowly it slithered down the tree. Unbelievable Mitsu smiled as did I! Once it stopped moving it became impossible to spot again! You can barely see the thing it blends in so well don't it? Natures camouflage.

Hey you lot Barry shouted! Standing next to Eddie and Robbie. Do the nature thing later but for now get

139

you asses up here! He's getting awfully friendly with them eh man? Ras says to me. Was just thinking the same thing mate but at least we speak their language so that's a bonus. Yeah man I guess. I don't think he is trying anything devious. We caught up with them and continued walking for another hour or so moving in a slight gradual incline all the time. Hey Aaron! What do you think Barry's up to, you know by befriending these guys? I was thinking the same thing Luke but let's just hope he has a game plan! Cool, at least were all on the same wavelength.

Sounds like a pair of giant denim jeans the length of a bus being ripped in two! Scooby laughed as he described the sound that dominates the jungle occasionally. Everyone paused to look up and see if it's going to land on them, yet another falling coconut falls from the top of a tree landing with a dull thud seconds later. Then again all is momentarily silent until the sound of the wildlife returns. That is if the animals birds etc also hear it and keep quite or some deep down thing from our DNA switches off all other sounds. We walk on paranoia lurks at every tree every stream behind every rock and mound! We must overcome not just these guys but Mother Nature too if we are to survive.

I smell smoke do you? Can you smell it Scooby? Nah mate! Look over there. A small trickle drifts aimlessly upwards through the pineapple trees into the clear blue sky above! Good nose Luke...Smell food too! Fish if I am not mistaken!

Now I consider arriving into a small secluded community in a remote foreign place one of life's unmissable experiences! Invited or not we were now about to have the cream de la cream of one of those experience's. As we came into the clearing for the first time the thing you couldn't help but notice was a pool.

And I am not talking about no out the back garden type pool but a full on Olympic sized pool! OK it was more a dyke mud wall type and it had no tiles obviously making the water look more dark than blue, but nice all the same.

Fifty or so feet away from that lay another much smaller pool. More Jacuzzi like! Behind that grew the biggest cannabis plant I'd ever laid eyes on. It must of been at least ten to twelve feet tall with about fifty large stems growing out from it. Each stem had dozens of golf ball sized buds clearly visible from where we stood fifty feet or more away! Smiling I elbowed Mitsu. Hey think they will let us smoke some? He elbowed me back. I looked at him and he nodded but he was not smiling. What mate? It was only then did I notice the three Thai women stood nearby menacingly holding machetes staring at us.

The shortest one was the first to let rip a torrent of abuse which was primarily aimed at the Eddie! This was quickly followed by the more slender and feminine of the three, who aimed her abuse at Robbie! Much to our surprise the two men began shouting back at them IN THAI! This tennis like confrontation continued for several minutes back and forth with the men seemingly from what we could gather defending us. The other woman, the third one occasionally put in her bit as well. During all this I noticed dozens of chickens running around our feet. Maybe they are running a chicken farm Mitsu suggested.

All the time the Thai women were directly gesturing aggressively at us but eventually they were pacified! By what? Who knows all we did know was it seemed to stop as quickly as it started. Scanning the faces around me I tried to break the ice by asking Eddie what's for dinner? He looked serious but then smiled. It's Friday

141

what do you think is for dinner? No you cannot be serious? I look at the others who are baffled. Its fish and chips! I grinned. Mitsu and Ras both smile and the others nod but I can tell its lost on them...Forget it just trust me it's nice.

I followed Eddie to where the smell was coming from and lots green banana leafs were creating the smoke. The leaves are atop of hot stones underneath which lay bundles of tightly wrapped fish in yet more banana leafs. They are slowly being steam cooked nature's way! Eddie tells one of the women, he calls her POW! To get a fire going under a barrel that's been cut in half and has oil inside. It is used as a deep fat fryer nearby lays the other half of the barrel this one filled with water and freshly cut homemade potato fries.

OK Yawl sit your lardy backsides down! Eddie said in a thick Alabama accent. We need to get a few things straight about this here place. Meanwhile Rob picks up a machete and began hacking open coconuts which he passed around for everyone to drink! Now number one thing here is yawl never ever get in the big pool. Pooh pee or even spit in it or nothing yawl get that? We nod! Good because that there my new found friends that's the only source of fresh water we have for miles around! What about the small one? Asks Barry. That's fresh too! But we figured from the start we could make better use of it to wash our clothes but the big boy there! We drink from it cook with it, wash from it plus it gives us an endless supply which we need to water our plants yawl understand? We nodded drinking the coconut water.

Where's it come from? Barry asks. Underground spring! Eddie replies. How come you guys didn't just make camp by a river! Because that's exactly what they would expect us to do!

Who? I inquire. Forces of evil that's who boy! Sorry

142

mate I didn't mean! Yawl didn't mean shit and don't call me mate Redcoat as I for one am not your buddy got it? Anyhow as I was saying after being in the jungle for half the day it's nice to be able to grab a bucket and give yourself a good old scrub down. So that's why we got to keep the other one clean or were fucked got it? Everyone nods again including me as I gulp down the water and try my best not to agitate our situation.

How long have you been here? Asks Sara! Five years says Eddie. You have been living in the jungle for five years? Shrieks Scooby....Or wait is that seven? Anyway give or take why boy? He laughs what's wrong with that! Nothing. Every few months we go back to stock up on things...diesel, cooking oil, cigarettes you know the essentials! And the girls like to visit their kin folk so sometimes we leave them take care of business! Business? I ask trying my best not to sound too noisy. Yeah the Marijuana business boy! You sell weed? Laughs Barry! Yes Sir we do! Eddie laughs. We grow more than enough of the finest so we exchange it with the Thai mafia. Regular moonshiners we are! Giggles Rob! Just got to watch out for the sheriff.

Cool Mitsu smiles and we all break into fits of laughter. And that's not all! Smiles Robbie.

We also have a little side-line in the Opium mano-fact-oring market. Eddie grins at Rob.

Gets better by the second man! Ras grins for the first time since the shooting! Is this all not dangerous? I ask. I mean here you are living in the heart of the golden triangle in this day and age of technology; you could be spotted by anyone and everyone yet your growing and exporting weed and opium to Thai gangsters? I mean of all fucking places mate... Thailand! Don't they hang people for that sort of shit there?

They look at each other with frowns then back at me

143

before crying out laughing like hyenas whilst slapping their legs..eh no Sir! Well actually yes but I think technically they strap you to a chair, putting your face into a big thick pad, yawl know to stop the mess. Then shot you in the back of the head! But hey fuck the lot of them punk ass mother fuckers man....they laugh, at me! So I laugh back. Err Luke is it? Yes....The girls do most of the business with their connections! Eddie tells me, besides all their friends think they're living you know the holy spiritual life in Laos. So they probably presume that's where they get it winks Robbie ...so you guys are in the clear? Barry winks back.

Number two! Under no circumstances must you ever... be seen. Yawl ever see planes Hide with a capital H. I mean you fucking run for it like a coyote is chasing yawl skank backside! No one is suppose to be here, always remember that. This area it's a sort of an unofficial DMZ and if one country were to see folks here! Well it could and would most certainly open up a can-a-worms....Such as? Aaron asks.

Look boy this here land, he says kicking his boot into the ground. Is of strategic importance to a number of countries in the region, but seeing as no one ever lived here then no cat could really stake a claim to it yawl hear what I'm saying? But you said the Laotians were here for......Here for ten years boy! Eddie says with that grin again. And that was on the lowdown hardly time enough to warrant calling it yours now is it? Or put it this way it's definitely not long enough under internationally recognised protocols at any wild stretch of the imagination...But but! Jesus H Christ boy may I continue? Sorry please do....

Thank you Luke...ok history lesson time. When the Burmese got their independence from the redcoats back in the day after world war two! He says pointing at me.

And with all the issues of the whole Thai neutrality thing yawl might recall during WW2 with regards the Japanese use of the prisoners? Err no we reply looking around at each other shaking our heads. OK River Kwai? Again blank stares. The old folks around your parts would recall but anyways forget it.... The Vietnam War? Yawl hear about that right? We nod! Good well it helped propel pol pot's Khmer rouge in Cambodia.

In a roundabout way of course. Now coupled with all the various political uprisings in Thailand in the seventies well the whole fucking region erupted into one great ball of paranoia, stronger than a bull elephant after being injected with amphetamine. Yawl know what the feds number one fear back in those days was? I swear yawl I'm not making this up but they feared a large scale drug attack! Like some sort of weed bazooka! Rob laughed. Or to be more precise some type LSD in the water attack, but with every military top cat suspicious of the next top cat around these here parts, well the whole place was one big bad acid road trip here anyway.

Does anyone ever even come here Eddie? Good question! Yes Aaron a few times a year they do. But always by helicopter! Robbie chips in. None of them and I mean none of them. I mean each country that is, would not like to be seen with a shit load of soldiers coming here by the other cats! Might start the bad paranoia trip all over again he giggled! So these helicopters they......Do they fly low? Yes and that's why it's very important you cats stay out of sight, hide in bushes ect whilst of double importance is that we plant the weed all over the land and not in no orderly grid type fashion.

Which is what they would expect us to do correct? Yeah...we agree! Eddie grins with a nod of the head that suggests he views himself supreme ruler. Yawl never in real life plant shit loads of weed in straight lines! No?

145

Hell no boy of course fucking not! Do you know how noticeable they are from the sky? Err. From a helicopter even ten Marijuana plants are visible once they are in a row! Where's this cat been sleeping? A fucking cave so it seems Rob! To my frustration Barry began laughing with them! This isn't corn on the fucking cob country amigo.

So plant them everywhere and anywhere once the sun is on them right? Correct brother! Correct! Everything else is just for the cameras? I ask laughing....The short answer is yes Luke. They never land helicopters to gather them up to burn them! That crap is for the media to make Uncle Fred and Aunty Jean feel safe in their suburban home knowing they not gonna to be overrun by flesh eating dobie smoking Shroom swallowing freaks.

Yawl ever stood under a flying helicopter? No why? All these cats got to do is fly down near the plants and they're ripped out of the ground by the pressure of the blades! Or at the very least they flattened! Robbie adds, Simple! One two three and they outré! Besides most places in the world they consider it dangerous enough to just fly near drug plantations! So it doesn't make sense to risk landing your crew and hanging around now does it? Guess not.

This place here though! Now that would be different, very different indeed. Why? Mitsu asked. Well when the Laotians agreed to leave this area back in seventy five and all the others agreed no one would occupy it as it really had no use! Hence the reason it became a national park. I mean who would of figured back then tourists would be so fucking stupid to want to come to places full of poisonous shit and sweltering heat? Sara and Nat both cast me spiteful looks.

Eddie and Rob both laughed. Anyway it became in effect a no man's land! So if somebody was to see life here they will think the others must up to something or worse still even....Watching them mon Ras injects. Yawl cats are catching on double quick Eddie smiled. Aren't they Rob? Uh huh... Anyways boys and gals geography or history or whatever the fuck lessons that was is now officially finished for the day and I believe yes sir I do that dinner is in fact about to be served.

POW as she was affectionately known begun handing out steamed fish and chips to everyone. After dinner nightfall crept upon us surprisingly quick! OK time to turn on the lights shouts Eddie looking around for POW! Lights I thought you said.........green lights Luke, can't be spotted through night vision! Oh..... Come on yawl get up let's show them the H-block Rob...what's the H-block? Barry inquires..... Yawl lodgings! We scrambled to our feet.

We walked after Eddie and Robbie yawl must understand in the seventies the government of Laos decided to build several 're-education centres par excellence' Rob described them as he giggled smoking a large joint. Which he passed to Eddie who continued. You see any cat they figured was after getting too westernised...yawl know like smoking weed wearing jeans long hair that sort of stuff? Well now those cats were clearly in need of 're-educating'.

One thing the commies didn't want? Was folks thinking for themselves. You mean thinking! Sara smiled....Yawl right there pretty gal. Thinking...exactly he smiled. Re-educating centres! Sara smiled. Par excellence Robbie smiled back! Long hair or jeans. Yeah or even if yawl wore glasses! Glasses? I laughed.Yes I fucking swear I am not making this shit up. Yawl ever see a dictator wearing glasses? Hitler, Mao, Stalin, Bush...what yawl cats got in common? None of these cats wore specs! They roared with laughter as did we.

As we walked along the worn dirt path leading away

147

from base camp and back into dense jungle! We had almost forgotten the purpose of the walk due to the shared jokes and passing of joints. Out of nowhere we stopped at a door! So sudden had it appeared that I walked into Robbie's back someone else walked into mine and so on behind me. We had only been walking seven or eight minutes yet it felt a million miles away from the camp Mitsui replied to me. Must be the new strain we're testing on yawl, giggled Robbie.

We give yawl home AKA the H-block! Eddie smiled opening it up. It was not a house door but a large school type door except made of Steel! In the thirty years it had been built it had been completely swallowed up and over-run by jungle foliage, weeds and roots as thick as an anaconda were draped all along from top to bottom! Eddie laughed as he told us how they had been sleeping by the pool for a month before he'd found it. And that was only when he went in search of a spot to grow some more weed.

Walking inside it was surprisingly clean with the floors and walls tiled. It even had beds a bit rusty n dusty but still beds all the same. One foot by one foot windows that were specifically designed to be too small for anyone to escape yet just big enough for light to shine through. These had long ago been taped up, so normal light could be allowed in! The light still made it in but once outside you couldn't actually see in. It was perfect and you only had a walk of around one thousand feet from the pool area to the H-block and that was lit up with little green lights which Eddie swore could not be seen by helicopters fitted with the best cameras.

The block housed a diesel generator which was used for lighting but served other purposes even though it looked a dorm type design from outside. Internally it was basically a cell format! Everyone had their own cells

148

allocated to them just like in a real prison! Eddie and POW had their cell Robbie and his girl 'mod' lived in another. Myself Barry Mitsu Aaron were allocated single cells each! While Ras opted to sleep outside on a hammock.

The girls shared a cell as did Scooby and Brett! The Thais joked finding that arrangement the height of good humour. As for Channarong? Well he had long since become a distant memory and I wasn't sure if he was even noticed missing by everyone. But rather than cause upset and stress by saying it aloud I choose to say nothing until the shit hit the fan! The last cell was belong to Porntip or porn as she was affectionately known! At first we found her name highly unusual almost amusing but later realised it is a hugely popular name in Thai culture! In Fact it was only at the very mention of porn that we found out about Franz.

Franz

Franz was a Berliner through and through! Eddie said looking at us. Though clearly upset by Porn letting slip his name now it seemed he was desperate to be the one to tell us Franz story. He is German and proud but a Berliner first and foremost. Kind of like folks from California yawl catch my drift? Robbie added....I looked at Barry confused but he just smirked.Now Franz always wanted to go backpacking! When he got his chance he did just that leaving Berlin in two thousand and four. First stop Goa where he chilled got a suntan and lost the jet lag before riding the trains across India to Chennai and onto the beaches of Pondicherry to meditate, study with Yogi's general hippy stuff yawl know. Before catching a boat to Sri Lanka for a few weeks, then finally flying onto Bangkok at the start of December.

As the festive season approached Franz found himself in the Deep South! Of Thailand that is and yawl will appreciate that when the crafty old cat managed to secure himself a room in a hotel on Patong beach that busy festive season! Looking around at us he grinned and spat into the sand. Well let's just say he was happier than a possum in the corn-crib with the bulldog tied up! Again we looked at each other as both of them feel about laughing, but we said nothing! Anyhow old cat Franz he booked it for as long as he could, till the start of January at least just to be sure he had accommodation! Yawl understand? So he could chill at the height of the tourist season without the fear of having nowhere to stay.

Now on Christmas night Franz had gone for dinner. Purchasing a German newspaper for company because he didn't like sitting around eating alone especially in the tourist ghettos! He said he always ended up making eye

150

contact with the two weekers as he called them. And they pitted him which he hated because in truth they we're the ones deserving of pity. Anyway the paper allowed him to busy himself while waiting for dinner.. Later on he went for some beers in a local bar, then he went to some other local bars and then some more. Yawl still with me? We nodded. Good Eddie grinned; boys let me tell yawl he got himself as rat assed as Cooter Brown on the fourth of July.

Next morning as you can appreciate folks he awoke with a mighty bad hangover. It was December twenty six! And boy was he sweating like a blind lesbian in a fish factory! As the air-con had stopped working. Next to him lay a very beautiful and very naked young Thai lady! As she slept he watched her golden brown skin illuminated by the white sheets beneath. Rattling his sore head he tried to piece together the previous night's shenanigans. Had someone slipped the crafty cat something? He pondered. Because if they did well now he wanted to shake their hands.

Now this here was to be the first time he ever laid eyes on Porn! No pun intended yawl hear me? I'm serious no taking the mickey now yawl understand? Well let's be fair obviously he must at some point laid eyes on her the night before but he was technically at a loss to remember anything about it. So as far as Franz was and is still concerned to this very here day. Well that very first morning was technically his first time ever laying eyes on her! She was the angel he had found in Paradise without even looking but would forever regard as his introduction to hell.

Yawl now should understand that for what Mother Nature give folks, she can very cruelly take away. Now whilst he was deciphering the previous evening's jigsaw he heard one almighty crash. The building shake's rattles then sway's as the foundation shook it like a tornado in Kansas. Then he heard the screams followed by the sound of water! Porn's eyes shot open as Franz dived out of the bed instinctively running towards the balcony! Pulling back the sliding door then walking out onto the set of what could have been a Hollywood disaster movie.

With porn by his side butt naked and the picture postcard blue sun filled skies above! They stood speechless as huge torrents of water flowed inches away from their feet on their third floor balcony! Sweet lord Jesus above he must of thought as Cars, Jeeps, Trucks, Trees, Boats Garbage and just about anything else you could think of including the odd dead body as well as some live ones all flowed past them.

Then they heard a lady bawl and cry, they looked down and saw her! With two little boys who were very obviously her sons. They were hanging around her neck for dear life an all. Robbie chipped in nodding with a grim expression! Yes sir they were in the torrent of water hanging on for their lives by a tread alright, with the momma shouting instructions to the bigger boy who was about five years old that he would have to let go and swim for it. It was his only chance she told him. She was planning on sacrificing the smaller one as she knew he couldn't make it! A decision no momma should have to make.

But then as if by di-vine intervention from the good lord Jesus himself Franz told me. He and porn could not believe their eyes, as of all the things you think won't save you in a disaster! In a situation like this! Somehow slowly moving along in the fast flowing torrent of water like a miracle came a god dam giant Anaconda! The length of a telegraph pole and about the thickness of lumberjack's thigh. It stopped next to the woman, its eyes staring intensely at her and the boy's yawl.

152

Franz swears the snake and the woman shared a message via the snake's Parietal eye. He and Porn were only feet away so they saw the lot! The snakes what? I asked. Third eye boy, don't tell me yawl didn't know snakes got them a third eye? Eh No where is it? On top of its head! Now Jesus H Christ Luke can you stop interrupting a perfectly good story? Sorry. That's the second time you did that shit so don't do it again or I swear I will feed your sorry behind to the gators! Sorry Eddie.

Anyway this woman as if by some telepathic message or as I said perhaps a Di-vine miracle of the lord. Placed the smaller sons arms around the snake and told the screaming kid hold on. Then the snake swam up to Franz balcony and just like a taxi stopped allowing the kid to be helped off by Franz, to the relative safety of the balcony! No way? We were all genuinely shocked gobsmacked and whilst personally I wasn't too sure if it were all true or not I wasn't about to spoil a good yarn. Nor upset Eddie to the point were he might follow through on his threat.

Franz told me he looked deep into the serpent's eyes! Its vertical elliptical dilated before him.

And then he saw it! Saw what? Aaron asked. The connection. That spiral of DNA that connects every living molecule but especially that reptilian human connection! Huh? I am lost.

Every human has around four percent reptilian DNA right? Err of course Aaron smiled. Only once the snake knew the kid was safe did it float away. The connection the evidence was all there home boy. The woman and her other son then swam over to Franz and he helped them onto his balcony were they sat for the next two hours in the hot sun without saying a single word.

When the water receded they simply all went their

153

separate ways like passing ships in the night, never even asked their names. Why what difference would it make Luke? Make it more human somehow I guess. You know years later you would think of their name rather than just their face! There are no humans forever burning in hell Luke just entities! True.

Now one of the biggest problems facing someone in a natural disaster is surprisingly a lack of cash! Why? Well because with it you can buy whatever resources yawl may need The ATM's were all down. As one would appreciate as were the phones so everything was down! Lucky for Franz he was packing some hard cash! Porn negotiated a local taxi to drive them to Surat Thani then when he got there he got paranoid and thought it was still too close to Phuket so told the driver to keep on trucking to Hu Hin. Then once there said fuck it make it Bangkok.

Thing was in Bangkok Franz was sickened by the actions of holiday makers and backpackers that had arrived on or after the disaster itself. So he and porn celebrated new years eve sitting outside a coffee shop watching tourists with the attitude of 'it's not going to upset my vacation' get drunk buy dodgy fireworks and fornicate. While just a few hour's drive south thousands lay dead and dying from injuries! Entire family's wiped out some never to be found. Others never to be identified. As well as the small islands that disappeared erased off the map forever as were whole Thai communities that inhabited them for centuries.

Yet all these folks wanted to do was party like nothing had happened! Their selfishness enraged him to the point that he felt like going on a murderous rampage. But what would it accomplish? Yeah I smiled nodding in agreement whilst looking over at Mitsu and Baz! So later that night they hatched a plan to go even further north. Away from everything and anything that reminded them of the evil selfish 'two weaker mosquito repellent carrying designer flip flop wearing travelling fuck-wads that they all was.

First stop Chang Mai! A few days there before they moved a bit further again! This time to Chang Rai. You see they knew the two weekers were catching up when they spotted familiar faces they saw in Bangkok. Once near the Laotian border Franz realised he had to do a visa run but Porn couldn't come as she had no passport, so Franz went to Laos on his own some and that my friends was how he ended up here.

Wow! Amazing! Cool story bro. Were just some of the comments I heard banded about by my fellow adventurers! We had only been kidnapped a few hours earlier yet they were now treating the whole episode like it was part of some bloody free extension on the excursion! An extra, where you got to chill with Hicksville's greatest Psycho's. No more thoughts for Channarong who had disappeared or Ayanna Breyanna Cyanna whom these nutters had casually slaughtered before having a fistfight to decide if we should perish too! Now these goons were behaving like we're all best mates.

He heard the same story I suspect you cats heard, Eddie smiled! What's that? Aaron asked. That no one had ever been here. That it was just a nature park! He smiled raising an eyebrow, nothing more nothing less. So he came to check it out as a place where he and porn could go live in peace away from the horridly materialistically intoxicated matrix society. Yawl know plus she would not have worries about a passport and he would have no visas to constantly update. All kind a perfect really don't yawl agree? Perfecto! Barry smiled.

Now I'm sure yawl can understand we were a bit

sceptical when he first came Eddie explained. But when he told his story! Well we felt the cats pain man. I mean here was a guy feet anyway from dying in Phuket! The guests on the floor beneath were killed as we're half the folks in town. Robbie here thought he was making the whole thing up as we didn't know shit about any tsunami at first and wanted to just feed um to the gators....he spat as they both grinned at each other.

But when we confirmed it...How? I butted in unable to listen to this clearly made up tirade of bullshit any further! Hell we got our ways Luke boy. Anyhow Eddie stood up with a cheesy grin, what could yawl do but accept them with wide open arms eh? So we told him go back get your gal and come on back real soon. Now shall we introduce them to Huey? He looked around! Fuck it man we showed them the H block why not huey? Eddie laughed slapping his hands! Are there any more people here than you told us about? Mitsu asked. Let's go yawl. You aren't going believe this shit...he said completely ignoring Mitsu question. I Looked at Mitsu and shrugged. I was hoping he would answer you mate I really was I whispered.

Once again we followed Eddie and Robbie like excited school kids out around the side of the block we went where a huge thick tree trunk grew. Strong sturdy chunks of wood acting as steps had been hammered into it creating a ladder! Oh great you guys built a tree house? Could be a look out post Bret grinned. Perhaps a watchtower? Aaron smiled. Nah has to be a smoking pad I reckon! Added Mitsu. Who cares can anyone see the top mon? Ras barked. No it's huge; Aaron said squinting his eyes as he looking up. Follow me Eddie shouts and begun climbing up eventually disappearing from sight into the darkness of the night sky above.

Ever so faintly his silhouette could be made out as his

shadow blocked the stars above. Robbie was hot on his tail as was myself after him! Slowly everyone climbed up. I had only gone about twenty feet when I heard Scooby say come on you slacker! Fuck you I thought but said nothing in case it encouraged him to hurl more abuse. Which would definitely cause me to lose my balance. I just moved a bit faster gradually losing my fear of falling.

Then out of nowhere Eddies hand appeared from the side and pulled me towards where himself and Robbie were waiting. Barry quickly followed then Mitsu and soon all of us were there. One hundred feet up a tree! In the middle of golden triangle added Nat, again at once we all burst out laughing, cool eh? A bright white light suddenly blinded us but dimmed after a few seconds! Then as we stared open mouthed whilst trying to get our vision back. When it returned fully we could only stare at each other.

We're on top of the H block which had been modified! A rounded flat loop had been built on it so it became a landing pad. The tree was just a way to get to it and sitting abandoned on top of it was a Vietnam War era American Huey helicopter! The huge tree had grown up the side and had long since begun leaning over the copter hiding it from passing planes. With crazy Eddie at the controls Robbie slid the door open spun around with a massive machine gun in his hands shouted get some at us! Bang bang! Get some baby.

What the fuck is this monster? Barry laughed rubbing and touching it like a horse. This here is a M60 quad capable of firing 7.62mm! I meant the helicopter Rob not the gun! Everyone eagerly jumped in but what caught my attention more than anything was the size! In the movies you normally have two guys flying and three maybe even four at most out back talking or shooting.

Eddie distracted me as he shouted something in Thai towards POW. The reality is helicopters are enormous! Words cannot describe how gigantic they are in real life! Looking around me I noticed Ras had jumped in the front with Eddie. Next to me sat Barry Mitsu, Natsumi, Sara, Aaron, seated across from which was Brett and Scooby. Soon to be joined by the three Thai's who arrived carrying a big sack of weed which I think was what Eddie had shouted at POW to get. With Eddie at the controls, Ras riding shotgun there still was room for more people.

Dam bro if these things are this size Barry say's. Then what size are those Apache helicopters they have nowadays? Don't worry be happy yawl Eddie bellowed in his thickest redneck accent! Now yawl want to get high? Yee Haw! Joints were built lit and smoked then passed around! Eddie whipped out an MP3 player and hooked it up to the speakers and it began belting out some tunes.

Is this the icing on the cake or what he laughed? I couldn't help but smile relax and enjoy myself. Even when Robbie took the joint and placed it in the slot of the M60 where the ammo is supposed to go in or come out I'm not sure exactly, before then turning the big gun around pointing it directly at my mouth. Then casually asking me, smoke Luke? In clearly yet another pathetic attempt to appear cool /act of bravado, call it what you will.

I closed my eyes prayed the gun wasn't loaded or that Robbie was such a totally fucked up goon that he might actually kill me for sport. Then strongly sucked deeply inhaled and kept the smoke down. I too joined in the bravado. The joint sizzled and glowed where it poked out at the top of the barrel as I sucked the smoke all the way down that barrel out through the nozzle and down deep my throat and lungs, till I felt like they're going to burst! Whoa take it easy there partner! Rob said. It's got to go round remember? Oh shit I cough...Err sorry I reply with my head spinning! Got a greedy one here Eddie! The boy certainly is Rob.

Then he waves it at the others. Mitsu and Barry push and shove for the right to be next in the firing line! Looking at porn she smiled. But with my head spinning I find it all too much to keep my big mouth shut and blurt out ignorantly 'where ya get such a funny name'. Doing so out of the feeling that I had to say something rather than say nothing over general ignorance. Her expression said it all.

Luke! Huh? Turning around I spot Eddie looking at me with a look of rage! I said no fucking jokes about her name! Err....sorry I was....You were what? I was going to tell her a joke that's all Eddie! Oh great myself and Rob here love us a good joke don't we Rob? Yup love us a joke we do! Hey Rob remember the time we pulled up at that level crossing in Mississippi and you said to that fat chick, well aren't you hotter than a mama cougar in heat running from my hunting dogs in August?. Yee Haw how could I forget that?

Seriously guys you don't want to hear any of Luke's jokes Mitsu laughs a nervous laugh! Remember that last story he told us guys? At which point everyone did laugh! Stories no. But Luke here has said he has a joke to share Eddie grinned. So tell it boy! Err em eh....OK alright! One day the boss of a big company needed to call one of his employees about an urgent problem with one of the servers! Because it was his day off he had to dial the employee's home number. It was answered by a child in a hushed tone.

Hello.

Hi, is your dad home?

Yes, whispered the child.

Can I talk to him please?

No.

Oh ok

How about Mommy is she around?

Yes.

OK can I talk with her?

No.

Oh ok is anyone else there?

Yes, whispered the child. The cops!

Wondering what a cop would be doing at his employee's home the boss asked.

May I speak with the police then please?

No, he's busy.

Busy! Doing what?

Talking to Daddy Mommy and the Fireman!

Increasingly concerned and worried the boss asked. What is that noise?

A Helicopter!

What is going on there?

The search team just landed the Helicopter!

Search team! What are they searching for?

Still whispering, the kid replied along with a muffled giggle. ME!!!!

The punch line caused uproar with virtually everyone breaking into fits of laughter! My joke went down so well even I was surprised! Eddie and Robbie high fived each other and even me and were repeating bits of it to themselves. I certainly wasn't expecting that Eddie laughed! Yeah didn't see that coming, added Rob. Luckily for me I had somehow thought of the joke on the spur of the moment and saved my skin.

Its short for porn-tip! This is my full name she said! Huh...oh yeah I'm sorry. No it's ok Luke in English it simply means 'to be happy'. Oh that's nice I smiled.

160

Only now were the full effects of smoking via an M60 hitting me full on like a ton of bricks.

What does Luke mean? My head was doing the full tree sixty like an owl desperately I searched for a half decent answer. It's an Italian name Aaron interrupts. Is it? Don't know Luke I'm asking you? Err yes I think eh yes yes Aaron that's correct! It's an old aristocratic name. Luke mon come here! I moved into the cockpit. Hey Ras what's up? Here take this man, he said handing me a joint! Yeah under pressure back there? Just a bit. We both laughed.

You see all around Luke? See what? If you look Eddie says pointing all around. You will notice the glow's from the neighbouring countries! This one here is Laos! Over there that is Thailand and that one over there is Burma! I faintly see a slight night glow from each angle around us in the distance! How far it actually was is another guess altogether but it was enough to give me a plan. Of sorts.

Eddie flicked a switch making the whole cockpit light up like a spaceship. Whopping and clapping broke out behind us! Think about today's helicopters guys what they must be like eh? Ras looks at me! Weapons of war, remember that's all they are! Sure Ras but...But nothing man they use these machines to kill millions of people over there beyond, he gestured across the tree tops! And further afield on every part of our beautiful home we name mother earth! I gaze out thinking about the reality of it...They pure evil these things man. Made by even more insane evil men. Sure from time to time they help people but the truth is these machines take far more lives than they ever save.

Suddenly a face lunges towards me from my side startling me. Passing the side of Eddies face screaming 'We got us a bogey at nine o'clock over repeat' Everyone

161

jumped as he startled them too..What the fuck! I yelled falling back a bit.....We got a bogey at nine o'clock over' he repeated bawling into my face once more, this time our noses only about an inch apart! His breath stunk of garlic and it seemed to cling to my skin as he paused to stare into my eyes.

Well dip my balls in sweet cream and squat me in a kitchen full of kittens if it isn't the man himself. Yee-Haw! Everybody I'd like to introduce yawl to a very special friend of ours, people I gave yawl the one and only Franz! Franz these here people are our new guest's and there going be staying around these here parts for a while ok. I nod at him but he says nothing, doesn't make any gesture he just gives me what is affectionately known in junkie circles as the thousand yard stare.

Eddie puts his hand under Franz chin gently cupping it. Jokingly he shakes it then in his best attempt at a German accent says! We have ways of making you talk! This makes everyone giggle including porn! A flicker of a smile comes to Franz face. But it is only token and not genuine. I'm starting to think these two weren't that bad after all are you? Ras says into my ear. I couldn't agree more, thou I still know none of them have our best interests at heart. Plus the way he said we're going to be staying like a decision has already been made for us.

Guten Abend comrades! He said eventually breaking the ice and eye contact with me! Then speaking to Eddie asks, tell me just how are you going to do that? Why I shall administer a truth serum, as he hands Franz a joint! Which he accepts. Oh Ja he smiles as he begins sucking on the joint! How are our international borders doing tonight? Eddie asks him, he stares back but says nothing just keeps sucking up the smoke! The western front? Franz how is it? Is good Ja is good comrade.

It's instantly clear to me that he is not mentally sane,

one can only presume porn don't notice this and in all probability considered him a rather eccentric westerner instead! Either that or she too is daft as a brush. Franz here is our very own department of homeland security! Robbie announced as he proudly holds his arm around him. Is that so? Aaron smiles. Franz stares intensely at Aaron sniffing him like a predator does.

When Heinrich Himmler announced the creation of the Gestapo it was initially named the department of homeland security! Oh err really? Ja. I never knew that. Ja he nodded. But the initials when, when spoke together sounded much too alike the Russian secret service agency! His face pushed closer to Aaron blowing smoke from his joint as he did! And Mien fuehrer had them change it to Ges-Ta-Po instead!

Scanning everyone's face in the Huey with a nerve wreaking stare I have never witnessed before or since. He continued talking focussing on no one in particular, but he certainly had the knack of unnerving people. Bet he wasn't the most popular guy in class eh? Barry said under a cough, to which all I could do was smirk. Ja...he turned back facing Aaron once more. He didn't like the idea of people thinking they how do you say in English? Copy them?

Huh Err ok! Mien Fuehrer never liked the idea of one man stealing another's idea! OK stop Bogarting the joint! Robbie tells him. To which he then drops it on the floor in spite and stamped it out! Zee was a sucker for how you say in English. Eh fair gamesman-ship? Looking up he grinned at Eddie and Robbie and they too begun to laugh! Laughing at our gullibility perhaps, but whatever it was I laughed too.

Should of seen your face Luke it was like awe huh, Eddie says pulling a face mimicking me. Better still were you lot! Eddie points at Aaron and Sara. I hadn't

163

even thought of them to be honest but when I looked at them they looked terribly uneasy. You learn something new every day eh smiled Brett! Sure do mate. I looked at Franz his long blond hair and blue eyes! Supported by a wafer thin body so suntanned he was barely visible in the night.

I was trying to figure him out when he turned and caught me studying him! He leaned over towards me gesturing I should come closer to him, which I slowly did thinking he was going to tell me something. Which he did but loud enough for all to hear as he stared intensely into my face! Social Genocide the new dark age is coming mein freund. Uh huh! OK I nodded in his direction holding eye contact with him! One hundred percent guaranteed it's the end of civilization, mein freund. No return to zee matrix.

He said all the while staring into my eyes as I found myself realising I was allowing him to drag me into his weird web like way of communicating.....or his world. I reckon if you were to hang out with him too long! Yes Baz? I said out the side of my mouth. Then it might just seem like the correct way to behave! Barry whispered nodding whilst offering me a small pipe he had put together. You read my mind mate! Of course bro I got your back.

If I thought Franz was a tad weird! What the hell we're the other's thinking? Still the fact remained pre-knowing Franz history albeit somewhat via Eddie and Robbie's story had cushioned the blow. The head-fuck the mental Spazoggle that was Franz. Me go lie down on the hammock now mon! It has been a long day! Err no sorry but yawl can't do that! Eddie informed Ras. Why not man? You're too high to climb down! Health and safety I'm afraid! What? I'm joking but on a serious note you might fall! Yawl know and hurt yourself then what do we do?

See we got laws around these here parts folks and they can't be broke! They are there for a dam good reason so yawl always remember that ok. Break your leg or break jack shit in fact out here and that is a crime that carry a death sentence! Yawl remember that and don't forget it none neither you hear. Young Ras here as an example if he were now to maybe fall break a leg then yes sir the gators sure are going to be having a feast.

But it's not all doom and gloom is it Eddie? No sir Robbie! Hey Ed what do you call a virgin from Mississippi? Chuckle, don't know Rob what? Why hell it's a girl who can run faster than her brother yee haw! hehe your funny Rob! Hey remember the time your uncle Joe was on the Jerry Springer show? Oh yeah remember that how could I forget? And so it became that we all had to agree to the law of Eddie and Rob or Eddie to be more specific. Rule number one whenever you climb up to smoke or party in the huey you took a full forty five minutes without smoking before you attempted to come back down.

Which made perfect sense. To be honest it was one of their few sane rules! I just didn't like the sentences handed out for breaking them nor the fact they came with no right of appeal! Ras begun humming a tune everyone swayed and rocked! An hour later were all safely back down and soon very asleep in our cell's, normally I always have issues with getting to sleep in new places, hotels guest house's even mates pads, getting used to the noises of the building, the street outside, the corridor outside my room! But here I went into a deep sleep, a kind of exotic warm wonderland within minutes, a pleasure dome.

The north African fishermen had guilty written all over their faces as they bowed their heads in shame

165

while they were handcuffed. The boat rocked from side to side in the choppy waters even though there was hardly a cloud in the sky! They were rocking from the wind generated from the helicopter hovering barely fifty feet overhead! Tell captain Wales his hunch was correct, these are bales of drugs all right. Said the royal marine balancing himself on top of dozens of bales of cannabis on the yacht in the middle of the straits of Gibraltar.

More marines jumped on board from the British ship that appeared soon afterwards and docked next to it. They handed over the two suspects shoving them up onto the main vessel before getting ready to tow the yacht into port. The second marine picked up his radio and made contact with the helicopter above. Breaker one nine breaker one nine come in over? Go ahead one eight! The Sarge said to tell congratulations to captain Windsor-over! Come again? Another notch on the bedpost captain Windsor the boat is fully loaded with drugs! We caught the bastards red handed-over.

Tally Ho. Tell Sarge it was my pleasure! One was only doing ones duty-over. The marine looked up gave the thumbs up to the Prince before getting the royal thumb back. Oi! Sarge prince sounds well cuffed mate! And well he should my lad! The Sarge replied as he begun hoisting up the first twenty kilo bales. Then as he picked the next one up he was momentarily startled! Underneath it a man is laying down looking up at him! Fucking hell! What is it Sarge? Talk to me the marine shouted as he ran over. What is it sarge?

The man grins as the Sergeant wrestles with his holster in an attempt to get his pistol out.

The Sarge's eyes dart down the man's body. He is wearing a suicide belt! As the marine moves forward raising his assault rifle...Sarge Sarge move move! He remembers Captain Wales above oh shit. Sarge unclips

166

his gun from its holster as they both scream! So does the man. Allah Akbar.............he detonates the bomb before either man can fire a round! The explosion sends the marines flying into both the air and sea in flames. As boxes, wood, bales of dope and debris fly upwards with a twenty kilo bale smashing directly into the helicopters rotor blades. Dozens of nine ounce blocks of solid resin create a meteor shower of projectiles. Creating the perfect IED.

Immediately causing it to spin violently before plunging into a downward trajectory.

The crew of the ship stand back up after the explosion and can only watch in horror as the helicopter with Prince William at the controls desperately trying to gain control but to no avail. It slams sideways into a wave causing a massive explosion and fireball! Within seconds it disappears beneath the pale blue Mediterranean sea. No no a marine bawls out.

NO...........................AAHHHH. I screamed louder than anyone else! Swim William swim water uh uh William swim! Luke! Yes William? Luke. Luke can you hear me? I open my eyes. Sara? Standing over me! Barry and Mitsu poke their heads out from behind her, are you all right there bro? Huh? We heard screaming Barry says. So we came in and you're lying on the floor! Mitsu added! Err what? Looking around I see I am indeed on the ground. You had a nightmare? Sara smiles! I did? What else or how else must you of fallen out of bed? Eh good point I guess. As I try to get up I discover a lump on the back of my head. Ouch that looks like its hurts! Barry winces...Just a little. Jesus I wet myself too? Looking at the soaking floor beneath me.

Bad dream huh? Mitsu says to me. Yeah! What was it about? Eh err fucked up just real fucked up mate! Don't worry about the wetness bro! Barry laughs! Do I look worried? Well personally I would if I pissed my pants! Whatever...Luke chill I chucked water over you to wake you up! You did? Jesus mate I thought I really had pissed myself! We had a little laugh at it as they got me back on the bed. Now come on tell uncle Barry what was the dream about? Helicopters mate. Lots of helicopters.

Well I suppose we were in one last night and that was some strong weed we burned huh? Yeah... guess so I said rubbing the back of my head! Think you're ok? I mean can you get dressed and walk? Sure, cool see you outside in a minute, breakfast is soon so don't miss out. Any idea what's on the menu? Not sure heard something about Rice noodles! What the fuck's rice noodle? He shrugged turning around looking at me. The fuck I should know bro just rice noodles! I stared at him. I don't know Luke honest but the Thais are cooking it and are adamant we give it a try, apparently it's what they have everyday here and it's a delicacy, so we can't very well go offending them now can we? No we wouldn't want to offend our kidnappers mate! Can't we just have eggs?

I know but seeing as were guests! Guests? Barry have you fucking lost it? We we're fucking kidnapped at gunpoint yesterday! Hello anyone home? His eyes looked glazed. They um probably don't have anything to go with eggs Luke! What? Have you not heard a thing I've just said? No bread they need flour for bread Luke and they grow weed here not flour! What? Look just try the rice noodles smile and shut the fuck up, were not in a holiday resort remember? He said lowering his head as he turned and walked off. Holiday resort! Fucking fuck wads...you useless cunts call yourselves adventures? I yelled after him. Pricks can't even handle a scary story! Knew I should have dumped the lot of you after the ship episode...Oh my head.....rice and noodles.......for breakfast! Just when I think these freaks couldn't surprise me anymore.

Five minutes later we're both staring into a coconut shell. Inside is a creamy off white colour substance that vaguely resembles what can only be best described as a thick pasta looking dish! Eddie, Rob, Franz the Thai's are all sitting across from us happily slurping away at this apparent delicacy. While looking over at us lot like were spoilt children. As we're all just playing with it! It looks like bloody vomit! Brett moans to Scooby under his breath! Yeah mate looks like something you might see on the street in Bondi at seven am on a Sunday morning! My heart warms to the fact Baz is now upset after being so nonchalant about it minutes earlier.

Eat up yawl! Robbie barks...its granny-slapping good! Aaron and Sara give it a try! Hmm this is yummy guy's tuk in, they smile at our jailers! This here has a taste of more if you know what I mean? Yeah it's really good ads Sara. Doing her bit with such convincing realism that I personally couldn't work out if she seriously liked it or was genuinely acting or being overly polite and has all but forgotten we are actually hostages here. Her response is rewarded by having the Thais talk and laugh amongst themselves at her! Barry slowly puts some in his mouth, then me! A little bit first then some more! Not bad for lunch but breakfast.... I don't think so! It does the trick Eddie growls, plus whatever they cook it with? The spice's yawl know? Well they seep back out of your skin! Charming! Smiles Scooby.

Well the mosquitoes hate them! Eddie says in between slurping loads more of it down his throat. Plus it makes you feel full all day long! You don't say, is all I can think looking into the bowl. Honest... It's a bento! Says Mitsu, what's that? Rob asks. What Japanese call an all in one meal! This is the Thai version then? Now I know your taking the piss Eddie. Honest brother I am not! Hey Porn tell him is this or is this not what Thais eat after a night on the moonshine? She nods! See? OK Eddie I believe you, but seriously can't you just give us some eggs? Would yawl like hash browns with that? Look nothing else beats this, sure have an egg have a dozen in fact! Now just how long do you think you will last you boy?

Look I know yawl had a nasty bang on the head an all this morning as the cock crowed but hey you're going to have to learn to adapt here or else. Or else what? Eddie yes Rob? Let's go it's time. But! Well we're off to the opium garden folks to check the opium field if any of you! Whoa did you just say to check the opium field? The OPIUM GARDEN! Everyone shouts looking around at each other! Ganja farming is one thing but Opium gardens as well. Now this was 'even I had to admit' something I didn't want to miss.

The Farm

I'm overcome by a sudden urge to gulp down my remaining rice noodle as quickly as possible so to catch up with the others as they leave camp. We giggled and joked like school kids on an outing! The landscape was strange, I was only now fully appreciating its splendour and beauty, its size and the noises of the animals. The sheer relenting indescribable magnitude of the humidity! Visually it looked like any other jungle except throughout it we would come across small little earthy sand like areas where no vegetation seemed to grow! Like our keepers had been planting there for so many years the soil had perished. The sun's rays illuminating through the tress was something you never forget after visiting a jungle.

I lost count of the amount of huge Marijuana plants we passed. We were fascinated looking at them in their natural habitat. Laying idle gently swaying in the humid breeze! Looking so tranquil waiting in fact just begging to be cut cured and smoked. They're seemed to be an awful lot more of them growing than Eddie had first mentioned! In fact they seemed to be growing everywhere! Robbie suggested they were a good way of finding your way back to camp.

In case you ever get lost. As for the smell? It was saturating as it was intoxicating to the senses! Clearly of a skunk verity, the herb stuck to you to the point that you forgot all about it. The jungle seemed to be one giant incense factory.

As we stopped! Robbie and Eddie put down the five litre bottle of water they had brought.

Eddie did an initial examination, proclaimed in his good old boy accent that 'it's so god dam dry Rob these

171

here plants would bribe my hounds to pee on them! He then began to gently water around the ground where the poppies were growing carefully avoiding the plants themselves! All we could do was watch.

So this is it? I asked Barry who shrugged! Guess so. This boring plant is what I have heard so much about all my life? Yup! Eddie says looking at me! But if it's a picture the government want to put up to warn the kiddies about drugs then it won't be this one! It won't be a poppy brother! No? No sir e. What picture do they use then? Aaron asks confused! Why they stick a picture of a Marijuana plant up of course, what else boy!

Hell Rob I bet Aaron there is just about as welcome at his in-laws as a hair in a biscuit tin! Eddie laughs as Robbie nudges him who then spits onto the ground. Both then break into fits of laughter once again! That's true you know ads Ras. They demonise the herb, so this is..... em what I mean is this where you actually get heroin from mate? Brett asks. Yup Eddie answers still laughing at his own joke! Ok he grins at Scooby. But don't forget your good old friend morphine now ads Robbie. Something yawl be dam glad of its help at some point in you or your loved ones lives.

What about paracetamol and codeine? Barry asks. Codeine is made from coke! Mitsu says. Uh huh no sir he is right! Eddie nods at Baz. It's derived from opium and made directly from poppy plants! It affects one's perception....of pain! Rob says titling his head with a grin on his face.

Eddie begun slowly stroking the plants with the back of his hand, talking and smiling at them like they were his patients or children even which I found bizarre yet soothing. So kind and attentive which made me begin to question my own sanity. Here was a guy that was trying to shot me yesterday, now less than twenty four hours later he is seducing all of us with his compassion for a drug! 'What the actual fuck'. To be honest Eddie I think in a beauty competition the marijuana plant wins hands down every time. Barry said snapping me out of my self-induced hypnotism.

Depends on who the darn judge is! Rob answers without looking at him but staying focused on Eddie staying focused on the plants instead. Then he looks up at Barry from his kneeling position by the plant. Yawl know Baz I guess it's like a beautiful female except the fair maiden is a bitch without a soul, no personality, nothing boy nothing it's... it's just a slut! He snarls. Yup that's what the marijuana plant is! Yes sir e. She is a total slut always remember that boy. Why? For she will go with the highest bidder every time! Any john with the hard cash is her daddy yawl understand that? He says looking around at his assembled students.

Yawl see the poppy here she frets! Oh hell yeah he nods, she worries stresses and panics too.

Don't she Rob? Sure does Ed he nods sadly making his lower lip quiver. Why? Asks Natsumi and Sara at the same time. Why? Because she hopes she ends up in a good home of course why else. And to folks most deserving of her I should add. Okay I mumble and nod, in tandem with the general consensus all around me.

Now my mental response at this point is not one of deep philosophical idealism or pondering the creation of the universe, but more leaning towards the what the fuck is this fruitcake talking about! Stressed out opium plants worrying about where they're going to live! They're not puppy dogs there not humans, their fucking plants you fucked up fucking hillbilly.

Bad enough they're a bunch of chronic weed smoking gun tooting red neck adrenalin junkie, hostage taking baby elephant killer fuck-wads. But are now also

173

adding talking to their opium plants is a good thing to their CV! So what you're saying is that the opium poppies have got personality or feelings like individuals? Barry asks. Yet again waking me out of yet another daze! Hell yeah! He snaps his fingers smiling, that's exactly what I'm saying Barry! That's it bull's-eye amigo.

These guys lost it a long time ago dude Mitsu whispers in my ear! I know I nod back, probably before they even came here! Yeah dude first the guns then the rules, then Franz now we got Opium poppies with feelings. What next jungle meth labs selling online life insurance? Next the poppies will have human rights! Look everything on this land is alive is it not? Robbie stands up waving his arms around scaring us for a second. Well yeah but! No buts Barry no buts! But fucking yes bro I got some buts here if you don't mind? OK then yawl go right ahead Mr.

Thank you! That coconut tree over there is alive correct? Yeah good example Barry. I edge him on pretending to be engrossed by what is now a clearly visible scheming plan by Robbie and Eddie. A type of mind manipulation technique! Well you get water from it and it keeps you nourished does it not? That's true very true in fact! Never thought of it like that before baz. But if you get shot or bitten by a rattlesnake in the bush on a dark night you're not going to be screaming for fucking coconut juice are yer now? I guess. Or if you get bitten by a shark, shark bites being mighty painful an all! Who the fucks talking about sharks Rob? Eddie injects. Are we Pirates? Yawl at sea? You know sometimes when I hear some of the shit you come out with I think the wheels still turning but the hamster's dead!

Look Eddie all I'm saying is heroin is used by junkie down and out fucking thieving no good hobo's who break into people's homes to steal their TV and snatch old ladies handbags that's all ok! That's because it's E-Legal Baz my man. Hell I bet you never even tried the lady have you? Have yawl ever even had a turn on boy? What....what do you mean take heroin? Hell yeah never did myself or the robster here no harm did it Rob? Nope, none what so ever Ed. No eh no of course not look don't even go there with the whole peer pressure thing ok! Heroin is used and abused by filthy dirty scumbag's, end of conversation bro.

So what does yawl know then baz? What does he know Eddie? Fuck all Robbie, sweet fuck all if yawl ask me he laughed as he coughed and spat on the ground! Well I don't if I...If what? Would try some? No.....yawl too pussy boy aren't you? He smiled clearly manipulating Barry into a corner he couldn't punch out of. No it's just stupid that's all, everyone knows! Everyone knows jack-shit boy......Just one hit and you're addicted? They laughed...Oh lawd Jesus above why yawl send me this here fool? Look spare me the lecture Barry yawl probably couldn't handle it anyway! Probley think yawl be sticking needles in your arm next huh? Eddie says accompanied by his sarcastic grin! Well there aren't any needles around these here parts son.

I pitied Barry as I watched this unfold but I'm helpless to intervene! I am outside the ring and there is no referee. Eddie is clearly on a winner however toxic that may sound. His augment just grew stronger with each sentence he threw at Barry in the head-fuck mental boxing ring. Baz had now got himself in a corner with a heavyweight and couldn't see the light and like most fighters was too stubborn to chuck in the towel.

Bullshit brother! All fucking bullshit government propaganda the whole dang lot of it! Go to war in Afghan I stan, fight the Taliban in Pak I stan, smuggle some Opium from where ever the fuck I stan to

Amsterdam. Then after yawl destroy the poppies help the grannies, build some schools for the little ones and set the fucking chinkara's free! Huh? It's a type of gazelle Luke. Oh! Yes sir but get shot or blown up in the process and before you can bawl out I love you Mary-Jane.............the government will have you hooked up for life brother for f-u-c-k-i-n-g life! Comprendre? Trust me yawl those mother fucking sons of bitches will fill your veins with as much golden brown as you can handle! Yes sir E bob...the powers that be will fill you up with more shit than bullshit given half the chance and that's the truth.

Knockout ding ding ding. He's got a point Ras acknowledges! I know I know Barry says as he finally succumbed to defeat! I patted his back in support. You're correct. Morally I smile at him. No Luke he is not, Eddie barked "Condemnation without investigation is the height of ignorance" Know who said that Luke? Nope but got a feeling you're going.... Albert Einstein said that boy! Really mate? Yes sir he did! Well how about.

All that glitters is not gold! What the fuck this here boy talking about Rob? William Shakespeare......The Merchant of Venice! I grinned. Eddie stood up and began circling me! If you find from your own experiences that something is a fact! and it contradicts something some authority has written, then you must abandon that authority! and place your reasoning on your own findings.........Leonardo de Vinci. I stood speechless. ding dong knockout round two. Barry patted my back, cheers mate.

The assembled sheep began clapping and applauding this evidently clear display of mental malfunctioning obviously brought on by a concoction of drugs or/and rejection of mainstream society sunburn isolation and oh who cares! Their fucked I'm not I want out. Be damned if I'm joining them in their private hell! I decided there and then I had to get out ASAP, all alone if need be. All I knew was I personally wasn't running from nothing, plus the fact of the matter was I didn't really know my fellow adventurers at all except through the fog of weed and entheogens. Besides I only knew them a few weeks so owed them no loyalty and if shit hit the fan how much could I rely on them anyway?

Too long in this environment I whispered to Mitsu and a chap would be talking to salamander's opium plants and lizards! Uh huh...would that be before or after you develop Franz thousand yard stare? We shared a private giggle. Much to my relief some of us were still rational! Looking across I watched Eddie and Robbie smirk as they looked into my travelling comrades eyes! Dead souls lost in an enchanted forest of palm trees ganja plants and silver tongued opium swashbucklers.

But of course that's just our generation! Hell yeah Robbie adds and before us it was Vietnam! Notice the madness continues Mitsu says. I noticed. Did yawl know that after Vietnam in the good old US of A and Europe we had ten million more heroin addicts than we had before the war? I didn't know that I told him... to be truthful I was genuinely shocked at that inconvenient truth and it spelt a death kneel to any possible constructive argument any of us could now possibly have! Hour by hour slowly but meticulously they reeled us into their web until my former travelling buddies worshipped Eddie with a god like status.

Well they sure did and they sure as hell weren't all vets neither! Vietnam vets? Barry asks. Is this cat for real? Yup! Eddie I reckons that Canadian fellers so dumb he be about two sandwiches shy of a picnic! Rob says coughing up yet another load of phlegm! Pardon me ladies always like this for a few god dam hours come morning.

So where did those returning soldiers score? More bullshit propaganda my man. Secret government networks. The CIA M15 what do you think these cats all be up to when they aren't organising coups arming dictators and generally going round whacking folks huh? Making out with hot Russian spies? They and all the others smuggled that shit in to sell. But why? I ask looking for some sort of logical reasoning even though it all made perfect sense in the strangest way. I wanted them to think we needed more persuasion. To raise the funds they needed man! Needed for what? What the fuck you think for what the fuck for Luke. The other shit that goes down my man! Yawl never watch those secret agent documentaries? Those cats will take you and your entire families life's if you cross them man.

Take yawl Mr Bond as an example. Bond now you must heard of him right? Yeah of course! Well you know when the boss says shit like oh and if your caught the government will claim complete ignorance or yawl acted alone an shit? Yes....well there cannot be any trace of cash or anything leading back to the state or government involved now can there? So just like Mafia goons these cats keep it clean, all on the low down! They shit in someone else's backyard man. The governments involved they do bad shit in one place to fund more bad shit in another! Any examples? Mitsu asks.

Afghanistan! Is a perfect if not **the** blueprint example in fact of this type of shit! We I mean the US government admitted it funded the mujahedeen during the soviet occupation in the height of the cold war correct? As far as I know I was little then so I. Well look here yawl I wasn't and believe me if one fucking agent was caught handing over money or weapons by the commies it would have been' hotter n' hell's basement on the day of reckoning' World War Three! Kaputz the end so long it was nice whilst it lasted ...Cooter Browns famous last words....Robbie added grimly staring at the ground before hawking out yet more phlegm again.

So what did they do Eddie? Barry says. Ding dong round four! Hell boy yawl don't give up? Told you Ed boy's got about as much sense as god gave a goose... Rob sniggered! Shit Rob I don't mind I'm having more fun that a tornado in a trailer park! He replied as they high fived each other! Look let me make it real simple Mr A gave money and weapons to Mr B via Mr C's government! Simple.

So if it went all pear-shaped and hotter than a Billy-goat with a blowtorch they could say 'it wasn't me. So what your saying is there is this giant conspiracy orchestrated by the government! Via proxy... yes sir e I do........Deep stuff man. Yes sir it is. Now look folks I haven't time to go on all day but just listen here one more time. Ever hear about the CIA's secret war on Laos? No! Yawl just been there right? Uh huh we nodded. Been there but never heard of...

Well this is a fucking fact man, the US Military dropped....more bombs.....more fucking napalm on Laos than they ever did on Vietnam. Hell that's a country they weren't even at war with! I could sense Barry was seeing stars at this point and he badly needed someone to chuck the white towel in the ring! Really? Is all the poor punch drunk could muster up as the ref went for the ten count with him! Yes Barry you can take that to the bank home boy! Eddie laughed! Knock-out ding ding ding.

Ho Chi Min! Ever hear of him? Yeah man! Ras suddenly piped up getting involved.

Well old uncle Ho his brother was only the biggest fucking heroin trafficker and warlord this side of the

Mekong! Was he? Hell yeah and who is in charge of Afghanistan today remind me folks? Err Hamid something! Whose brother is?...Err...only the biggest fucking smuggler since Alexander the great! I didn't know that man? Alexander was a Ganja smuggler? Pips up Scooby.

He scans our faces intensely, history repeats itself always remember that! History repeats itself! So do I seriously have to spell it out? No we mumble unanimously shaking our heads. Now where we're we? Oh yes a nicer sounding name for sure is of course morphine to err facilitate that processed packaged consumer society we are forced to live in. Your very own personal and very fucking real matrix! Shit folks don't even want skin a fucking chicken before they eat it back home now days! Not to mention kill a goat. The Slaughterhouses are tucked away! Kept miles from prying eyes.

Numbed out perception of reality, what's real what isn't? So stop believing everything and anything that comes on the news yawl know why? Because it isn't the truth. A fantasy world of make believe where war is upheld as a peaceful endeavour. Where power struggles and invasions are called humanitarian interventions! But he has a point about addiction! I say to Eddie supporting Barry! That's a bit rich coming from a redcoat! He snarls. Reminding me his volatile side can and does appear in an instant and without warning.

Huh? Huh my ass boy. You're Queen Vicky well she had no qualms about sending your navy to war to supply the Chinese with all the Indian Heroin they could handle and today just where are the British army Luke just remind me if you will? And for what supposed reasons are they there? I laughed and nodded just to make him think I too was under his influence, as one by one they continued to zoom in on each of those present to manipulate their thought process. To focus detect and test each individuals strengths and weaknesses.

Look here yawl.......Do not insult the lady! Robbie said! That's all were saying ok just don't. I am not insulting the..What lady? Boy you couldn't hit the ground if yawl fell twice could you now? Huh? .....Mary-Jane Luke who else? You're talking about it like it's a person! I couldn't help myself from starting to argue with him. Even though I realised the conversation had turned so bizarre it couldn't possibly be taken seriously by otherwise rational people! But this was no rational situation nor was it a rational place to have it or rational people to discuss it with. So all rational behaviour goes out the window.

But I needed to dissect their minds if I were to manipulate them! Figure out the weaknesses in their armoury, what made them tick? If I didn't do that, then perish the thought I may have stay here forever, thus the only way was to pretend to allow them to think they were in fact manipulating me. It is a lady! It's not! It's what then Luke a what a plant? Well yes! Technically maybe but to us here it's alive and it helps us stay alive.

Like how? It gets us cash to buy stuff we otherwise could not afford...but the Ganja? Asks Ras. The slut get you nothing man look yawl don't get it do yee? Yawl in the middle of the golden triangle here brother, you won't get jack-shit for weed around these here parts. Now there isn't no point in beaten' a dead horse...course can't hurt none neither! But the best yawl can wish for is food, maybe some shoes or fishing gear but money yawl crazy if you think you get cash out here.

But Mary-J here will help relieve the trauma of child birth for a female! Make a dying soldier's last moments

181

as pleasurable as possible! Or for anyone when near death it will soothe and make it less traumatic all round for all yawl in-laws as we enter the 'astral' on that finale lonesome journey back to the promised land! Back to where we came from and all must surely return! The place we call home! Hallelujah brother! Yes sir the lady will indeed get you what you need when it's most in need! Eddie smiled! Praise the lawd! Rob added.

You know what? What? I want to try some Mary-J now! Oh for fucks sake Barry I feel my head is going to explode when I say this! Well yawl can't! Huh why the hell not? We got us some fishing to do. But. No buts Barry! Guys. Yes Luke what is it? Where has Franz gone? He disappears all the time no one knows where to. Now come on guys and as for you sweet ladies yawl go back to the camp now you hear, to help POW and the girls! What? Sara and Nat both look at us. They then say nothing but reluctantly sulk off towards the camp as instructed. While we go towards some river.

Eddie can I ask you something? Sure you can Luke! You know women are equal to men nowadays right? Thought you were going to tell me you couldn't fish boy! Huh err no! No what you can't fish? No I can but yes they are you know they are equal. Look Luke! Eddie stops walking and faces me. You're young and just because you hit it off with Mary or Pammy or whoever down the local discotheque does not make you expert on the female of the species! Word grins Robbie. Cooking and cleaning is about all they are good for if yawl ask me! Spiting he continues, and hell sometimes they aren't even good for that neither.

Now we will fish with spears Ras laughs. Like in the days of Solomon! Wasn't he in a desert? Scooby says to him! Nah man back then Africa was as lush and green as the fields of France. We got us some proper rods Eddie

182

says taking two out from under some bushes. We then walked for about an hour until they located the river. We cast our rods chilled as best we could whilst our glorious leaders preached lectured and generally ranted like the psycho hillbilly fuck-wads they were.

Conspiracy after conspiracy was touted until thank goodness we caught some Mekong catfish or I should say I caught a catfish, a big one too and could thus leave! But not until Eddie confirmed yet another wild conspiracy on how the Mekong catfish was actually a hybrid of African catfish brought in by the you guessed it US army! Then bred out the native catfish. If you ask me he was jealous of my fifteen seconds of fame and wanted the limelight back on him. It wiped out the native catfish during the Vietnam 'adventure' as he constantly referred to it.

When we got back to camp I sat in a yoga posture chilling whilst I practised some meditation I learned a few years back. I didn't feel anything from it at the time, but now figured it would be a good to give it another try! I recalled the teacher placing major importance on breathing and how in normal everyday living real breathing isn't practised and it should be done via the nose for it to get into those hard to reach places.

I felt alone, it was a nice feeling, my first real time feeling that in the jungle. At one point I opened my eyes and I thought I saw Franz head suddenly pop up behind a bush but then when I went to investigate there was nothing where I thought I'd seen him. Not that I wanted to see him, must of been a jungle version of a mirage...a jungle mirage.

After about an hour chilling I felt the spiritual feeling I'd not had since I had left Nepal return, which was nice. This time it was much more powerful....Luke! Luke huh, hey dude wake up! The hand shook my shoulder so

183

violently it nearly pushed me over! I was seriously pissed off at being disturbed just as I felt my inner self awakening.

Well maybe not exactly but I had heard people talk about the Kundalini.......the invisible powerful energy that lies deep within each one of us, at the base of our spine which can travel to our pineal gland in the brain via the spinal cord! Once the Kundalini is awakened, an evolution of the mind body and spirit occurs. Leading to a higher state of consciousness and spiritual awareness...one where you know and understand your purpose in life, the afterlife and so on.

Do I look asleep? Huh what? Know what your problem is Barry? What Luke? You're a major league fuck-wad! Want to go clubbing tonight Luke? Go fucking what? I shook my head in disbelief! A club it's called the Opium den and it's right here in the jungle... Isn't that just wild dude? You know what? Your problem is not the problem Barry......Oh ok cool bro. The problem is your attitude towards your problem! Huh? Nothing Barry... nothing mate, yeah I'd love to go clubbing!

Eddie said some of the opium poppies are ready for tapping and we should come and watch him do his thang! Barry laughed. Want to come? Yeah why not eh, Baz Yes Luke...What's tapping? Oh shit sorry dude! It's when the poppy is ready and they make these tiny incisions with a blade allowing the raw opium to just ooze out! Sucking his lips as he said ooze and with desire glazing his eyes whilst holding his fingers up reminiscent of Italian chefs the world over.

Oh I see! Yeah wild huh? Err sure yes em amazing! I smile. I knew you'd love to see it done Luke! It's a skill that can only be passed on Robbie said. Just like cooking then! Huh? Look over there Barry, at the girls....oh yes the Thais are showing Sara and Nat how to cook Thai style! Sara catches me watching her and gives me a wave calling me over. Barry have you got a smoke? When did you start? Start what? Smoking ciggies! Oh eh I just feel like one every now and then, you know due to all the excitement earlier on. Yeah of course here you go! He says taking one out of his pocket! Thanks mate. I'm going to talk with Sara! Awesome! But make sure to call me when you're off to cut those poppies! Will do Buddy! I walk over to the area where the ladies are busy preparing food.

Hey Luke! Hi Sara hard at work eh? It's not hard actually it's quite enjoyable. Got a light? I ask holding the smoke Barry gave me. No sorry POW have you a light for Luke? She hands her one which she passes to me. Lighting up I inhale before passing it back. I heard all about your David and Goliath moment after we left you this morning! What the catfish? I never thought about it like that but now that you mention it.

But that is a cool way to describe it, thou it were nothing really! Nothing? Have you seen the size of the thing? Of course I caught it remember? Sorry my English I was trying to say....Hey of course Sara! I'm only teasing I understand what you were getting at. The Thai ladies have been talking about you all day. They have? Yes! She leans in close, they said the men never caught a fish that big before but shush she says putting her finger to her mouth, do not say it! Err ok why not? Eddie and Robbie they are em how you would say it very competitive in a non gentleman way! Does that make sense Luke? Yes Sara that makes perfect sense. Are you going to go with the boys to learn about the poppies? Might as well not much else to do.

Sara...yes Luke? Tomorrow after breakfast I was going to go down by where I caught the fish would you like to come with me? Sure why not...if this lot are flexible, myself and nat are still not really in the clear of what is or is not expected of us here! I have an idea but I will keep it to myself at the moment? Why what is it? Oh nothing in fact that's another thing I'd like to discuss with you. OK in the morning give me the sign when you're ready...Will do.

I stroll over to the pool area where the guys are lounging passing joints and chillums around! Rob is semi submerged in the water! Howdy, he says to me...Alright there Rob! It's a bitch trying to get that stinking catfish smell off yawl ain't it? Does a bear shit in the woods? I respond in my best southern accent...Yes sir I believe he does and its slicker than greased goose shit too! Everyone laughs. Here cool man Luke! Ras passes me a joint..Thanks mate! You deserve it mon.

Fish supper tonight all thanks to you! Robbie says as I Inhale the first of many a lungful for tonight! So what time are you guys off? Don't do time round here! Matrix invention, he winks! Really? Yup he nods. Yawl ever hear of Horus? What as in the Egyptian sun god that did battle with Seth the lord of the underworld every night? Aaron asks! You betcha well he rose every morning in the 'horizon' and the sun rises in thirty degree blocks giving us the 'hour' Horus horizon hour interesting don't yawl think? Yes Err very. Need to study yawl Etymology boy! Eddie thought me that! What's etymology? Scooby asks. The studying of the origins of words.

But it's a safe bet when Eddie come o clock would be about that time! Where is he gone? I ask taking another deep drag on the joint! Then I realised I didn't really want it as I'd had more than enough excitement for one day........For a sheet Luke......... Oh nice mans got to do what a man's got to do eh. That's right son, he ran over yonder with arse cheeks looking tighter than a skater's ass in a nose dive! Again everyone laughs at the originality or simple-mindedness of his slang. I wasn't quite sure which so I passed him the joint...yes sir got that! He said with a smile as he took it from my hand.

Well speak of the devil! What's that Rob? The good town folk here well they yawl getting restless to go see Mary-J juices flowing! OK give me a minute in fact just leave me talk with POW and I'll be back! After a few minutes Eddie returned. Let's roll! Following our glorious leaders once more we silently marched. With little talk from my fellow hostages I allowed myself to succumb deep into a mental abyss of mind body and soul. Looking around me I saw flashes of beau-jest like confusion among this rag tag collection of adult sized but mentally childlike soldiers that were my comrades.

The silence how the silence was deafening. But ours was due to strong weed and not the thought of imminent death which was almost a certain outcome. For if there was only one thing certain here, it was that unless we escaped we would surely all perish one by one at some very near point in the future! It seemed lost on most of the others that this wasn't the holiday Eddie and friends were presenting it as. We couldn't simply be released or let go now, we knew too much!

The motive? Questionable...but my hunch was they needed slave's mule's workers or whatever just as and when we happened to of strolled into town! Either way get as many of us as possible onside seemed their plan! Then utilise the classic divide and rule technique and whoever's left outside the circle will vanish in the night. Just like Channarong had vanished! The ever lurking ever menacing Franz. He seemed to man an outer ring we didn't yet notice or know about. They pretended to tell us everything but in reality they weren't telling us shit! I bet even if we made good any escape past Eddie and Robbie then Franz would be the hardest obstacle of all.

Then I saw them we all saw them! Dozens and dozens of these peculiar yet pretty in their own way. Green bulb like flower tops growing on the end of thick stems. A mild breeze flowed down through the jungle canopy and filtered through the landscape. It cooled the back of my neck as we studied them in trance like awe. Sitting on top of these green bulbs were what can only be described as a small yellow crowns! Some were still in the flowering phase looking more like tulips than Poppies! So many! Barry remarked like a kid in a candy store! Rob smiled like a granny looking at her grandkids. They like companionship he said gently stroking one.

Companionship? I repeated! Yes companionship! You know like...Don't tell me........like people? Hell that's exactly what I meant Luke! That's exactly what I meant. How did you know? I winked at him! OK Ras, Luke, and Barry! Everyone yawl gather round! Eddie said. I noticed the aroma floating throughout the air in the area. Growing more intense as the senses picked up and analyzed it registering it in my brain! Obviously emanating from the plantation itself. Not an unpleasant one! I couldn't quite describe it but in fact quite the opposite of what you would expect from such a vilified plant.

Everyone crouched down listening to Eddie give a lecture. I stared upwards at the treetops, then heard Luke! Huh? Boy the engine's truly a running yawl but nobody's driving! Now yawl want see this or not? Yes of course I said walking over to where they were. Sure boy? Yes then tune in because this is hard to do! Oh ok I didn't know. Well it is. It'd be like trying to put peanut butter up a wildcat's ass with a hot poker! No seriously yes I would love to watch you at work Eddie! Keep telling you Ed if this here boy's brains were dynamite, he couldn't blow his nose! Heard that Rob heard that! Now sit the fuck down and pay attention boy...

With one hand he gently held the base of the bulb which sit on the top of the plant and with a very sharp box cutter he very carefully made two small incisions down the side of the bulb towards the ground. Then he moved about an inch or so and made two more incisions before finally repeating the process a third time before moving onto the other side of the poppy. A tiny little trickle of white sap appeared were he'd sliced them open. Talking all the while as he slowly showed us the protocol to follow.

This here pop pay dropped its leaves about oh two weeks back I reckon! It's best to wait at least two weeks before yawl drain um. If you slice them too deep it will just pour out onto the ground and hell we don't want that now do we boys? So what do we want? Mitsu asked him. We want it to trickle out over the next few hours, bout a day or so should do it.

Now look here boys as the sap oxidizes it turns brown and forms a resin yawl understanding this? What do we do with that? Aaron asked. This we will collect tomorrow, well most of the time you collect it next day.....Sometimes the day after.

Over here is one I prepared earlier he joked. Well two days ago to be precise! As Eddie walked over to it everyone including myself followed! Lawd Jesus its hotter n' hell's basement on the day of reckoning up here today aint it Rob? He said wiping the sweat off his forehead. Yup must be like record heat we a getting here today! Yes sir hotter than Death Valley I'd be reckoning.

Nearing the plant we see a thick brown resinous sticky tar like substance has seeped out. Rob took out a plastic eggcup and with the sharp knife scrapes and scoops the resin from all around the bulb before carefully placing it in the eggcup.

So how much is there? I ask. They both just look at me! I mean how much in weight on average would a guy get from each bulb? You know just curious about the actual financial side of things that's all! About a gram a bulb boy....WHAT? That's it a poxy gram! All that work patience risk and love of course for a fucking gram? Eddie stared at Robbie before turning to face me! Well now just how much was yawl expecting Luke? Don't em know but. Well that's all yawl get boy! OK no wonder it's so precious I say faking my best fake smile no wonder indeed! Now where was I before that fool started jabbering on?

Oh yeah I can show you some that I prepaid earlier Eddie and Robbie then broke into wild convulsions of laughter again as they walked off leaving us the sheep to meekly follow. What did you make of that Luke? Barry asked me looking rather impressed as we strolled back to camp! M1 Junction eleven! Huh? What Barry says looking at me confused! Oh nothing mate just talking to myself.

No man seriously you said M1 what's that? Sounds like a gun or some type of weapon bro, you're not planning anything stupid are you buddy? Stupid no it's just the name of a motorway that takes you out of London that's all! Oh what's a motorway? Err what you guys call a free-way. I think, but don't quote me on that. Anyway it's just a name I gave this footpath.

Whoa ok time out dude stop turn around. OK what do you see? A footpath going where?

Don't know! North! It's going north from the camp OK how you know that? Because the huey is over there I point uh huh and last night the North Star was up there beyond those big trees! I add pointing towards the river! OK now as you already know every so often other footpaths go off in different directions. Err yes sure ok. So I just thought in my spaced out head that it would be a good idea to you know to have like....Landmarks. Fair enough Barry said walking away.

Looking around I notice were still alone so I grab Barry by the arm. Where the hell did Franz go? Barry shakes his head! He is a strange one though isn't he? Must have that post traumatic stress disorder or something from that tsunami experience I mean that sounded like the ultimate bad acid trip dude, imagine that shit....a fucking Anaconda.....Quite ssshhh Seriously Barry I want you to tune in for a minute! Are you ok Luke? Listen I say staring into his eyes! OK go for it brother.

This isn't any huge mountainous snowy Himalayan Andes shit sort of place we're stuck in you do understand that don't you? Yeah sure! So where the hell does he keep disappearing to?

What's going on? Is he digging a tunnel or what? A tunnel? Oh who knows Luke the guys a loon he is......No Barry there is more to it than that! Huh, such as? Like they do not care where or pretend not to know where he disappears off to but if you ask me they know alright, know what I think? No but go on! They are pretending their showing us everything but...Luke? Yes? Relax dude chill it's all cool bro.....here, he pulls out a joint and lights it up and goes to pass it to me.

No I fucking won't chill out! I say in a hushed tone through gritted teeth! And neither should you! Do you remember what the waitress told us back In Laos? Can't recall what Eddie told us five minutes ago dude. About the guy who came here several years ago and was never seen again? Holy shit you think its....Franz! Of course it's fucking Franz Barry who the fuck else is it? He grabs both my arms with a startled look...quite shush. I put a

191

finger to his mouth before looking around to double check no one is listening.

Look mate everyone here seems to of become suddenly intoxicated by this whole fantasy scenario we have found ourselves in. I can't explain it so don't ask but the others seem to think it's all going to be fishing sunbathing and getting stoned. Whereas in reality these guys seem very fucking keen on turning everyone here into some sort of stoned spaced out zombie drug plantation workers or something!

We are kidnap victims but right now if the cops from whatever country we are officially in we're to come here! What do you think they would say? That is to say this bunch of desperados doesn't actually start a fucking ok corral style shoot out with them! Err dude. Do you seriously for one minute they might consider we are victims too and not involved in this business? Of course not! They would see a bunch of westerners surrounded by shit loads of drugs and fuck knows what else and then for all we know this lot could frame it on us.

Shit bro...Have you even noticed that much? Tell me you have for fucks sake Barry! Well err sort of...And there will be no point in saying shit about dead elephants because the insects will have fucking ate them by now! So you or we will have no proof to back up our story. Plus am I the only one getting a real bad feeling in my stomach about Channarong? What about him dude? Jesus Barry that's what I mean. Huh? Nobody's seen him since yesterday and I think ...You don't think they...Don't know Baz mate I just don't know what to think any more. Sure you don't want a smoke bro?

Look for all we know they might have cut a deal with some paramilitary outfit in one of the countries around here, you know set themselves up as vital drug kingpins go betweens or whatever, you just don't know. If that is the case say we escape past them past Franz see the cops and they.....Bring us right back? That is what I'm thinking Barry. Their bandits outlaws, go back a century and there would be wanted posters dead or alive of this lot up stretching from Alabama to Arizona.

Jesus Luke were their slaves? Now you're getting it. Look I really don't know the score but make no mistake about it these guys were ready to kill us yesterday. Don't forget that plus they have destroyed our only way of getting out of here. Completely disorientated us with strong weed and walking around in circles. Locking us into a drugged consciousness where we are incapable of rational decision making. Which makes it almost a certainty they've got rid of Channarong! But they didn't kill us why Luke what reason do they have to keep us alive? Well they want us alive for some reason mate. And I'd rather not hang around getting fat like cattle waiting for the farmer to turn us into a double with cheese. Too right bro, too right Luke you are so right he says stamping out the joint.

OK Baz mate here's what we're going to do, tonight were going to get high with them and play it cool ok! Awesome! Awesome plan brother..Then again it's not like we have a choice is it? No guess we do not Luke do we...No and that's the way it's going to be for as long as we're here don't forget that either Baz. The more drugs we take the less likely we are to resist and if me or you or anyone else seems reluctant or protests well we will probably just you know.... disappear.

In secret? Yeah. I reckon as I don't think at this point they would actually kill any of us out in the open in case it started a revolt. My bet is they would just entice us off somewhere quite where you know they could do a shallow grave job, then when asked they'd shrug and claim not to know, he must of got lost guys or ran away they would say. Classic divide and rule technique but either way what's clear as day to me is there's no way they want us to leave EVER.

Shit Luke what are we going to do? Don't panic tomorrow I have a date. Huh? I mean a meeting with Sara so I will talk with her and find out what or if she's learned anything from the Thai women. You can also bet Natsumi is freaked. Yeah she didn't even want to come here! Neither of them did. Man were all fucked Luke...they been here seven years, seven freaking years bro! Yup and if we don't hatch an proper escape plan now while we are still mentally strong and physically fit enough to do it we might just be here for a long time too.

OK let's get back before were missed now remember we must play it cool Barry ok! OK bro...If the opportunity arises tonight try to find out what way Ras and Mitsu are thinking. OK Luke what about the others? I think watching Brett and Scooby today. We lost them already...Shit bro and Aaron? Fuck knows mate could be he's playing them us or maybe he thinks the whole thing is the result of some spiritually divine karma shit. That's another good reason I want to spend time with Sara tomorrow because....LOST GENTELMEN?

Whoa Hanz you scared me man! Shit bro you can't come creeping up on people like that!

Franz not Hanz! Now I asked are you lost? Err no you lost Baz? Nah you, nope I'm good. Then why are you hanging about in so very much criminal like fashion? Huh. We looked at each other confused then back at him! Around here hanging around suspiciously when zee camps are surely that way, he says pointing! Ok mate you got us were lost Ha ha! Yeah bro haw haw just didn't want to admit it! Follow me! Franz escorted us back to camp.....lucky his English is not so good Baz hissed though clenched teeth once we were a few feet

194

behind him. Yeah I nodded, real fucking lucky.

After a dinner of deep fried catfish and crispy vegetables we found ourselves yet again hanging around the pool. Where smoking copious amounts of weed in the most imaginable of ways possible seemed like an obligatory task! It was a good natured environment with nothing sinister about it and you could see why some had succumbed so easily so readily to the wish that everything was fine.

The only giveaway that not all was right was the fact that Eddie positioned himself at a higher vantage point than everyone else, with Rob at his right side. And sure enough as I suspected Brett Scooby and Aaron we're practically sitting at his feet! Giving him the god-like hero worship he so evidently desired! Hail Eddie Caesar.

THE OPIUM DEN

Franz had grabbed himself some food after bringing us back before yet again doing a Houdini on it! Since our encounter with him I was now absolutely certain he was always lurking monitoring studying everything, all of us! He was never too far away...a sort of border guard keeping watch on both the outside and inside. Or maybe it's all an act and we're all fooled and he is the top dog! My only question was the various levels of loyalty? If one dropped would the others fall and if so, then who really was the man? It certainly pointed towards Eddie! Fucking hell mate you got to give them credit I thought looking around me, they had hoodwinked everyone good and proper and with such speed. Guns, Ganja, Opium, Helicopters Fishing and now apparently a night club! A stoners nightmare but a backpackers dream! Even I couldn't wait to see this 'nightclub' I must admit that. Mitsu was across from me nodding silently while Ras and Barry sat together and in close conversation. I was so relieved to know I had not lost Barry. Plus I knew this gave him a chance to get inside Ras's head. In between listening to and feigning sorrow at Eddie's tales which I must admit he did a terrific job of. Then Rob produced a set of bongo drums and began slowly tapping away on them as Eddie spoke.

Personally though once I'd heard the words gangsters guns etc I lost interest as I knew it would be some crap where he could portray himself as some kind of hero of epic Hollywood proportions. So it was great to know Barry was at hard at work faking it. Oh shit really Eddie! That's awful how ungrateful he was after everything you did for him! Were just some of the stomach churning comments I heard in response to this gun tooting, sadistic ego maniac's outlandish tales.

The others we're clearly becoming more indoctrinated by the minute! Mitsu how are you doing? Alright considering. Considering what mate? Considering the compete bullshit these guys are coming out with, he said quietly passing me a joint......Ha ha ha, I faked a laugh out loud and nodded at him, hoping it didn't look too obvious. Say what you want about the lot of them. But Eddie is the sharpest tool in the box alright and as such had naturally swam to the top of the food chain! Eddie *was* the man, had to be.

You have noticed? Mitsu asked as I turned my face away from Eddie's stare. I winked yup talk later ok I whispered as I passed him back the joint! Darkness had fallen when Eddie stood up, just as Rob suddenly stopped playing the bongo drums and with arms outstretched and a full moon in the clear night sky behind him, Eddie loudly proclaimed. In Xanadu did Kubla Khan an Opium dome Erect!!!! I half expected to hear wolves to begin howling but all I heard were hushed tones and muffled comments interspaced with excited gasps.

Pointing in the direction of the Huey. He jumped down and took off marching towards it like a man possessed! Resembling more a hybrid cyborg wizard in a sci-fi movie than a kidnapping desperado. Followed by a bouncing Robbie himself reminiscent of a modern day piped piper. With their zombie like initiates in hot pursuit it was a struggle not to laugh. Especially as the warmness of the indica strain we had just smoked began to creep into my system. The feelings of stress nausea aches and pains all melted away and were replaced by those of relaxation and giddiness. It was then I realised it must be the herb that was making them all resemble characters from movies.

I shrugged and nodded at the sane section of the camp as we begun to follow the pack. Conscious of the Thai women who were watching our every move, any little slip up no matter how small might be justification to be reported back to Emperor Eddie! Although I suspect everything was being reported back regardless. Plus Franz oh how could I forget where was he? Big brother the human CCTV was most likely up some tree watching.

I half expected a bolt of lightning to fly out his finger Barry joked. I didn't reply for fear of encouraging him, only for him to later on when high say something off the wall and maybe get us all in a serious predicament. Even though nothing was actually planned! Be cool tonight Bas I mumbled. No matter how tempted you might become to say shit well... do not say shit! Any shit at all got it? Aye captain. Cool but I mean it ok our lives depend on it......we followed them around to the back of the building following till we got to the far side where the Huey was.

Rob began sweeping away leaves and dirt revealing a cellar entrance. A double trap door which when unlocked and pulled back revealing a void darkness from which a putrid stink seeped out...Phew wee! Rob waved his hand about his face! Smells worse than the shithouse door of a shrimp boat don't it folks.... he said before suddenly jumping down into it laughing like a hyena...Eddie was laughing too but more demonic! Yawl ok down there Rob? Yeah give me a second Ed! He lit a lighter and we stood there with Eddie till he somehow got the lighting working, only then did we follow him down.

Eddie had of course ensured the light bulbs were junkie must have Red! If nothing else they helped hide his features I thought as he perched and got comfy on a big old rocking chair that was his throne! Scattered around the cellar I noticed big cloth sacks about the same size as oil drums but perfectly square in shape. They were bound tightly by duct tape in a cross pattern ensuring that whatever was inside could not fall out! Mitsu noticed me looking at them and asked jokingly is that where they keep the bodies Luke? Shut up I hissed out the side of my mouth. It's a joke bro! I know it's it's just giving me the hee-bee-gee-bees! Huh? The what? Nothing mate.

Robbie disappeared and several moments later a small speaker perched in the corner of the cellar suddenly sprung to life! Shaking and vibrating the dust off it as it hummed low playing some unusual Asian/Eastern style ambient tunes. Then he returned with a small fan which he also managed to somehow get up and running after fiddling about with it. Placing it in a spot that as it whizzed it served the entire room! This was welcomed by all of us myself included as it not only rid the room of the 'shrimp boat air' inside but also fought a running battle with the sweaty sticky south east Asian humidity.

How's that bitches? Robbie laughed satisfied with his work! Everyone nodded and agreed it was much better. Yawl were sweating like whore's in a church just now! I could tell. Welcome friends make yourselves comfortable! Eddie smiled as he cast his hand slowly out across the room. Like a sultan welcoming dignitaries! Except Eddies palace looked more like a dirty illegal rave than a palace! And Eddie the gangster was running the show. He clapped his hands and Rob retrieved a small box that was sitting on one of the crooked shelves that lined one of the walls. He placed it on a table that sat in the middle of the room! Know what he needs? Barry asked Mitsu. What? A few little green helpers! Or blue....They broke into giggles...shut up you two I hissed

199

frowning.

The table consisted of a large square box with no legs but had an opening on one side so one could if wished hide stuff inside! Rob opened it and took out a three foot long bamboo pole. On the end they had very firmly fastened with duct tape one of those tiny square whiskey bottles that holds about enough for a shot. At either side they had somehow managed to drill two perfectly aligned tiny holes.

Then moving his attention to a small box that he took from the shelf. Opening it he took out something about the same size as a cigarette packet. Carefully unwrapped it revealing its contents. A chunk of what looked just like temple ball hashish but I knew better. It was O, raw Opium in its purest form. A lump of it the size of a golf ball. He then picked up a needle scooped off a little dot sized bit of Opium onto the centre of the needle. Then pushed it through one of the holes in the bottle till it sat firmly inside the whiskey bottle. Cocked and loaded Eddie.

Who was swaying his head to the music as he sucked on a fat joint that appeared from fuck knows where! On cue he spoke as though he was performing a ritual. As this is your maiden voyage with the lady, he smirked! There are a few things you need to understand my friends! The Robster here will spark up the 'goodness' held within his safe hands! And shall keep the flame burning inhale continually until it's completely e-evaporated and don't waste none either yawl hear.

Now it may, to the uninitiated resemble hashish! But I can ashore each and every one of yawl cats it ain't and neither does it burn like it so yawl listen up. You only get one chance yeah hear? Once that burning begins keep smoking yawl keep inhaling, till it's gone.... understand? Now who wants to be first? Scooby and Brett's hands

200

shot up like kids in kindergarten eager to impress the teacher.

The bottle is gently heated by a candle which he waves carefully underneath from a distance of several inches. Doing so just long enough for the tar inside to bubble and fill the bottle with smoke. Scooby then placed his lips on top of the bong and sucked in the smoke. Before Rob quickly moved over to Brett as Scooby fell back. Next up was Aaron! Rob took out the needle wiped it on his arm. Scoops a fresh bit on to it and repeats the process before kneeling in front of him with the bong, enjoy!.......what mother nature herself has provided children, grinned Eddie as he continued with the ritual.

He repeated the process time and again. Then approached stopped and knelt placing it directly in front of my mouth! For the king who fed us all with one fish! He says giggling. Yaba Yaba do.... Eddie roars laughing watching me like a predator! Watching judging my reaction, looking for a crack or chink in the armour, any form of weakness, fear bravado anything! I looked at Eddie and Rob both their eyes dilated like owls at night they stared innocently yet intensely.

I looked at the others, their glazed eyes telling me all I needed to know! So without wanting to give the game away I placed my lips over the bong as Rob waved the candle in slow motion beneath the bottle. Looking at me grinning as he did. I watched as the tar inside began bubbling and immediately the bottle filled with smoke. On cue I inhaled deeply. A super sweet taste engulfed my mouth; my senses went into hyper drive as it cruised through me. First stop, my lungs where it paused before it rushed further inside seeking out new crevices like a flash flood in a cavern.

The beautiful sweet incense like smell returned to

engulf all around the outside as I tilted my head backwards blowing the smoke out. Before turning my head upright again grabbing the bong and wrapping my entire mouth around it in an act of bravado! Repeating the whole process inhaling even more, holding the smoke down even longer. I sat there holding it long after the tar had disintegrated and fumes evaporated. Until Rob began to tap at my fingers indicating for me to let go. Gripping it I realised I was gone.

He moved on to Mitsu who I watched through glazed eyes. But Eddie studied my reaction! My head flopped back and forth as I gazed at Aaron Brett & Scooby who were on the floor not saying a lot. Spaced chilling too stoned to move or talk. Just smiling at the music. Smiling at the music? Am I on fucking drugs or what? Must be because this shit definitely isn't an entheogen nor is it illuminating but fuck me it feels nice. Anyway who am I to judge because I'm not feeling too talkative myself but I am alert enough to realise…. I'm in a fucked up situation! But hey man such is life I tell myself giggling. Yup I'm high as a kite all right.

How does it feel….Is it nice Luke? I hear someone whisper! I don't flinch or reply just stare ahead! Is Papa Verine relaxing your muscles? Huh…Yes Luke…What? I turn to see who it is and he is right next to me sitting crossed legged like a yoga guru! He seems calm smiling reassuring almost loving but I know it's an act! Huh? I respond even though I had heard him, desperately I tried to clear my mind enough to figure out what he is up to. How to respond as it's clear he's thinking my guard is down and I'll tell him exactly what I am thinking.

Your muscles no longer feel tense do they Luke? No I stutter dribbling a little, my head flopping forward. You see that is an effect of the drug…papa…verine at work! Yawl understand that don't you Luke? Of course yawl do. You see Opium in its raw form is a combination of oh well over forty drugs! Yeah forty I think it was when I last read up on it.

Were 'as heroin! Well H you see gets you addicted to…well just to heroin he laughs. But Opium is like getting hooked on forty fifty different drugs! Codeine morphine and so on yet naive backpackers think it's all a game! Eddie…..slurring my words.. my heart beats slow. Depending on which continent you score on of course, he continued laughing at me. Bastard who found this I mean discovered it Eddie? Don't worry about yawl heart beat Luke. As for the truth regarding its discovery well the Opium trades discovery has been lost in time.

It zig zags through the early civilizations from China to Babylon eventually finding its way to Europe! Where groups of early cave dwellers found the poppies growing wild discovered that when you smoked or brewed it. It well it took the edge off living in a fucking cave hiding from predator's I guess, he grinned sparking up another joint.

All the problems in your head are going away now aren't they Luke? He said blowing smoke in my face! All I could do was nod! Your muscles are relaxed all those negativities, all those stresses of life have vanished! Yawl feel on top of the fucking world right about now don't you Luke? Like you could accomplish anything yawl wanted. Look at this lot he laughs pointing across at the others, your different from them you're a leader not a follower I can sense it Luke. I hear Robbie giggling in the background as he had just finished giving Barry and Ras their respective hits. Causing them to melt into the sacks beneath them. I realised they're of no use to me tonight! Man even I'm of no use to me tonight.

I gaze over them, poor paralytic heaps I thought! As Rob brought the bong to life again. This time its Eddies turn. I spot the huge lump of tar bubble as Rob heated it. The music seemed to grow louder as Eddie sucked the thick smoke down in one go, sucking all of it till the hot glowing amber tar faded. Taking a hit big enough for three men! He outstretched both arms and as if on cue Robbie removed the bong from his master's presence.

Eddie slowly allowed just enough smoke to trickle out so he could breathe! Robbie then prepared himself a hit as he sat down in front of the small table giggling and proud of the condition he had gotten everyone in. Eddie stood up and proceeded to waltz about with an invisible partner in a slow circular motion for a few seconds as the last reminiscent streams of opium exited his nostrils. Suddenly coming to an abrupt halt on his knees in front of me.

Does yawl head feel light? I nod. Awe does it now Luke? He asked as he sat cross legged in front of me. But I pretend to not hear him as I feel the eyes roll back in my head. Perhaps a little sleepy huh? He tilts his head sideways looking at my face mockingly, staring into my eyes laughing. This cats rushing with endorphins Robbie! Huh? Oh yeah I do believe young Mr Luke Steel here is rushing his god dam head off.....That is what is making your body pulsate with pleasure right now Luke he says pointing at my chest! That is what is slowing your heart rate boy. Endorphins! Why hell what else can it be what else? He roared laughing.

Bet yawl feel no pain now do you Luke? The euphoria is intense is it not? You're now the happiest and warmest you will ever be in your life because all your feeling right now, is pure unadulterated pleasure! Forget your past it don't mean shit no more. We are your family now! No stress no strains no hunger nothing. Not now nor ever again ...but only if! If what? I ask turning and facing him. He smiled. Only if you want it Luke! Do you want it? Want what? To be the natural born leader you where meant to be? I smile but before a word can pass my lips to my horror Barry begins speaking.

Its takes Eddie's focus from me. I look over and Barry is rambling....It's it's like a wave Eddie! Wave after wave after wave after wave bro! What kind of wave yawl talking? This might sound strange Ed but it is kind of like waves are being produced inside my head and every time a wave comes! Well they feel like an um eh like they're rushing through my system and my body is err.....Oh I don't know wave after wave bro! Well ride um cowboy. Ride that giant wave like you're the surfer King of Wai kīkī beach. You the man Barry and aint no one going to stop yawl.

Wow how did you.... Know? I know everything Baz! Don't I rob? Yes sir! Queen Opium is beautiful my friends. Truly a beautiful gift from the creator himself. For she is far from the recklessness the harmfulness self destructive family destroying evil that is liquor! He hisses his face contorting with contempt at the very mention of the word. Or the lubricated jaws of the habitual cocaine user and E party head. He laughs mimicking the chattering teeth of someone on ecstasy making all in the cellar laugh. Nor will you get the mystical misconceptions of the psychedelics! The shrooms Egyptian lotus African ibogaine! Yes sir pound for pound Opium is right on up there with the big boys! Cause yawl gotta admit guys, she's one hell of a ride isn't she? His grin now reaching epic proportions.

No one replied! Subconsciously I think we all expected him to ramble on and on! Yawl making a joint? He barked over his shoulder at Rob. Yeah! Good I'm dying for a toke! Class A always does that to me yawl understand? Makes a man smoke like he's on death row In Indiana! Brett, Barry, Ras suddenly sit upright and began rolling joints...Where was I Luke? Huh. This is all Barry's fault I tell myself! He was the one that kept on about getting wasted on or giving Opium a try but now Eddie is all over me. And what's all this do I want to be the leader shit?

It's ok Barry I say looking at him, I forgive you....Huh? What the hell yawl talking about? Eddie said staring into my face. Yawl feeling ok? Shit I actually spoke the words and not the telepathic message bit I planned! Oh ha ha yeah sure I'm great..Forgive what? Eddie smiles looking at both myself and Barry...Eh....for calling me fat! Barry says! Fat! You called Barry fat Luke? That's not nice! But still its good he apologised isn't it Rob! Hell yeah..Cruel comment's of that nature must upset the poor feller, not to mention leave a lasting psycho-logical effect! Its fine! Barry smiles.....Well then, glad that's sorted out! Eddie says slapping his leg.

So, so what's it like in tea? I put a coherent sentence together to try and change the conversation....What slop? Ugh disgusting Luke just disgusting trust me! Really? Yeah plus it lacks any form of romance! Romance? Yes of course the queen is very romantic you know? OK I nod with a grin. This err romantic bit would be after err after the companionship stage? Why that's exactly what it's like tell him Rob. Yup sucking slop is colder than a mother-in-law's love, and yawl knows what that's like don't you now.

Yes sucking slop through a straw hardly has the sexiness one imagines when they think of the red-light pleasures associated with an Opium den! Guess so Ed! See Rob, Luke is a catching on mighty fast, mighty fast indeed. Let's play a little game! Now Luke I want you to visualise, its sunset a beautiful beautiful golden rainbow sunset in the orient. Hot and humid so hot the sweat is forming across your upper lip with tiny little droplets

206

trickling down your back! Your hearts beating fast as you reach the door of the secret club you've been told all about....yawl knock.

The hatch slides and eyes stare at you before the door opens allowing you inside! Immediately you notice the white plumes of circular smoke swirling overhead. Faintly it drift's through the air in slow motion. Gently pushed by the fans in the dimly lit room hitting your nostrils with stunning effect...mmm you breath it all in. Your excited but your cool. Yawl take the seat your offered next to the other smiling gentlemen present! And proceed to take a hit from a bong you're offered by...........the geisha girls...their aplenty as they catch your glazed lust filled eye's! He says mimicking a slender females curve with a grin! I nod and smile.

As they gracefully sway past you with a natural rhythm not unlike that of a dolphin...Its smiles all round from the other customers....no bad vibes anywhere here my man as the good times are rolling. You're served marijuana joints on silk cushions! The Shan-Gri-La girls dressed in nineteen thirty's style red silk knell bow and cater to your every desire! Every..Single.... desire boy... everything you can think of Luke.

Shangri La! We we're there man..............Bellows Scooby shattering my illusion before collapsing again. I am stuck for words Eddie. Well I don't know about you Luke but I would consider that the height of romance my man! Eddie says laughing as he lays back into his rocking chair and grins as begins gently swaying back and forth, sucking on a joint passed to him by Robbie.. Everyone's idea of romance differs I shrug. We we're in Shan-gri-la though weren't we? Interrupts Mitsu trying to boast, but no one pays any attention to him.

As I turn to talk again I'm interrupted! Did you know that Jesus took the silk road Eddie? Asks a totally out of it Aaron. Ahhu uggg Eddie chokes on his joint as the smoke goes down the wrong passage. Uh huh stuttering and spluttering over Aarons comment! Yawl right there Eddie? Yeah yeah Rob....Eh come again there young Aaron? Yes sir J C took the silk road......Oh really? Yeah.....I'm intrigued Aaron! Did you hear this news Rob? Yup he replies laughing. Well now do tell me more Aaron. I'm hanging in there like loose teeth waiting to hear this. What about you Rob?

Yup to say this boys gotten me intrigued is an under-statement Ed.....Ok time out where do I start err well look basically when a boy Jew used to reach thirteen back in the day! Bare with me here I'm a Jew! Eh ok..... Eddie grins at Robbie......Well that was when we would traditionally take a wife you see, and the bible of course, well it stops writing about Jesus at around that age right?...Yes that's correct! Robbie grins! So the story goes after hearing about his various shenanigans, you know regarding the temple Scribes and Pharisees etc well I'm sure his name would of gone around the Jewish social scene like a virus, as you can Imagine? I guess it must Aaron yes.

Yes....err em anyway his parent's house which coincidently doubled up as his father's workshop and the carpenters' store! Are you still with me? Uh huh Eddie nodded. Well it begun attracting all sorts of rich and Nobel men who wanted this guy Jesus to marry their daughters! Ah I see yes marriage. Obviously they could tell now this here feller is going places correct? Eddie remarked! Well more let's just say he was already celebrated for his edifying discourses in the name of the almighty! Eddie looked smiling at Robbie. Edifying discourses...they slowly repeated to each other. I do believe I just had a moment of epiphany Rob.

So Jesus decided to clandestinely leave his father's

house, leaving Jerusalem to join the merchants who travelled east on the silk route. Why that route? Asked Rob! So he could go and study the teachings of the Buddha and perfect himself in the divine word! Buddha yawl saying? Correct! But.....I Know...Look Eddie, Jesus took parts of Hindu culture namely patience, love, forgiveness, vegetarianism and when he returned he preached it and they.....The Romans and some very very powerful Galileans crucified him for it. Well I be a son-of-gun! Shouts Rob! That was what all that was about? Only thing Aaron says Eddie scratching his chin! What's that? How did he know about the Buddha very existence if he was in Jeru salem all his life?

Good question no great question actually! Remember at that time it was eye for an eye...so when he came preaching all this far out peace and forgiveness stuff, well it didn't sit too good with certain people. I'd imagine it very well would not of boy! Now mind me saying here Aaron but your story don't add up! Why not? What do you mean? Well if the top Jews were all over him when he was a kid? How come they killed him as a man? And yawl still didn't answer my question about how he heard about the Buddha.

Err well obviously he heard of it.......Yawl know what I believe? What? Destiny my friend. Destiny what will be will be! I don't believe in any man in the clouds that can see the shit I do every minute of the day. Yawl know why Aaron? Why? Because it's all astrological the whole darn thing, every last bit is based on the zodiac. Therefore making the bible a registry of astrological phenomenon, nothing more nothing less. With J C being Julius Cesar! Who imposed upon himself deification in order to expand the Holy Roman Empire. Hence the first Reich.

The shortest day of the year! The winter solstice! It's on December twenty first! Now the northern hemisphere at that time of year gets dark about four pm....and up to this point the days have been getting shorter and shorter until it stops bang on this date every year! But only for three days! Then on the twenty fifth....Christmas Day the sun rises one degree north.

Beginning the cycle of days lengthening all over again....Christmas day is simply the point where days begin to get longer! December twenty fifth is the day that even the Vatican themselves admit to placing Jesus birthday on because it was a pagan holiday called Saturnalia that they needed to eradicate! So if they done well lie about that, then what the hell else yawl think they lying about?

I noticed Mitsu stare at me and look towards the door.... he then stood up and said he needed some fresh air! Hey Bro are you ok? I asked! Yeah just feel a bit stuffy my chest feels a bit tight as well! Let me come with you I offer and stagger like a drunk after him... Eddie notices this in between his conversation with Aaron. Chest tightening huh? Don't yawl worry. All be cool in thirty minutes, nothing like a little hyperventilating....just chill with him in the fresh air for a bit Luke he winks, he be alright once he get some air.

Outside Mitsu asks me if I remember the Wi-Fi gadget he bought in China? The Yoga? I think so why? Yagi not Yoga but yeah look I'm sure that if we get it rigged up to the Huey we might just be able to get online and.....What are you talking about? That helicopter is over forty years old I laugh.....You can no more hook it up to that than I could charge my MP3 on it. You think it's got a USB connection I laughed.

No it's a 2.4 Ghz device Luke! I only speak English and you're talking Dutch mate! OK it's like a surveillance camera in so it can stretch for miles around! Huh? It's a Yagi! I know you don't understand techie stuff but imagine a telescope but for radio waves? Look trust me once we can get a signal going someone might just pick it up. Well seeing you're that convinced who am I to argue, let's go before it's too late.

Hang on what did you say about an MP3? I said I couldn't charge it on.....You got an MP3? Like on you now? Yeah well no well yeah it's in my bag why? Let's get our kit we haven't a second to lose! Why? He took off running and I have too as well to keep up! Within a hundred feet we're both out of breath hands on our knees panting! Stop fucking running Mitsu. If the Thais or Franz see us they will guess something's up and I've already had a slight run in with Franz tonight already.

Holy shit I'm out of breath. Me too. Must be the Opium Luke! No shit genius. Come on we must keep going! Tell me what you were saying back there? You can send email via some MP3? Don't know why I didn't think of it earlier. What? Yeah so we just need to get the Yagi up and running Luke.

Ten minutes later after a quick stop to grab my MP3 the waves of Opium were hitting their peak making us so stoned out of our minds it was difficult to function! We clambered up the tree and into the front seat of the huey. Man what are we doing here? I moaned. Imagine Franz jumping in the window and slashing at us with a giant Rambo knife or worse! Mitsu you listening to me? We know nothing about this mate. We should just go chill with the others. Luke your falling apart Mitsu says suddenly grabbing me! We stare into each other's eyes and I see his pupil's dilate back and forth.

I'm sleepy Mitz so sleepy I yawned. Luke the trip you're on bro, our central nervous systems are feeding both our brains the drug right now. It's flowing though our veins into receptors in and shit our emm....cranial nerve endings and oh I don't fucking hell know what I'm talking about Luke! I'm stoned too but all I do know is I need you! So get a grip bro I'm sleepy too ok. Own it don't let it own you fight it Luke. You're right mate I'm out of it...I'm so fucking out of it.

Hey! What? Tune in! Mitsu say's suddenly pointing at a wire coming out from under the dash. See that? My eyes follow it slowly tracing it as it goes down through the floor! I bet that's the connection Rob used to hook the music up down the basement! You think? Definitely brother I've heard advertisements come on in between the music like it's some local radio station or something we are listening to down there. Ads! You heard advertisements? Luke do me a favour! Sure. Try finding a black or brown wire as I can't see any! Ok...err like this one I inquire pulling up the first one I trace. Coolio he smiled and began twisting it around the Chinese Wifi Yagi gadget thing.

Your MP3 give me it. Huh oh here you go mate, sorry it's the Opium! Ssssh be quite Luke! He connects the MP3 to the power source via the Yagi and sure enough it comes to life! He smiles. I smile back. Then he places it in my hand and nods! What? I don't know your password bro! Err I will give it to you! Do I need to do everything Luke it's a fucking email, send one to someone reliable and do it fucking quick.

Huh. Err like fucking who bro? Don't know Luke it's not my email....No eh.. you can email someone you know from my account its cool.... I smile? No good won't work! Why? If Japanese see English names on their email they think its Nigerian scammers and will delete it without reading it I guarantee you. We need someone you know and trust bro. As I begin logging in my mind scrambles as I try to think of who to email....Could write to dad but.

Hi Dad, trapped in the golden triangle with drug fiends not sure exactly where, send the SAS the Calvary the French foreign legion and anyone else daft enough to want to come rescue us....All the best your son Luke............... not sure it would do anything other than give him a massive heart attack bro, and everyone else I know would think I'm messing them about! Shit Mitsui says looking outside. What? We got to move quick as we don't know when we will get this opportunity again! Might be a week or.......Hang on a minute I pull out my money belt! There's this one guy I have his business card! OK great who? A stranger I met on the flight over to Kathmandu! Here it is.

B.HuckBuck@hotmail....A strange American you met on a plane? Yeah so what? Nothing just asking chill bro. Look if you think he will come through go for it. What? Just its just Eddie and Rob are American that's all...we both giggle. Nah this guys sweet mate, trust me.

Brandon it's me Luke! Luke Steel from London. We met on the plane to Kathmandu and you gave me your card. I'm kidnapped actually we're all kidnapped some friends I made that is...Not joking I'm deadly serious. Please contact my embassy ASAP? I'm with other travellers in the Laotian section of the Nam Ha national park in the Golden triangle, not sure where exactly but it took about two days to get to where we are. I repeat THIS IS NOT A JOKE, Luke Steel.

When we clambered back down into the den it was like we hadn't even left, the discussion was still in full swing. I noticed a pile of vomit in a corner as we descended, but no one was offering to inform us of events since we had been outside! Look Aaron I heard Rob say in an not so friendly way. I said to Mitsu it's not looking too chilled now is it? He shook his head.

Remember the story of Moses coming down Mount Sinai with the commandments? Yes! He was gone so darn long that the people had begun worshipping a gold bull? Do you remember that Aaron? Yes of course I remember that. Well I mean the biblical story bit yes.....Wanna to know what that was all about boy? Go ahead Eddie. It was Astrological pure astrological that's all it was boy. Every twenty one hundred years or so a new sign of the zodiac falls into place! Now Taurus the bull? Which was from thirty three hundred BC to twenty one fifty BC was changing over to Aries the ram. How hard is that to figure out?

You see the cycle was in play at work in motion. Bit like how the Chinese got the year of this or the year of that and all! Well no not exactly like that but sort of like that if yawl catch my drift? Smoked too much eh Rob? Nah yawl doing mighty fine there Eddie! OK it moves but not exactly you get me? Err well no. Same same but different Robbie laughs. As they say in Thailand Barry winks! Yes sir Rob smiles back. Anyways everyone back in those days was expected to changeover..Kinda like analogue to digital? Bret joked to which everyone begun laughing..But they didn't some folk well all those folks stayed with the bull, Taurus.

Now old Moses here he was the cat trying to convince every-body to change! Point is Eddie?

Point is they 'Rome' pick and chose various bits of stories to brainwash the masses Aaron!

Jesus H Christ boy that's what my point is! Yeah but.....Yeah but yeah what boy? Rome stole the lot down to the bloody great big Obelisk that sits in saint peters square today. As for Lions don't get me started, now yawl tell me which here part of Italy Lions come from? Eddie stands up clearly on a rant. Don't look like we were missed I smile at Mitsu who just grins.

Then twenty one hundred years later right on cue J C bursts onto the scene happily ushering in the age of pieces! Single handily debunking Krishna, Buddha, Isis, Mithra and just every other cult that came before him. Oh coincidently Aaron what is the sign of pieces? Don't know! Two fish! J C feeds five thousand with two fish. When he begins his ministry he befriends two fishermen who follow him! Lent begins in February when the days begin......lengthening...lasts until the equilibrium or what the Jews call Passover where the sun passes over the equinox, see where I'm going with this boy?

Think about it Aaron three day's then rises! Search out the hidden signs, there all staring yuh in the face boy. that's why I for one plus Robbie Franz and everyone else round these here parts want nothing more to do with the outside world! We were born free independent sovereign human beings and that's how we plan to spend the rest of our days or yawl help me god for I will take the life of any man that comes and tries to force us back into a life of servitude, hell yeah Robbie says clapping as do some of the others laying on the ground.

A co-rupt evil manipulative mother fucking machine that goes against everything humans were designed to do! It's a prison out there can't yawl see that? We weren't created to work all day every fucking day of yawl lives, why do that? For bits of fucking paper? Humans were created to hunt gather eat and dam well chill and philosophy for the good of the human family. To seek and understand our divine purpose. Know what the number one regret almost ninety nine percent of folks with a terminal illness had when asked? Not spending enough time with family, and too much with work, think about that!

Slavery? Barry asks dazed! Bankers or whoever the

fuck it is that sits behind those yawl curtains pulling our glorious leaders string vests! Obey god or be condemned to hell they yell! Obey your government or go to Jail! Rob passes me a joint making me smile! Why would we want that eh people and for god dam what? To be a manipulated fool void of self-thought belief and determination?

Self-reverence, self-knowledge, self-control, these three alone lead a man to sovereign power.

Alfred Lord Tennyson! A famous British writer and poet said that I mumbled as I passed the joint along. Self reverence knowledge and control Eddie slowly repeated to himself....I like it Luke I like it. See yawl Brits always were masters of Err......anyway who wants to be a victim of lies and propaganda? Is that what you want Aaron? Is this what yawl want?

Over population yawl want to know how big a scam that is? The square mileage of Australia is quarter million miles! Multiply that by six hundred acres in every square mile and hey yawl get two billion acres! Presto enough for every human alive to have a quarter acre of land and still have room for more! Exactly my brother exactly! Ras says adding you got enough room for a home a big garden for chickens and grow veg! Each neighbour can grow a different fruit tree! Ads Rob...yuh know to swap stuff and all.

The matrix is fucking real, so real you better believe it or one day soon yawl going to be sweating like a hooker in a church wishing yawl became a believer when Eddie told yawl it was the gospel! For I can show yawl the door.....'But are yawl man enough to walk through it' I say finishing his sentence. He stares at me with a demented grin! That's right master Luke. Yawl feeling better? Little bit! Got any jokes to cheer these freaks up?

Err nope, Pity boy...Actually hang on a minute if you choke a Smurf what colour does it turn? Don't know....Pretty fucking blue! I don't get it says Rob! Yawl not supposed to get it fool. Morphine! Huh sorry mate? Morph....was named after Morpheus the god of sleep! Really I nod! Bet yawl didn't know that huh? Nope! Guess what Luke? What Eddie? As soon as you leave this place....this enchanted forest. Your back in it man, he grins scratching his chin....Leave this here yawl place and you re-enter the matrix with a vengeance amigos. Only here is where you can be truly free! Mother Nature has shown us the way! A lifetime of sweating to pay bills awaits nothing more....

Ever hear about the third dimension mon? Yes Rasta of course! But of which do you speak? I mean ghosts! You talking walking through walls and shit? No man E.M waves! Huh? Electromagnetic wavelengths! Err Nope...you're going to have to educate me on that one Rasta! E.M waves they are all around us, everywhere you go every minute of every day no matter where you are man. Point being? Say's Rob as he prepares another round of Opium.

Close your eyes man now picture in your mind, a small wave....on a beach then imagine that same wave the same shape but this time it's in the air floating along, but invisible because its air correct? Yes of course Rob answers. Well we are surrounded by these same waves and we know they exist! Huh? Mobile phone signals! Oh shrugs Eddie! Plus WIFI to name but a few.

Look me brother five hundred years ago mankind thought the world flat mon! A simple one dimensional world you sail far enough yuh fall off! Until Columbus proved to them the world was round! Now maybe someday someone somewhere will make the break though so we will be able to see what we now cannot see

217

yet know is there! What only the dogs and cats can now see and hear what the Lion feel and sense or how the Shark smell blood from hundreds of miles away.

Err hat recht! Boomed the deep German voice shaking us up as we turned to see Franz's shadow covering the hatch door! Excuse my manners friends at times I think I'm back in Deutschland he laughed stepping down into the cellar...he walked forward taking the joint out of Robs hand! Dragging deeply on it as he sat down cross legged and stared around the cellar. Interesting story Ja! I was listening outside.

A few years ago I myself had the ultimate misfortune of being in the wrong place at the worst possible time! Dec twenty six two thousand and four Thailand, Phuket, Patong beach I'm sure I do not need to tell you anymore about that! But what I can tell you is this. In zee days afterwards all the media reported the same thing from the local population! The locals pets dogs, cats, the birds, monkeys, elephants every animal you name it about one hour before the wave hit! They fled they all automatically went to the mountains.

Why? You ask he stands up and strolls over bringing me the joint! Instinct? Maybe Luke but who knows for certain! But when even the fucking birds in the threes knew what was coming! Then you know you know for certain something not of this world is at werk! While the most dominant creature on earth the top of the food chain most sophisticated sticks its ugly head in the sand like a dumb ostrich! Everyone burst out laughing.

Rob began passing around more Opium! Grinning wildly he said 'round two boys get it while its hot' everybody took hits including Franz. We got so out of it with and the good versus evil debate going on I felt my eyes closing and I no longer fought it! Until all I could hear was no more words just soft sweet music.

Burma

The officer in the comms room noticed the discrepancies almost immediately! He printed it. Ripped a copy and studied it before he walked over to the man's desk where he left it. The man stuck out. Middle aged shaved head! Several deep scars crisscrossed the right side of his head Continuing down onto his forehead till they reached his face. Only stopping near his right eye. A white man his face deeply tanned he looked out of place among the spotlessly clean shaven Burmese. When he spoke he held a tone of authority that was listened too. He looked at the print out then stood up kicking back his chair! Quickly he strutted over to the man's desk and called over another officer.

See this? He barked in a broad Irish accent? Yes Mr Know what it is? No Mr! Well err yes Mr I know it's not normal but.....Too fucking right it's not normal. It's a fucking signal. Ok Mr.......See this? He said pointing at a graph....Yes sir! That's a beacon.....OK Mr......Know what that is? No Mr ...This type of signal only comes from US military hardware of some type or other! Ah American? Yes I'm not sure which but it's defiantly American...Ok mister.... Stop giving me the ok mister shit I'm tired of hearing it o fucking k? Now can someone any one in fact kindly tell me why the fuck we got a signal coming from an American plane ship or helicopter or fuck knows what within...

What is the problem here? Asked the general marching into the room making everyone stand to attention! A solid square shouldered man with dark olive skin gelled jet black hair and moustache. A large Black Hand gun dangled from the belt on his hip. The new radar equipment has just picked up a signal. A beacon coming from a piece of hardware only used by the US military. I see, this could be bad news! Well if you think that's bad news wait till I tell you this.......ITS LESS THAN 150K FROM RANGOON.

OK smiled the general unwrapping a sweet which he popped in his mouth. Don't worry Mr Gerry! Well I am going to worry seeing as they have a price on my head! Plus perhaps you too should worry as I'm sure it wouldn't exactly go down too well in Washington if they knew. There are no ship's Mr Gerry it is all land! The IT guy said which they both ignored as they stared each other out....Can't be a plane either as there's no airport for hundreds of miles! Must be a helicopter then, smirked the general! Black Op's is my bet! Gerry replied. Fuck, fuck, shit and fuck I knew I.. Relax all is cool my friend. The Americans are not about to begin a new Vietnam for you! The general laughed.

Black op's can and do get in and out without no one knowing a fucking thing. No bodies no witnesses. No proof evidence not a fucking thing! These guys do whatever-the-fuck they like general! Know what I think? Tell me? I think you would you like to fly out there am I correct Mr Gerry? What? He replied nervously. Yes I can arrange for some…some helicopters right now plus say thirty men! Leaning forward the general whispered, just so you can satisfy your curiosity Mr Gerry! See if the Americans really are invading Myanmar after all! Both their eyes locked onto each other....Gerry grinned back at him. Let's fucking roll.

One by one the waves of Opium had gotten more intense. Eventually each one of us slipped into a deep slumber. Sometime around dawn I was having a brilliantly lucid dream when a sharp sudden poke in my ribcage jolted me awake, opening my eyes I struggled as a hand clasped over my mouth! I zoomed in on the face.

Channarong dude. I silently muttered. He placed his finger on his lips indicating for me to stay silent.

I nodded. Acutely aware I was higher now than when I fell asleep. The dream's Opium had given me sure as hell seemed real. It filled my heart with joy knowing our friend was not dead. But the happiness upon realising I wasn't dreaming was about to come to an abrupt end. In fact I was about to discover this was in fact a waking nightmare! Whoosh! Was the sound the hunting knife made as it flew past my face! Huh I gasped momentarily stunned.

Unable to turn my head as fast as the knife travelled. I followed the sound of the whoosh and cry. Locating it just as it ripped into Channarongs arm directly between his bicep and triceps! Splitting it right down the centre he winced in pain as the blood spew outwards landing on the sand floor. I turned away to see the others awaken one by one from their drug induced slumbers! What's going on? Ras groaned. Party's over mate.

Slush....came the sound as Channarong tore the knife from his flesh! Eddie begun panicking thinking he was going to to get the knife back I suspect and desperately searched like a man possessed for his gun screaming at Franz and Robbie. Overturning the table he began ripping everything like a human tornado.

Turning around all I saw were Channarongs feet disappearing up the steps. I then noticed the blooded knife in the sand and contemplated grabbing it but for what? What the fuck Dude? Barry yelled rubbing his eyes! Was that what's his name? Bellowed Scooby.... Channarong! Mitsu answered looking at me grinning that grin. Get up you lazy fuck tards and get that bastard now! Bawled Eddie smashing open a box and pulling out a few pump-action shotguns which he threw at Robbie and Franz! Now finish the fucking job this time. He screamed with veins bulging from his neck all the way into his temples. His hair electrically stood upright with eyes so bloodshot he could have been mistaken for the devil himself.

Come fucking on! Robbie roared passing on the abuse he himself had just got by kicking Scobby, Brett, Aaron as he marched past them clicking and readying the pump action as he did. Time yawl earned your fucking stripes. I jumped up as did the others not wanting the same treatment! Up the steps we went and out into the blinding morning sunlight! Franz was first to spot his trail. Look this way JA! He whispered pointing and took off in that general direction.

When I turned around Robbie was pointing the pump action directly in my face! In times of conflict any yawl sons of bitches disobeying orders shall be fucking well deemed thy enemy and subject to the rules of war! Slowly turning he pointed the gun and fired a blast into a pile of nearby boxes! Boom! it exploded reviling various assorted tools. Pick yourselves a weapon boys we got us a hunt on. God dam Eddie I did tell the stubborn son of a bitch we should of bought us some hounds ages back. Any way let's go boy's yee haa.....

Yanking open the box revealed the oddest assortment of weapons I ever saw. I grabbed the nearest thing turned and began running after Robbie running after Franz! Not to hunt down Channarong but to try stop them killing him! Only once I was running did I realise I had picked up a medium sized cross-bolt with about a dozen ten inch steel arrows cello taped to it! It's practically a gun I thought to myself! I was neither calm nor agitated but definitely demented. Looks like he is headed for the mangrove swamp boys come and hurry up! Rob yelled as he disappeared into the bush ahead! Yahoo! The what? Barry yelled. Ignore him mate, mangroves are near the

222

sea! This could be our chance. Chance for what? To escape! Oh cool bro...But we got to get their weapons first! How Luke? We kill um all.

Out of our minds we bolted through the jungle. This enchanted forest without an ounce of fear...the effects of the Opium made the world around glow and seem very strange! No longer did I notice the air or feel the heat and only felt the sweat once it begun dripping from my nose! The natural dimensions were long gone! A surreal video game world had developed out of thin air and the main players were us. Kill them! Are you fucking serious? I mean what if we miss or. Look guys we get one shot at this and one shot only. Yeah but the fact you only got one life too seems lost on you Luke and were all drugged up here I mean we got to think this thru.

Has it not occurred to you? Barry asked. Has what not occurred to me? BOOM....BOOM .....BOOM the shots rang out in quick succession from deep within the jungle! Reverberating deafeningly as automatic gunfire ricocheted dat dat dat dat! Boom Boom Boom! Instinctively I hit the dust with Barry falling on top of me then the others...Boom shah-lock-lock boom he giggled! What? I said wiping earth out of my eyes! It's a rap tune Luke ......Get the fuck off me you.... You what? Go ahead say it! He said though gritted teeth. In a flash his demeanour turned with pupils huge and dilated I knew this wasn't the time to argue with him. Plus if I am honest he scared me! The whole fucking thing scared me! I was scared half to death expecting the other half to make an appearance any second.

The fact he was holding a fifteen inch long three inch wide serrated blade gripped tightly in his hand confirmed my decision. Ok the fact is we are all off our heads on drugs and it is now more than ever crunch time. We got to stick together Baz or it will become survival

223

of the...... Don't you get it Luke? There are no Marquees of Queensberry rules here it's like some fucking weird zombie mutation chemical has clung to everything! Mitsu laughed making us look at him. One bad fucking trip bro that's all I know! Except normally people aren't supposed to have bad group trips I nod, just individual ones. Nor do bad trips tend to involve guns and extreme violence Barry grinned.

What you got Ras? Machete! Mitsu? Bagged myself a samurai sword bro. Aaron Scooby Brett showed cudgels of various sizes some with nails and studs embedded. Ok here's what we're going to do......out of nowhere we heard a blood curling scream, women's screams followed by gunshots! Sara....screamed Aaron who took off running in the direction the screams were coming from.

Natsumi! Mitsu added his eyes wide and fearful. He too then began running after Aaron. Guys I shouted after them. And with no other option the rest of us then ran after Mitsu running after Aaron. As we rounded a corner and came into a clearing we froze in our tracks as we saw the bodies! The blood made my face ice cold in a millisecond as it drained from me, as the sight of the three Thai girls lying sprawled in pools of blood with a fourth attempting to crawl away sent shockwaves up and down my spine.

As she pitifully lifted her head a wet mess of hair and blood. Slowly she outstretched her arm towards Mitsu standing just yards away! A soldier immediately walked over and shot her again this time at point black range in the head! BOOM. It was Natsumi! Our Nat! In slow in motion I saw Mitsu scream and run towards her and Aaron towards his sister, who was being pulled by another soldier. Simultaneously Scooby Bret and Ras appeared from a bush to the right all charging forward, taking the soldiers unawares! What the fuck? Barry yelled next to me.

Like warriors in some medieval battle they charged screaming and waving their armaments overhead as they ran. Momentarily stunned demented from drugs panicked and in just all round total confusion. We were not sure if we too should join in the charge? We turned facing each other open mouthed, we had frozen. Then in that very instant before our brains could make the decision and react accordingly the Burmese soldiers turned their weapons on our friends.

Simultaneously whilst this happened I noticed a man retreat backwards into the jungle screaming at the soldiers to open fire. The silhouette of his gun facing directly at me allowed to catch a glimpse of his face. In a microsecond he became chameleon or ghost like disappearing into the camouflage the foliage of the jungle offers! Emotionally and physically exhausted trembling and dazed I turned my face back towards the battle charge. In an instant the slow motion effect not only stopped but went to into maximum overdrive. As they were cut to shreds from the bullets of the automatic weapons that began ripping into them.

Nooooo I screamed as Barry dived pulling me down with him! Closing my eyes the sound stalled, for a moment stopping completely! We looked at each other is it over we pondered? Then a wave of firepower so fierce came rippling through the jungle like a tsunami of death and destruction. Metal bullets shells all rained down with such ferocity the jungle itself began to melt and disintegrate before our eyes. Our hearing came back with a vengeance.

This caused my already fast beating heart to begin thumping so powerfully I began to see the skin on my chest heave up and down! Trees trunks fell sliced into half's quarters, eights and sixteenths before finally landing in tiny bits. Coconuts popped from tree to tree like a pinball machine until eventually exploding into millions of glistening white snowflakes.

It seemed to stop as quickly as it started, once the smoke began to evaporate we could see soldiers retreat into the jungle after the ghost. Leaving a single figure a mystical figure among the chaos. Sara! Standing in the same position frozen to the spot she had somehow miraculously by way of divine intervention, not been touched by a single bullet! Neither a graze nor cut, nothing, speechless she stood.

The others were less fortunate! Heaps of bodies lay scattered most with such horrific injuries we couldn't bring ourselves to look at them. Blood gore limbs. We decided to rather not play the game of wondering who's what belonged to whom. I thought it best to look at Sara instead of my dead friends. Hang on those bodies aren't just our friends Luke! What Baz? It was then we noticed the figures slowly manoeuvre in the background dressed in dark combat clothing! We're not alone I hissed looking at the ground. Huh?

No longer able to decipher fact from fiction or understand who what where was on whose side. With ears no longer able to help hear or a brains to comprehend our visual reality! We slowly staggered towards Sara! We hugged and grabbed each other tightly. Is this the end? Barry mumbled. They seem to be ignoring us I stuttered. We might just make......then we heard coughing and noticed blood sprouting out someone's mouth! Its Ras Barry yelled. Over we rushed, kneeling down I saw his eyes wide open as his body heaved up and down as blood pumped out his mouth.

Where're you hit bro? Barry asked holding up the back of his head trying to comfort him. I could see three large holes all of them oozing blood from his upper torso! Luke mon! I'm here Ras I'm here I said as I held his hand.....Me go Zion now you nuh! He winced in pain but still managed a smile...Ras your....No listen, me a go now man. The reaper the duppy him a soon come mon but you! As he began coughing a huge lump of blood mixed with yellow bile flew out his mouth. But you will ah..Again he cried out in pain as Sara wept.

Promise me something? Anything mate anything......Yuh nah go back Babylon promise? Me serious mon! There's no going back you can't go back. If Eddie was correct about just one thing! Look Ras its cool! Me go home now he smiled. I'm going home man I can feel it they're coming...he nodded smiling. Who Ras I turned but saw nothing? Then his body stopped convulsing and he gasped. He's gone Barry sobbed! Guys! Hey guys look! Sara screamed. Mitsu? No I don't fucking believe it. He was struggling to push bodies that had fallen on top of him off! We smiled and went to walk to him. DONT FUCKING MOVE yelled the voice.

I turned and looked at the man screaming dressed in black with green paint streaked across his face. Brandon? Is that Brandon Huckabee from Detroit? I don't believe it you got my message! Wait hang on what are you doing he is our friend Brandon! I screamed sensing he was about to squeeze the trigger! Are you sure he is not a Burmese soldier Luke? No his names Mitsu and he is my mate. He is Japanese for crying out loud.

Bravo two we have secured the area. Huh? Confused I looked at the others who shrugged. What are you talking about? Then I saw the ear-piece! This way he barked at us, simultaneously motioning at some dark figures we hadn't noticed in the bushes, via some secret hand gestures. Don't look at the stiffs just keep walking. We left the area with him whilst he refused to acknowledge me. Slowly doing a full three sixty around himself pointing his weapon all the time.

They em those stiffs back there...are our friends Brandon! Are you going to come back to...Do you want to join them? He grunted! Eh no sorry I stuttered! Then follow my orders. First order shut the fuck up ok. He held the ear piece! Incoming he yelled diving as did we. Out of nowhere came the sound of an incoming missile followed by a huge explosion which rocked the jungle. What the fuck was that? Barry moaned! Enemy chopper! Brandon replied spitting onto the dirt looking around nervously. Don't know how many more there are of these bad boys! We got to keep moving until we get to our rendezvous point. Rendezvous point? Mitsu shrieked. Yeah that's good real good Barry agreed. Me too I said smiling at Sara. I like the sound of it don't you? She said nothing.

Enemy chopper! Mitsu mimed at me. Don't know I mimed back. Within seconds we heard the sound of more helicopters in the distance! We looked at each other then Brandon smiled reassuringly 'the good guys' he said with a wink. Ok assholes and elbows people not far now. After a few minutes more hiking we reached a clearing and we're told to crouch down.

Suddenly a giant helicopter appeared! Hovering less than twenty feet overhead! Again my hearing failed and I could only stare in awe of this alien like creature from a sci-fi movie. It seemed to float effortlessly, studying us as it swayed left to right before centring itself! The thunderous violent vibrations emanating from this monster engulfed our all our bodies. Holding us to ransom. Trapped in an invisible beam it gloated in its power at our helplessness! Whilst it spat dirt and twigs in our faces and terrified all Mother Nature's creatures. My central nervous systems rattled to the point of collapse! Unable to respond or move, trapped like a fly in a web. Our destiny long gone out of our hands we sat in awe.

A ladder was lowered and within minutes were on our way out of the living nightmare. The machine groaned as it violently shot upwards...Simultaneously banking sharply to the left at break neck speed. The sheer volume of drugs cruising my system convinced me that the machine had metamorphosed into a hybrid alien creature! Part machine part physical. She's communicating with the pilot she is telling him he is pushing her too hard I imagined. I cracked the code guys I yelled laughing! Brandon looked at me but said nothing just spat out the open hatch door he manned. It is their language and I can speak it! Then I felt like I was going to vomit.

It was my first time flying on a chopper, maybe that was why I felt the urge to vomit or was it because I had just seen my friends bodies literally being ripped to pieces by creations created by the very same people 'Babylon' as the one I was now trapped in the belly off! Or a combination of both? I guess I will never know. What I did know for certain was drugs didn't even come into the equation. It couldn't be the drugs.

Sara gripped my arm tightly as she sobbed and numbly stared into space with the vacant expression only a war veteran gets! To my right was Barry! Any-time I looked to make eye contact smile or nod, to acknowledge that we had made it, all I saw was the back of his head. Maybe he was genuinely interested in seeing the lush green landscape beneath us, but my guess was that he didn't really want to talk.

Besides what could we of possibly talked about?

Surly the story of how we had been held hostage in a drug induced haze in a remote isolated jungle cut off from the world by a crazed Opium smuggling psychotic international gang. Only to be caught up in a bizarre Mexican style stand-off between them and an unknown army. Which was abruptly ended with the arrival of American Special Forces that led to a ferocious gun battle during which several of our friends and acquaintances lost their lives! And now we, the survivors, were being flown by helicopter to a undisclosed location somewhere. Nah that would be boring.

So what do you talk about after that? Football, the weather. Perhaps talking was my way of dealing with it. Was I being selfish? Maybe. Hang on a minute where the fuck was Eddie Robbie and Franz or Channarong for that matter? My mind cleared as the adrenalin rush receded as did the urge to be sick. Slowly it dawned. They had all disappeared or at the least I don't recall seeing their bodies.

As evil as it might sound I hoped they had been on the receiving end of some of that firepower not Channarong of course he was cool but the others yes. The fact I couldn't recall seeing their bodies bothered me or was this the Opium? Was total confusion part of the come down? Flashes of the Aussies. Aaron and Ras stiff corpses hit home making me shiver. Now the adrenaline had gone the Opium was flushing my system. A minute or two later I gained control of my body. Best not to dwell on the dead or at least try I told myself.

Across from me was Brandon Huckabee! Our knight our saviour! Looking as poised and content as a car rental clerk who had just closed another deal thus hitting his target and instantly upping his monthly bonus! Rather than a secret undercover god knows what he actually was! A solider? A mercenary? Who knows or cares. There certainly seemed little point in trying to tell him about Eddie and friends as he seemed to think he knew it all. Then again maybe he did, maybe he knew a lot more.

He was being spoken too via the microphone thing near his ear as his eyes gave away the fact he was listening! Either way he looked a million miles from the innocent drunk that sat next to me on that flight that night. Occasionally he would talk back but because of the noise I could never hear exactly what was being said. I couldn't complain he had saved our lives. Seated next to him was a shocked and numb Mitsu! I felt his pain bad! Yes Nat was his buddy his travel companion but she had also become my friend.

Whose idea was it for them to go backpacking? I hoped for his sanity it wasn't his! Then I got a flashback to the last time I saw a guy with that facial expression. It was at a party in Camden a few years ago. The guy had candy-flipped! Which is when you take two drugs like acid and ecstasy at the same time. Now this should only ever really be done by someone who regularly takes both these drugs and it goes without saying must be done in the correct surroundings. Preferably in the countryside and not in a city and defiantly not in a nightclub in a city! In fact I wouldn't recommend it anywhere as you can well you can quite literally flip over the cuckoo's nest so to speak.

The shock from that amount of enlightenment can sometimes be too much for the pineal gland to handle, as instruments for attunement is what the glands primary purpose is or points of contact between the spirit and the body if you like. These glands are the gateways of the spirit into physical consciousness and manifestation. The functioning of these glands are of course primarily

231

dependent upon the quality of motivation and dwelt upon by the imaginative forces of the individuals mind! This guy was clung into the corner of the room looking like a terrified rabbit. Wild eyed and sweating profusely all he did was stare up at the ceiling and look back down. If you caught his eye he would give you a grin that was neither passive or aggressive evil or friendly but it just made him seem…unapproachable.

I knew I wouldn't get any rational form of communication from him! So I didn't bother. Mitsu now had that very same look on his face! I hoped it didn't become a permanent thousand yard stare as had Sara. But I did wonder what was going through their heads. We'd all been through a lot. But just like Entheogens some folks handle it better than others. He had Nat on his mind; Sara had her brother who just gave his life for her! So maybe I was being harsh as all I had was me and I was safe.

Or well I felt relatively safe. I admit shook up most defiantly. Then again the slow come-down effects of the Opium session had me so chilled nothing could phase me. No dought that would later on change. Hey what we all really need is a big create of beer to chill us eh guys? I shouted. Brandon looked. No one replied.

After what seemed like the longest ride of my life but couldn't of been more than an hour or two we touched down on the centre of a deserted runway. We had past a metropolis of huge skyscrapers twenty minutes back. Which I presumed was Bangkok so we were definitely not in a city! Which was confirmed as we stepped out of the chopper? Looking about all I could see were lush green fields and palm trees galore! No sea breeze here Luke huh? Shook out of my thoughts I turned around, it was Barry. He was back!

Where do you think we are? I was going to ask you

the same thing! Is that the only reason you want to talk to me? When I want something? Yeah! You just stole my line Luke. How are you feeling? Fucked up but hey we survived so we must be thankful for that. Yeah true mate! Did you see what happened to our glorious leaders? Those scumbags? Yup! Nah people like them those types that live on their wits always slitter away! Yeah the old street wise self preservation instinct kicks in! Yeah I guess. Better known as fuck everyone else syndrome. So much for the all in this together crap.

Hey we're at U-TA-PAO! Barry said pointing up at a big sign on the airport roof. Looking up I saw the sign welcome to Thailand! Half a dozen helicopters were lined up two large regular passenger type planes, lots of smaller models of various shapes. All machines of war, of death and destruction. All grey in colour. All bearing an American flag! There was even one of those small puffed out overweight kiddie looking planes with propellers! A few large closed hangers prevented us seeing inside as we walked across the tarmac following Brandon.

Once inside a Thai Officer dressed in a sparkling white crease free uniform sporting shiny black shoes meted and greeted! Sawadee krup Brandon said to him. No further words were exchanged and with the officer seemingly counting us, he produced a notebook, wrote a few words in it and that was it! No passport check! No fingerprints. No eye scan. No record of us entering the Kingdom nothing we just strolled on in.

Follow me! Brandon ordered as we sauntered through what must have been at one time an arrivals hall. All under the watchful eye of the Thai Officer. And then Brandon stopped. OK guys listen up and listen good. On the other side of those doors, he said indicating towards a tinted glass door. Is your freedom but your country's respective secret services are outside waiting to talk to you! What you tell them is your business. Sara your brother is amongst the deceased I'm lead to believe correct? She nodded. So they will at a minimum want a statement from you. I reckon same for you Mitsu! How did you.........

But not yours, he said shocking Barry and I! Drugs come down hangover afterglow however you want to describe it. No one ever wants to hear the words your country's secret service wants a quite word. No way bro why? You two neither lost anyone. You're free to go and if I were you I would not do anything stupid. Such as? Like walk into a police station voluntarily once back on home soil or call a TV station and opening up a can of worms you later can't close.

In fact if I were in your shoes I'd sit down here for a few minutes before that nice kind Thai Officer over there opens the door to let you out. Have a little chat get your story right and never ever deviate from it! There is a water dispensing machine over there. Good luck! Then he turns and begins to walk away! No no no....this can't be it! This isn't right? After what we've been through this guy is practically telling us to lie piss off and shut up. To just all round fuck-off like nothing ever happened? No fuck this shit guys! Hey Brandon! Luke forget it bro and come back Mitsu yells.

Brandon I shout after him catching the eye of the officer, he pauses then turns with a sigh. What happened back in the jungle? My job is done! Fuck you we have just seen our friends slaughtered today for what? For Nothing! His abruptness took me off guard! Err no Brandon it was for something we were kidnapped I sent you an email. What email? Huh? It doesn't exist! I don't exist. Your camp in the jungle no longer exists. There is no Brandon Huckabee! Don't yawl get it kid?

We may all just be kids but we're not gullible enough to swallow that such a big military rescue was done just to save our weed smoking asses. Besides you just confirmed every fucking suspicion I had! What's that Luke tell me? This shit was bigger than us wasn't it? Look......No Brandon you look! Sara there lost her brother. Aaron his name was in case you're wondering? My very good friend Ras was among the dead I counted four large holes in his body! It could of been me or any of them standing over there that died today.

Look I'm sorry! He says gesturing towards Sara but really there's. So what's going to happen to the bodies? Your embassies will take care of them. What about us were alive? What about you Luke? I'm glad you came to help and all that but....Luke take it easy get yourself together man you have been though a very traumatic experience! He says putting his hand on my shoulders. Plus I can clearly see you're under the influence.......What? Now when you're adequately rested I'm sure someone will call on you asking do you know who this guy show you some pictures etc...

You know to help ID the bodies which are currently on their way to Chang Mai! They are? Yes but for now you really need to get some rest get drunk high visit a church a temple just do what you got to do man! But firstly you guys must sort out a story. Chang Mai? But what about the evidence? What evidence Luke? The camp the opium den the pool the huey? You're clearly not listening! To what? Me!! It's gone all gone Luke! Gone where? The whole place was fucking napalmed after we left! We were never there, you were never there, it's a black Op mission for fucks sake! Do I gotta spell it out? Now as I said go concoct a story.

Fuck you and fuck the story! You lied you didn't come for us did you Brandon? What are you talking about Luke the drugs are fucking your head up! The guy with the Burmese the shaven headed white guy that's who you were after wasn't it? I saw the way you guys went straight after him like he was public enemy number one! He was the reason you guys arrived so quick. I figured that maybe after about a week there was a small possibility a search and rescue party or maybe a few local cops might arrive! But not the US Calvary! So spare me the bullshit who the fuck is he?

He is no one Luke! Yes he is someone, someone important enough for the US government to send you guys in. Wait a minute, why were you even on the plane that night? I laughed as the penny dropped! You were on the lookout for him even then and.. Suddenly Brandon got so close to my face I could feel the heat of his breath! You don't want to know kid do you understand me? Fuck you! No fuck you you're correct this shit is bigger than you kid so you can just take your skinny ass and fuck right off out that door and continue on our silly little gap year like nothing ever happened.

After our friends lives were snuffed out? Oh yeah I will go get high laugh and say what a funky helicopter ride, what a freaky shroom trip. What a nice guy he was and weren't we lucky old Brandon Huckabee from Detroit Michigan came to our rescue! Numb out the reality till I'm old living on Prozac to hide the flashbacks! Good boy now you're getting it! We didn't want this shit Brandon but I be damned if I'm going to walk off into the sunset and have questions for the rest of my life that need answering right fucking now.

What do you want from me Luke? Err an inquiry would be nice or better still go after the people responsible or... Listen for the last time it was a black op mission not a fucking drive by shooting in the hood! No crime scene fingerprints no DNA no hero fuck detective!

Everything that was there is gone forever! They lost a lot of men and a helicopter this morning so I'm pretty sure there pissed. And you think our government are going to call up and say hello em any chance we can have someone handed over? Whoever killed your friends is dead got it? And the United States certainly is not going to go to war for a bunch of kids that got themselves kidnapped by venturing too far off the beaten track. Hell yawl lucky to be alive as it is. Tell them yourselves! What? I point over towards the others.

Brandon walks over to the water machine pops in a few coins! Grabs several bottles then walks past me towards the group and passes the bottles around. Breaking open one himself he takes a swig...OK you want answers fine. The place was destroyed as soon as the foreigners' bodies I mean your friends and loved ones were located. Now every other last thing is gone, like it never existed. My team and I were dropped off about twelve hours ago, we had just about made it to you when we saw the Burmese helicopters moving in. Then we knew something was about to go down so we got there ASAP. The guy with the shaved head! He says looking at me. His name is Gerard Slone! One of the most wanted terrorists in the world.

He was one of the greatest engineers the IRA ever produced! After the peace process got rubber stamped he disappeared underground! Became a soldier of fortune! A ghost. He popped up in central and South America's in the late nineties, slipped the net before we could catch him! Catch him for what? Why do you guys want him? He was training groups to build bombs. The type of bomb that can take down an entire city block. Nothing for several years, then he re-surfaced, in Iraq.

Whereas in the Americas it was the old Marxist ideology he once held dear now he was willing to work for who-ever would pay! A rebel without a cause. A dictator with money no problem! A terrorist organisation with money no problem. How do you know for sure it's him? Mitsu asked! Every bomb is unique every bomber leaves a fingerprint of his work so to speak. The actual design themselves the way they are made! Put together, even after they explode the experts can tell if this one was made by the same guy as another one. Eventually they get a brake and find something linking the bomber with his crime. A bomb went off in Laos outside the Thai embassy last year killing dozens of people! A warning to them to stop being too friendly to the US after the cyclone that devastated Burma.

It was telling them to back off! Agent provocateur? Barry grinned! Not exactly but near enough.

They called in our experts and they found a perfect match for a spate of bombing attacks that occurred in Kirkuk, northern Iraqi. Which occurred over a year long period. Not one arrest. Thousands perished in those attacks. He was the prime suspect. Also suspected of training rebel groups in the area funded by the Iranians during the conflict. It was all Mr Slone.

Now the government in Laos knew if those responsible for the attack on the embassy attacked again it would make them look weak in front of their people! They knew they could not beat the Burmese government the same way the Burmese know they could not beat the Thai's! So they attacked their embassy instead! How did he escape or get out of Iraq? Sara asked. Who knows, the SAS went after him then but he got away... again. M15 are after him big time for some conspiracy to murder some politician in London.

Yet next thing we know we get Intel he is working for the Burmese junta. So yes Luke you're correct we have spent the last two years out and about here getting boots on the ground ears eyes etc open making contacts! We had Intel during the week I met you on that flight. We had undercover officers on every flight out of the UK going to Asia that week keeping watch! Every single airport in Asia had a man waiting. But nothing.

Now there's talk of friendship, of bridge building with Burma so it's hard to tell if we will ever get him. So that was your last chance to catch him huh? I said drinking the water. I've said enough. So out that door over there, he smiled pointing. Your embassy's will issue new documents for you, complete with entry stamps into Thailand once you contact them. So you will be able to leave when you're ready to do so! It's up to you should you decide on going home or staying here, they won't force you.

They have been briefed so it will be just routine stuff they might ask do you want to call anybody, do you want to go home, stuff like that. I must go now so please do not mention this conversation to anyone. Especially any of those bad boys outside he laughed....Hey Brandon! Yes Luke? Thanks man....I forgot my manners there for a little while and if I don't say it now you know if you had never given me your card well......I know Luke! I know buddy.

We turned and walked in opposite directions. outside a black 4x4 was parked, out of which got some lean mean Mossad looking types! I swore they were brothers they looked so alike. I hugged Sara tightly holding her for as long as I could. Prey for me Luke she said. Of course I will. I wrote down my email and told her keep in touch! A hug from the others then quick as a flash she was gone! Strangely it was like she had never even existed, then more jeeps came.

Pattaya

It was THE place to be! He said before adding that the in crowd were all here! In fact there's not a US soldier alive that hasn't hit the mean streets of downtown Pattaya Luke! So popular the US army even opened a re-enlisting centre here at one point! Can you believe that? The infamous walking street where all the drunk GI's could act macho in front of other drunk GI's and hookers and sign up to fly straight back to 'Nam' for another year of slaughter before returning once again if they survived for three more months of R+R. What debauchery! What idiots eh? The ultimate self flagellation really wasn't it don't you think? I nodded in total silence. The intelligent ones did their time, enjoyed some fun in the sun and got the hell out of dodge, but not these idiots. Rumour has it some of these guys did four even five tours before managing to get their sorry asses killed.

My brief, handler, I didn't know what to call him was waffling on about this rubbish in his posh oxford accent without even offering me his hand. All I knew was I was being driven at speed to some secret location! They're still here you know? Huh I replied transfixed looking out at the thousands upon thousands of girlie bars in neon signs as we speed past! Some of these wrinkled grey haired hippie biker looking chaps you notice sitting about drinking beer for breakfast with an anorexic hooker never too far away....been here since the mid seventies he nodded. Forgive me I seem discourteous at times Luke, my name is William. Anything you need let me know OK! Err yeah sure will do Will.

The Jeep screeched to an abrupt halt outside a non descript building surrounded by a corrugated iron wall! Standing at least fifteen feet, it looked imposing to put it mildly. Blacked out windows hid its interior as did its purpose. Not much was in his big office! A plain table, a few chairs and a large mirror on the wall. There were some other guys present who all greeted me with the fake kindness that seeps from indoctrinated civil servants and council administrators on a global level.

I nicknamed one cheesy chops and the other sweaty pits both for obvious reasons. I got a sense that an overwhelming amount of bureaucratic bullshit emanated from within these walls! Luke my poor boy do have a seat! Sweaty pits smiled whilst gesturing for me to sit on a seat he had pulled out! Eddie suddenly sprung to mind and I almost laughed in my deliriousness. As cheesy chops began a vain attempt at questioning me whilst I recalled Eddie's trailer park accent saying something about 'sweating like a hooker in a church' as cheesy ranted on with sweaty standing by. Like he was giving cheesy telepathic messages to ask me.

You have been through such an awful time Luke we know all about it! You do? Yes he smiled with awful teeth! Tea? Huh.... Nice cup of earl grey? Oh so you know? We know everything Luke! Sweaty said with the condescending grin of a cocky prosecutor who never made the grade but got this gig instead! And knew in his heart it would be the highlight of his career! Simultaneously letting his guard down allowing me to see through the double act! No I'm good with this I smiled shaking the water bottle! Have you guys called my parents? No we only got the news a few hours ago so we didn't have time to go tracing your home number.

Plus you're an adult it's your business if you want to inform them! Good I don't want them to know 'So much for we know everything but don't know my home phone number I thought' we understand Luke! You do good! Of course why worry them correct? Yeah... why worry them

241

I nodded at cheese. I was expecting a big fat no we must call or something like that. These guys were fast beginning to sound like not to mention actually remind me of the Eddie and Robbie show with the bad double act and it was starting to freak me out. Shit man what I'd give for a beer and a joint.

Besides it's none of our business what you tell your relatives! Yup. OK Luke! Said some guy I hadn't noticed in the shadows of the room suddenly appear. Making me jump as he revealed himself. Removing a packet of slim cigars from his pocket he 'much too cheesy and sweaty discomfort' lit up...Cool.....Our man in Havana was an average sized chap with brown hair. I had the feeling I had met the man.

I am not here to bullshit you Luke! Good opening line but just who the fuck are you as I've had enough bullshit plus dealt with more than my fair share of vipers this week. They looked at each other but the harsh truth was I was wearing a dirty t-shirt shorts in a cold room on a major cold mistress style comedown, penniless with no passport and these people sounded like me looked like me. I wanted so badly to trust them believe them to even like them but would I loan them a pound or tell them a secret? Not a hope, slippery bastards.

Surrounded by social workers who clearly thought they were 007 in waiting tasked with gathering informants to glean information! They studied me like I had the key to the Vatican vaults but all I knew was I was in desperate need of a beer a joint a sleeping pill. Then wake to a shit shave shower and extra strong coffee. I desperately fought the urge the scream you can fuck right off. OK Mr no BS do you mind telling me who you guys are?

We're M16 Luke! Said a female answering for him! I swung around dropping the bottle of water as a fifty something woman appeared from behind the big mirror! First a man from behind a curtain who wasn't the man. Now this. Dark curtains mirrors tinted windows sound proofed walls as well I presumed and populated by more social workers than you would find in a Soho bar on a Friday night! Cheesy Sweaty Havana-man and now mam appears from behind a giant mirror. If I were you I wouldn't tell a soul about this! No shit amigo I reply retrieving my bottle and taking another gulp of water! Nor should one most definitely speak over the phone, ever! These people the ones that got away today Luke! Uh huh I nod! They are part of a ruthless international terrorist organisation who could if they pleased wipe out your entire family back home.

Fuck off I laughed. Looking around I noticed everyone's solemn expression. Really? Yes really Luke! Do not tell a living soul you care about she said so close I could feel her breath. You know I really have had enough of people getting up close to my face I think to myself but understanding a game was at play I decided to play my part. Taking another sip of water I replied. Well I don't ever want to talk to a living soul about this mam. In fact if my parents knew what had happened they would order me back home immediately and I don't want that. What do you want? Sweaty pits asked. To continue my gap year with my friends! The Canadian Japanese and the girl from Israel? Says Havana-man reading from a list of nationalities he held! Uh huh I muttered shaking my head as I finished off the water. Only problem is I am strapped for cash and....

Could do with a............Instantly I'm cut off by Cheesy 'we can only assist you with flights home Mr Steel' and/or minor expenses like hotels for a few days if you don't want to go back! Hotel sounds good I smile. Until I get a replacement credit card from my bank. We have been in touch with your bank already! You have? Yes they have a branch in Bangkok and they will be sending your new card to this hotel! He says pulling out a recite with reservations in my name! Sounds like a nice hotel I say to no one in particular as I read the flyer. Yes they beamed like they paid for it.....You're booked in for one whole week! After that you're on your own! Added mam. Weeks good! A week's good Mam.

My friends err...If they so choose to stay it is very likely you will find them on the streets! Pattaya is not a big place! She smirked looking out the window! Is that it? Yes that's it you're free to go. I stood up cheesy opens the door revealing Willie outside. I smile at him... Oh Luke! I turn around. Yes mam? This conversation never took place! What conversation? I turned and proudly walked past Wills into the heat of the afternoon. I don't think that's the last we're going to hear of Mr Luke Steel mam, sweaty pits announced as they watched from the top floor window. Me neither, but I hope he makes it.

After I'd checked into my hotel I couldn't sit still. I had a shower but that was no good as I still felt the need to just be back outside in the fresh air. Get some alcohol yeah good idea I thought! I didn't get a hundred feet before I stopped at a roadside bar and got myself a beer. There I sat chilling watching the sunbathers hit the beach across the road as the sound system played. Some old American guy with a long beard and a beer smiled to himself. I thought maybe he was one of the few remaining ones Wills had spoke about.

Whereabouts yawl from? London you? Sacramento California names Randy! Luke, Pleased to make your acquaintance. Likewise. Just then who should walk past? Barry! I yelled out and we bear hugged! Not long after Mitsu appeared and we were united. They knew what they were doing as they had placed us in neighbouring hotels it transpired! We drank and toasted the fact that we now had the greatest adventure story ever of how a group of backpackers had first set foot in Thailand just like Brandon had promised me that night on the flight.

Enjoy the sunset Randy. Will do brother. We laughed as we walked off into the night. Then we got on the main strip and had to fight off the bar girls all dressed up like it was Saturday night in the club. Then I knew my adventure, our adventure as I looked around me was only just beginning. After what seemed like ages we found a spot with no one trying to usher us inside. It was an English theme pub so we grabbed a table outside and relaxed with beers and people watching.

What do you think of this place Mitsu? Wild bro! Hey Mister.......a youngish well dressed Thai with a leather briefcase introduced himself. No thanks I don't want sunglasses or watches Barry tells him. No sunglass, working for travel agent mister! I organise excursions to Kampuchea....Where? I asked. Cambodia!! We got the sales pitch big time and before long was offering Angkor Phnom Phen. The killing fields or the raw mean lawless Battenbang.

Up for more adventure? Are you joking Luke? It's like Thailand yes? I asked. Yes mister same same but different! I looked at Mitsu who looked at Barry who looked back at Mitsu. Then both of them looked at me! They got ganja in Cambodia? Too much Mr too much he laughed. I looked at them and smiled. Yawl heard the man. We got us two roads; one goes home the other is going to Cambodia! You choose and placed my fist facing down on the table! Mitsu placed his over it looked at Barry who looked at me.

Shikata Ga Nai laughed Mitsu, Barry smiled as he too slowly placed his hand on ours.

Shikata Ga Nai we shouted together as we lifted our

drinks in a toast.

Holiday in Cambodia here we come baby, here we come.